JULIANA GOODMAN

THE
BLACK
GIRLS
LEFT
STANDING

FEIWEL AND FRIENDS
NEW YORK

A Feiwel and Friends Book
An imprint of Macmillan Publishing Group, LLC
120 Broadway, New York, NY 10271 • fiercereads.com

Our books may be purchased in bulk for promotional, educational, or business
use. Please contact your local bookseller or the Macmillan Corporate and
Premium Sales Department at (800) 221-7945 ext. 5442 or by email at
MacmillanSpecialMarkets@macmillan.com.

Library of Congress Control Number: 2022901697

First edition, 2022
Book design by Veronica Mang
Feiwel and Friends logo designed by Filomena Tuosto
Printed in the United States of America

ISBN 978-1-250-79281-5 (hardcover)
1   3   5   7   9   10   8   6   4   2

For Elena Marcia Gross AKA Fat Baby

CHAPTER 1

THERE'S PINK LIQUID IN THE SOAP DISPENSER. It's not the automated kind where you stick your hand under and get a glob of foam—it's the old-school kind where you have to press the button to get a gooey string of soap.

As I try to wash my hands, I can't wrap my mind around the strangeness of a toilet in Warshire's Funeral Home. It's weird that I can pee, flush, and wash my hands while my sister's body is lying in a box a few rooms away.

When I leave the dirty bathroom, Deja's waiting outside the door. Like I asked, she's wearing her thick, jet-black hair in a tight doughnut bun on the top of her head. There's no makeup on her face either. The last thing I want is my uncles and cousins eyeballing her and asking who she's kin to.

"You good, Beau?" she asks, leaning up against the wall.

"Yeah, I'm fine," I say.

We're both in matching baby-blue sweatpants with "R.I.P. KATIA" spray painted in pink and purple down the leg, and baby-blue hoodies with Katia's face screen-printed across the chest. I drew the sketch myself a couple days ago, trying to copy my favorite tagger, Bexley O's, style. I'm nowhere near as good as her though.

"I really don't want to walk down this hallway," I say, shoving my hands in my pockets and trying to remember how to breathe. *Inhale, exhale.*

"I know," she says.

Dad's old friend Wheeler is a goddamn liar. I've been to a few funeral homes and his brother-in-law's has got to be the shittiest in Chicago. The inside is dark and outdated. Old musty rugs lining the floor, dingy brown walls that were probably white once upon a time, fluorescent lights with a bunch of burned-out bulbs that buzz like flies and leave most of the place in shadows. It's a nightmare, but it's free so we had to take it.

The worst part is this long creepy hallway that leads to the back chapel. It's lined with mini chapels, three open caskets inside each one. All these bodies laid out in one place, the heavy scent of potpourri and death, it makes my stomach start to knot up.

"Hold on to me and close your eyes," Deja says, holding her arm out like she's my prom date. I link my arm through hers and let her guide me down the quiet hallway of death.

There's gotta be at least twenty people in these rooms from when I counted earlier, but we're the only live ones, and the light rustle of our sneakers on the carpet is the only sound I hear.

When Deja tells me I can open my eyes, we're back in Katia's chapel. There's pink and blue mini spotlights that give the drab wood-paneled room some color. The obituaries are already laid out on the pews, although there's at least fifteen rows and I doubt we'll need that many.

"Dejanae, would you mind moving my car out front? I'm double parked, sweetheart," Wheeler says. He's huddled in a circle in the back of the room with my parents and, like, a dozen other people I've never seen before. They're all dressed in black suits and dresses even though I told them Katia's favorite color was blue. *Disrespectful asses.*

"It's *Deja*. Give me your keys," she says, holding up her hands as Wheeler tosses them to her.

"Be right back," she says to me before kissing my cheek and turning to leave. It's really not like her to be taking orders from anyone. The regular Deja would have told Wheeler to shove his keys up his wrinkly ass, but helpful Deja is doing everything anybody asks her to do today.

But I only came here for one reason: Jordan.

As Wheeler starts going over the order of the "celebration of life" with my parents, I walk to the front of the chapel slowly, like a bride about to meet the love of her life at the altar, but there's no altar here. Just a closed white casket with shiny golden brass handles on the sides.

I walk up to the shining white box with my sister's body in it and place my hand on top where her head is. Heat, vibrations, a genie to pop out and grant me three wishes? I'm not sure what I'm expecting to feel, but it's like touching any regular old object. I don't *feel* Katia's spirit.

I don't think she's in there.

From the photo they keep showing on the news, Officer Peter Johnson looks like a stand-up guy, with his blond son on his shoulders and his blonder wife at his side. But I know he's a cold-blooded murderer. It was 4:00 A.M. and he says Katia was trying to break into his house. Bullshit. All I know is the bullet entered her face just above her lip where her Monroe piercing was and came out the back of her head.

Suddenly, I feel a hand on my shoulder, just as light and jasmine scented as Katia's hands. I whip around, beaming, but it's only Deja.

Just like that, someone turns the light off inside me again.

"Do you need anything?" Deja asks, leading me to a pew like I'm a glass figurine that might shatter at any second.

"I think so."

"What? Some water? Coffee? I can run down to the Popeyes and get you something to eat. Tell me what you need."

But I just shake my head. We sit down next to each other in the front pew, and I lean against her shoulder. I pretend it's a dream, that any second I'll wake up in the hospital after having hit my head or something. The doctors will say I've been out for days. Katia will be sitting in the chair beside my bed. She'll look at me with her glowing black skin and fake gold bamboo earrings and say, "Beau, don't you ever fucking scare me like that again!" Just like she said that one time I spent the night at Deja's and didn't tell anybody where I was going.

The cops asked us if Katia was on drugs, what she was doing on that street, why she would break into this cop's house. We said:

she wasn't,

we don't know,

and she didn't.

Because that's what *we* know.

At least, what we think we know.

I keep my eyes shut as tight as I can, pretending to have fallen asleep on Deja so people arriving inside the chapel will leave me alone. It works for a while. I hear some of my aunts and uncles, sniffling and talking to Deja about me. I even let out a fake snore or two so I can keep my head pressed to her body and hear the deep vibrations of her voice as she explains to everyone that the past few days have been a lot on me.

"Poor baby, I know she's tired," Aunt Nisha whispers.

"That cop gon' get what's coming to him. Believe that!" Uncle Kolby says.

I hear a *whap* and then Aunt Rachel's voice.

"Don't talk like that! Last thing we need is your ass getting arrested."

I hear Momma somewhere wailing and asking *Jesus why?!* As if he's going to come down here with a flow chart and explain why Katia had to die. I hear Daddy say, "It's gon' be alright, baby," but then he collapses into sobs. Then I hear three loud thumps and some gasps, but I still don't open my eyes. I don't wanna see any of this. I don't want it to be real.

"Do you see him yet?" I whisper to Deja, my eyes still closed.

"He's not stupid enough to show his face here. There's these two goofy-looking white dudes standing near the door. Cops," she replies.

"To catch Jordan?"

"It's a few Onyx Tigers in here. Cops probably just here in case somebody in here thinkin' about shooting."

Katia and her boyfriend, Jordan, left the club together that night and Peter Johnson says he saw two people on his porch, but that the guy ran away before he could catch him. That was eleven days ago. No one's seen Jordan since. And if they have, they're not talking.

Way more people than we expected show up for the memorial: Grady Park people, Black Lives Matter supporters, a gang of bikers, a *gang* gang. There's so many people that we run out of obituaries and Wheeler runs to print more. It's standing room only, and there's so many people that Mr. Warshire has to push all the other services back because there's not enough room for any of the families to get in.

At 1:50 P.M., fifty minutes after we were supposed to start, the service finally begins. Deja moves to the pew behind us while I'm squished between Momma, Daddy, and the rest of our family.

"We gon' be aight," Daddy says, kissing me on the forehead and leaving a greasy smudge from his lip balm. But that's just something people say at funerals. It doesn't make me feel better at all.

I scan the room looking for Jordan, his block-shaped head and his signature fade, but he's still not here. Officer Johnson's on paid administrative leave. Our lawyer, this red-haired lady named Ms. Anniston, says the district attorney needs a witness testimony before he'll even consider criminal charges. We need someone to say, *Katia didn't do anything wrong.*

"In this here casket! This CASKET! In this casket is DUST!" the rent-a-pastor who came with the memorial package screams into the microphone. His brown bald head is already sweating, and he uses a cloth to wipe it.

I know it's only Katia's body in the casket, but it's the body that she used to live in, the body that I touched and slept in a room with for sixteen years. He can go on somewhere with all that hollerin', because there's a big difference between Katia's body and the dust that's always on top of the blades of the ceiling fan in our room.

"We gon' be alright, baby, we gon' be alright," Momma keeps whispering to me.

I should be crying, too, but I can't for some reason. It's like my ducts are all blocked up and the tears are dripping down my insides instead of my cheeks. *Katia, why didn't you just stay home with me instead?*

It's after the pastor sits down when the real clowning begins. They open the casket so people can stare at my sister, so they can see for themselves just how dead she is. Identifying her in the morgue with Momma was enough for me. She was gonna do it alone because Daddy didn't answer his phone in time. But I didn't want her to be in there by herself. Momma didn't want me to, but I know she needed me to. That's why I can't look at Katia now. I can't see her like that again.

The rest of my family gets up to stand in line for the viewing, and then Aunt Pepper faints in the center aisle. She did the same thing at Grandma's funeral a few years back, complete with a pencil roll across the floor. People were already crying; now they're screaming and wailing because grief is contagious.

"Lord Jesus, help her!" Aunt Rachel cries, cradling Aunt Pepper's head as her brown eyes roll back.

An usher with big hips in a white dress and nurse's cap runs over to help. Uncle Kolby gets Aunt Pepper back in the pew, but she's gone limp and everyone around her uses their obituary to fan her sweating face.

When Aunt Pepper finally comes to again, the service continues with Katia's best friends, Monica and Clarice. They're wearing the blue R.I.P. Katia sweatpants, too. They almost didn't get them because they let her leave the club alone with Jordan that night. If they'd had her back and gone home with her, none of this would be happening.

I twist around in my seat to see the crowd of what must be at least two hundred people. Deja was right. Jordan would miss his girlfriend's funeral to protect himself from the police. I don't know a lot about him, except that he's got a record, his father's been locked up for murder since he was a baby, and he's spent the last two years lying and cheating on my sister.

My fists tighten and I start bouncing my leg to satisfy my need to get up and do something that actually matters right now. Like snatch the microphone outta Monica's hand and tell everyone to get in their cars so we can start looking for Jordan. Sitting here crying isn't doing anything.

After a long speech, Monica leaves a letter for Katia in her casket and then screams how sorry she is. Clarice only has a split second to catch her as Monica passes out. She misses and there's a loud thump as Monica's head hits the floor. Two more ushers rush to tend to her. About six more people pass out, and you gotta give it to the ushers, they are *on* it, making sure nobody dies on their watch.

"Beau, baby, do you need a tissue?" Aunt Pepper asks from

the pew behind me. She's back to her senses after her fainting spell, but her eyes are bloodshot.

"I'm fine." Katia's funeral is just *one* day for her, for everybody here. But for me, it's for the rest of my life. When I get out of bed in the morning, when I go to sleep at night, Katia will always be dead. This is forever.

The knot in my stomach tenses when I hear the opening notes of R. Kelly's "I Wish" playing from the sound system. Mr. Warshire, the funeral home director, motions to our family. My parents, aunties, uncles, and cousins all gather around the casket, one hand each on the lid. Mr. Warshire slowly and gently folds the white ruffled blanket over Katia, as if she and the damn ruffled blanket aren't going to be shoved into an inferno once this show is over.

Momma starts howling from the deepest pit of her lungs as the lid makes it midway.

"Oh my god, not my baby! Katiaaaa! Please lord please please lord!"

She's straining against Aunt Pepper and Uncle Kolby, who are the only things stopping her from climbing inside the casket with Katia. She wants to be dead with her.

This is my last chance. If I don't look now, I won't get to see her ever again. After this, Katia will be cremated and all we'll have left of her is a bag of ashes.

I do it quick. I look down at her and then look back up at the lid.

I instantly regret it.

She's bloated, ten shades darker, and her chin is touching her chest like she doesn't have a neck. Or like they stuffed her full of tissue paper. They've draped her in a thick white net and placed a lacy pillow over the side of her face where the bullet tore through.

This isn't Katia, I tell myself as the lid is about to close. *This is NOT your sister.* I don't want it to be her. She looks disfigured and broken, but this *is* Katia and she's lying still in her casket not doing anything as we press the lid closed on her forever.

———

I stay in my pew until the chapel empties out and the funeral home director wheels the casket away to the dark place in the back where they incinerate people's big sisters. When the police officers lingering near the door finally leave, I accept that Jordan's not coming.

"Miss?"

I jump out of my seat when I feel a hand touch my shoulder, but it's only Mr. Warshire in his navy-blue funeral suit and the tackiest red bow tie I've ever seen. "Sorry, I didn't mean to frighten you. Do you need help carrying the arrangements to your car?"

He motions toward the big pink and blue flower arrangements that rested on top of and beside the casket.

"Um . . . actually is there any way you could donate them or something? We don't really have space for them," I say. Even if we'd had the space, who would want funeral flowers just sitting around reminding you?

"Absolutely, miss," Mr. Warshire says. "Is there anything else I can do for you?"

"No, but thanks."

Once he's walked away, I start sifting through the floral

arrangements, just in case there's any cards or something. Then I notice something that wasn't there at the beginning of the service. A baby-blue teddy bear holding a single red rose with a piece of paper rubber-banded around the stem.

I slide the note off and unfold it. It says:

FOR MY BABY GIRL, KATIA.
LOVE, YOUR FOREVER, JORDAN.

CHAPTER 2

BEFORE

RAIN FROM THE THUNDERSTORM OUTSIDE POUNDED against our window the night Katia told me she was running away. She was sixteen and I had just turned ten. I was standing in the middle of our dark bedroom, silent tears rolling down my face as Katia shoved clothes into her gym bag. The clock on the wall read 2:37 A.M.

"Would you go back to bed already?" she whispered over her shoulder. She had her micros tied in a high pony and she was wearing her black jacket with the knockoff designer logo on the chest.

"Why—are—you—leaving?" I choked out between sobs.

Katia pulled the strap of her purple gym bag over her head and across her shoulder.

She knelt down in front of me and took both my hands in hers.

"Because I have to, Bozo."

"Where are you going?" I tried to do everything Katia did back then. I wanted to wear my hair like her, dress like her. Sometimes I even ate the same food she did, even if it was nasty. But if Katia left, what was I supposed to do by myself?

"I'm just going for a walk," she said, looking from me to the door like Mom or Dad might bust in and catch us awake.

"Tell me where you're going."

"I don't have to tell you shit. You're just a kid, go back to bed."

"Katia, tell me!" I whined.

She clamped her hand over my mouth and told me to be quiet.

"See? That's why I can't tell you anything. I haven't even left and you already about to wake the whole damn house up."

"Just let me come. I promise I won't annoy you or anything!" I said, bouncing on my toes.

"I said no," she said, standing. She lifted up our bedroom window as the rain outside sprayed her face.

I was right behind her.

"If you don't let me come, I'm telling Momma and Daddy right now," I threatened.

"Ask me if I give two fucks," she shot back, swinging one leg out of the window.

"Then I'll tell Momma you stole that twenty dollars out her purse the other day."

Katia sat still on the windowsill, half in and half out of our room, and looked at me like she wished I didn't exist. After a full minute of staring me down, she asked me a question.

"How much birthday money do you have left?"

It wasn't enough to buy two bus tickets to New York, where Aunt Pepper lived and said we were always welcome. It wasn't enough to buy a bus ticket anywhere. Instead, we walked the dark streets of the South Side and caught three trains to the outskirts of some suburb we'd never been to.

On one train, a white nurse wearing pink scrubs, sitting across from us and looking dead tired, asked us what we were doing out at this time of night.

"This is my daughter. We're going to visit her father in prison," Katia said sarcastically. The lady's eyes went wide but she dropped it and didn't speak to us again.

I was terrified but mostly excited. I loved being out at night because Momma and Daddy never let us out the house after dark. They were afraid something bad would happen to us, but the nighttime was the best part of the day. No crowds, no loud talking and yelling, no crying babies, no school. But it was also the scariest time of day, where dark parks and black storefront windows hid monsters and perverts.

I knew Katia wouldn't let anything happen to me though. She knew Momma and Daddy would put her on punishment if she ever did.

"I'm hungry," I said as we walked down a street lined with bars and liquor stores. We were soaking wet, and it was only getting colder outside.

"I am, too, kinda. Let's stop up at this place here," Katia decided.

An old-fashioned restaurant was just up the road and looked like the only place open twenty-four hours. As Katia walked through the parking lot to the door, I almost tripped over something hard.

"This brick musta came off the building somewhere," I said, picking it up.

Katia held the door open and rolled her eyes. "Who cares, hurry up and get in here."

I walked toward the open door and that's when I saw it, a gap in the bricks just outside the glass door.

"Wait! I think it goes here!" I lined the edges up and pushed the brick into the empty spot. A perfect fit. Just as I finished, Katia grabbed me by the arm and yanked me inside.

Rosie's Diner was the coolest place I'd ever been to. There was a light-up sign outside with the name on it in hot-pink light-up wire letters. Inside, all the booths and tables were baby pink and baby blue, while the floor was black-and-white checker patterned. A jukebox changed colors and blasted sixties tunes in the back.

"Can we sit here?" I asked, scooting into the closest booth and picking up a polka-dot menu.

"Whatever," Katia muttered, looking around and drumming her fingernails on the table. She seemed nervous.

A skinny white lady with a blond beehive hairdo and a baby-pink dress came over to take our orders. I asked her if she was Rosie and she said Rosie had died ten years ago. We ordered cheeseburgers, fries, and two strawberry milkshakes. The waitress didn't ask what we were doing out so late, but she did ask if we had money.

"Duh, we have money. Why would we sit down and order food if we didn't?" Katia snapped. The waitress apologized and went to put our orders in.

"You think Momma and Daddy called the police yet?" I asked.

"I doubt it." She took out her pink lip balm and rubbed it across her mouth.

"Why did you wanna go see Aunt Pepper anyway?"

"I dunno. I was going so I could have somewhere to go," she said. As if that made any sense.

The waitress brought our food out and told us to enjoy. I bit into my burger and grease spilled down my chin and onto my green jacket.

"Dammit, Beau, just take the fucking jacket off before you get food all over it," Katia barked.

I took it off and gave it to her to stuff into her gym bag. She ate a few fries, but mostly she just looked out the window where every few minutes a car would pass by. She liked to do that a lot, watch other people or stare off into space like she could just think about it and she'd be somewhere else.

"How come you don't want to live at home? Momma and Daddy aren't that bad. I know kids whose parents beat them and don't buy food to eat," I argued.

"It's not them I wanna get away from," Katia explained.

"Is it me?"

"If it was, do you think I would have brought your annoying ass with me?"

I ate the cherry off my milkshake and tied the stem into a knot. "Yeah, if you were trying to kill me and go home and be the only child again."

Katia looked at me and then she busted out laughing. "You watch too much dang TV. It's not you I wanna get away from either. It's Grady Park."

"It's not that bad," I said. I didn't really have much to compare it to, but it seemed fine to me.

"Yeah, exactly."

"Huh?"

Katia shrugged. "Let's say you have two friends. One is amazing. The other is 'not that bad.' But you're only allowed to have one friend. Which one are you going to choose?"

I put my French fry down and tried to think hard. Katia rarely tried to explain things to me, so I knew it was important that I give her the right answer, make her think I was just as smart as she was.

Eventually, I came up with an answer. "I'd be friends with one for one week and then the other for the next week. We'd just switch, so I'd be friends with both of them but not at the same time."

Katia just rolled her eyes, and I knew I'd blown it.

"Just forget it, Beau," she said. "One day, you'll be my age and you'll understand exactly what I'm talking about. Hopefully I'll be long fucking gone by then."

I hoped she wouldn't be.

After I finished my burger, we counted what was left of our money. We had enough to either catch the three trains back home or order more food to pig out on and call Momma and Daddy to pick us up. The only reason I wasn't scared of getting in trouble was because Katia didn't seem scared. We were going to be okay. I knew that at least.

"I'm cool with whatever you wanna do," I said.

Katia gave me a funny look, like maybe she liked me after all. She stood up in the booth and flagged the waitress down behind the counter.

"Hey, waitress! Can I get two more cheeseburgers and fries over here? And cake!"

The waitress looked annoyed to be beckoned to like a servant. She took her hand off her hip and pulled out her notepad.

"What kinda cake y'all want?"

"Uhhh . . . whatever kinds y'all have!"

Our waitress sighed. "We have seven different kinds."

"Okay, gimme, uh, two of each!"

She looked at Katia like she was nuts. "Sweetheart, that's *fourteen* pieces of cake. Our slices are big, too. You sure you want all those?"

Katia looked at me for assurance, as if she even had to ask.

"Yeah, we want 'em all," she replied.

CHAPTER 3

I'M STILL STANDING WITH THE NOTE AND STUFFED bear in my hand, reading it over and over to make sure it's legit. Because if it is, that means Jordan was here today. We were in the same building, and I had no idea. How could I have missed him?

I hear the doors to the chapel creak open again and my old friend Breon sticks her head through the door.

"Hey, Beau. I was waiting for you to come out. I need to talk to you," she says, stepping into the chapel and shoving her hands in the pockets of her black cargo jeans. Not exactly funeral attire, but I give her a break because she's wearing one of those fake tuxedo shirts and it doesn't look bad.

Breon walks up to me, stares at the bear and note in my hand.

"Cute bear," she says.

"I think it's from Jordan. He signed his name," I say in disbelief.

"Really? He was here? I didn't see him."

"Yeah, me either. But he must have came in at some point, right?"

Breon tucks a curl behind her ear. "Maybe. Or he could have gave it to someone else and they brought it for him."

"I guess that's true . . . Anyway, you said you needed to talk to me?"

I invited her, but Breon and I haven't been friends in over a year. She still lives in the building across from mine and I see her around a lot, but we don't kick it like we used to.

"I was just gonna say I'm really sorry for what happened to Katia. I'm around or whatever, if you needed to talk or anything. Only if you want to, obviously."

I open my mouth to respond, but a voice replies for me.

"Hell no, that's what I'm here for," Deja says, entering the chapel and standing next to me like a bodyguard.

Breon groans in annoyance. "Deja, don't you get tired of being in everybody else's business?"

"Actually, I do. I wanna be more like you, doing nothing on the street all day. Now if you don't mind, me and *my* best friend would like a little privacy."

Breon turns to me, thinking I'll step in and say something to shut Deja up. But I don't have the energy to worry about these two on top of Jordan.

"Fine, whatever," Breon says. She gives Deja a cold glare before leaving through the chapel doors.

"Was she bothering you?" Deja asks.

"Nah, it's fine."

"Are you sure? Because if she doesn't know by now that our friendship is dead—"

"Deja. It's fine."

Sometimes it's hard to believe the three of us used to be best friends. We'd still be best friends today if Breon hadn't switched up on us. It was crazy how it happened. One day she was a straight A, Goody Two-shoes obsessing about being eighth-grade valedictorian, and the next day it was like she'd been possessed by Lil Wayne. Partying, drinking lean, showing up to school high off her ass. I think we could have dealt with all that if it hadn't been for the stealing.

"I don't know why she even showed up," Deja sneers.

"She knew Katia, too."

"Did you invite her?" Deja asks.

"What? Hell nah."

But I did invite Breon. It was stupid, but I'd been secretly wishing for that magical moment when the three of us all got so overwhelmed with sadness that we said fuck the past and started being best friends again. I should have known that was never going to happen.

"What's this?" Deja takes the note from my hands and reads it. "Where did you find this?"

"Under a bunch of flowers. Did you see Jordan come in or leave?"

She shakes her head. "No. He can't show his face in Grady Park with the Onyx Tigers after him."

"What do they want with him?"

"I dunno too much, but I heard some people saying that he was stealing money from the OTs. They didn't figure it out 'til he went missing, but they're gunnin' for his ass now."

This is bad. The Onyx Tiger name is attached to almost every homicide on this side of the city. There's a couple of them who live in Building A, their blue-and-orange bandanas a sign for the rest of us to get back inside before something pops off and we get caught in the middle.

"They're gonna kill him?" I ask.

Deja shrugs. "Hopefully. He doesn't deserve to live after what he did to Katia."

"But they can't do that!" I shout. If Jordan dies, I'll never know what really happened that night. I wanna believe Katia didn't do anything wrong, but I have to know for sure. I need proof.

"What are you talking about? You *don't* want Jordan dead?"

I open my mouth and then shut it. We need Jordan alive to find out the truth, but after that? I don't give a shit what the OTs do to him. But it's not like I can walk up to them and ask, *Hey, I need one of your opps to testify in court. Do you mind waiting to murder his ass till after the trial?*

"I don't care if they kill him," I say, "but he's the only one who was there that night besides the lying ass cop. He obviously knows something, and we need to find—"

Deja holds up a perfectly manicured hand. "Hol' up. Ain't no *we* in this. Now you know I'm the first one ready to jump up and box a hoe but playin' with the OTs is playin' wit your life. I'm not interfering with shit they got goin' on, and neither are you."

"We're not interfering by asking him some questions."

"But that's not all you want. You want him to go to the police about it so they can charge that cop, but I'm tellin' you, it's not gonna go down like that. You know people don't fuck wit Five-O. Especially not Jordan," Deja says.

"But this is different! I'm not asking him to snitch on anybody except the cop. If we find Jordan, I can get through to him. I can get him to tell the truth."

Deja throws her hands up. "No, you can't! You think you can, but you can't. If Jordan wanted to be honest, he wouldn't have ran that night. So why do you think talking to him is gonna change his mind?"

I hold up the stuffed bear in my hand. "This. Maybe he wasn't the one to leave it here, but I know it's from Jordan."

"So?"

"So this means he's probably feeling guilty or something. And if he's feeling guilty, he just needs someone to push him into doing the right thing." Katia was my sister. Everybody else feels bad for me, maybe Jordan would, too, and then tell me what I need to know. If that doesn't work, maybe I can bribe him with something.

Deja blinks. "The right thing? Do you really wanna spend the rest of your life ducking and dodging the OTs? Because that's what'll happen if we even think about interfering," she warns.

The code in the hood is that you mind your business at all times. But hood rules don't matter to me anymore.

"Deja, everybody thinks Katia was trying to break into that man's house. You didn't notice some of the people looking at us all sideways today? The police need to know that Katia didn't do anything wrong!"

"Why? Since when have the police ever given a fuck about what's true or who's innocent? Babe, I know you're upset. I know it hurts, I do. But you need to leave this Jordan thing alone. I'm not about to be going to your funeral next. I can't," Deja says.

But I'm doing this for Katia. She doesn't deserve for the

world to remember her as a criminal if she didn't do anything. We need Jordan's testimony, and that means I have to find him. By any means necessary.

"Deja, I can't—"

"I'm not asking you, Beau, I'm telling you. Not just for your own safety but for mine, your parents', your aunties and uncles. If you're in danger, we're all in danger, too. We can figure out another way to do this. Just promise me you won't say a word about him to anyone else."

She doesn't realize she's basically asking me to give up on Katia. Which I'll never do. But there's no changing Deja's mind when she gets like this. Plus, I'm gettin' tired of arguing with her. She doesn't have a sister, so there's no way she could really understand what I'm feeling anyway.

"Fine. I promise," I say.

"Thank God." She pulls me close, and I rest my head on her shoulder. "I know this is hard but it's all gonna be okay in the end, boo, I promise."

She's right. It's all going to be okay in the end.

Because I'm *not* going to stop looking for Jordan.

CHAPTER 4

THE GREEN TEA FRAPPUCCINO FROM STARBUCKS is so sweet my teeth ache a little with each sip.

"They don't have the thread I like," Deja says, looking at the store's massive collection. Two days after the memorial, we're at Beauty Supply Queen, a store as big as Target but filled with mostly haircare products and cheap clothes. About a million packs of weave cover the fifteen-foot-high walls, yaki, remy, virgin, Brazilian, Chinese, Mongolian. The floor of the store is divided into sections, wigs and lace fronts, shampoo and conditioners, holding gels, grease and oils, and then the section we're in, hair tools.

"Just get anything. They all look the same," I say.

"They don't all work the same. Choosing the wrong brand could be the difference between your weave looking like Blac Chyna's and having one of your tracks slip out on live television."

I hold my hands up in surrender. "In that case, take all the time you need, girl."

Deja is an expert weavologist and the only person I trust with my hair. I haven't been worried about my head too much lately with everything else going on, but I know I can't be at the press conference looking jacked up.

I'm not excited about the press conference or being on TV at all, but as long as we keep talking about Katia, as long as there are candlelight vigils and spray-painted T-shirts, it's like she's not fully gone.

Deja picks up a package of fire engine–red Jamaican curl hair and starts to read the label on the back. She loves wild colors and anything that sparkles or shines. Now that the funeral is over, she's back to her usual over-the-top outfits. Today she's wearing bright yellow Timberland boots with matching waist-high biker shorts and a cropped tee that says "Barbie" in pink lettering. Her hair is split into two honey-blond ponytails that drape past her hips and swing just above her knees. Strangers in the store keep staring at us because my best friend is just that glamorous, like a supermodel.

"You may as well put that hair back on the shelf. You know my mom doesn't let me do colored hair," I say.

Deja sighs and puts the pack on the hook.

"I know, I just thought maybe she'd bend the rules a little now."

"I wish. If anything, it's the opposite. She watches me like a hawk. Last night, she opened my bedroom door and just stood there for, like, ten minutes."

"Did she say anything?"

"No. I think she thought I was asleep." I don't tell Deja that

I haven't really been sleeping. Ever since Katia died, it's like no matter what position I lie in, I can never get comfortable. So I face Katia's bed and imagine her sleeping in it.

Deja is my best friend, but I don't wanna lay this heaviness on her. Besides, being outside in the sunlight today, Deja driving with her sunroof open and the warm wind whipping my face, I almost feel alive. I almost feel back to normal.

Once Deja picks out a needle and thread, we wander over to the clothes section. We look at cheap joggers with emojis printed on them, neon dresses with the sides cut out and stitched back together with titanium loops, and ugly belts covered in pink rhinestones.

"You want anything else out of here? These shorts are kinda cute," Deja says.

"Can't. Daddy only gave me enough for the hair."

"Pssh, girl, didn't nobody ask you what you had, I asked what you wanted." She opens her emerald-green Gucci clutch and pulls a fat wad of money out.

"Really, D, I don't need anything. But thanks."

She shrugs and puts her cash away. Deja would never call herself a sugar baby, but that's what she is. It's how she and her momma pay the bills. I've only ever met one of Deja's clients, this old dude named Casey who looks like Carl Winslow to me. But he's loaded and makes sure she never wants for anything. I don't ask what she does for him. I don't wanna know.

We're walking to the front of the store with four packs of 1B when we almost crash straight into this tall dude.

"Damn, don't you see us walkin' here, dumbass?!" Deja shouts, smacking his arm with a pack of hair.

"Sorry, my bad. Oh, hey, bighead." I know that warm and luscious voice. Champion.

"Hey, what's up?" I ask as Deja winks at me and goes up to the counter to pay. I haven't talked to Champion since before the memorial.

"Nothin' really. Still in training for basketball."

"That's cool, that's cool," I say, shifting side to side under the stare of his hazel-flecked eyes. I was shocked when he first sent one of his boys to ask me if I was going out with anybody. But then I went home and really looked at myself in the mirror and saw it. I'm starting to look more like Katia. I'm not gonna say I look like Tyra Banks now or nothin', but I'm definitely not a Clarice.

"Yeah, it's aight. Get bored of doin' the same thing all the time, but it's not too bad."

Everything's all screwed up between me and Champion because I'm the girl with the murdered sister. Neither of us says it, but if he asked me to be his girl now, everyone would think it's because he feels sorry for me.

"How you holdin' up?" he asks. Everybody asks. But Champion doesn't ask me like he's asking for the weather, like it's just something to talk about. He asks me like he cares, and the way his brow furrows, I can tell he wants to know the truth.

"I'm not sure? I mean, not good. It's not good at all," I say because this is the best way I can explain it when he's staring at me and turning my insides to liquid.

"I figured. If you ever need to talk to someone, someone who's not your family, and not ol' motor mouth over there, you can text or call me. Anytime. I'll come get you and we can chill or somethin'."

"Yeah, that'd be cool."

We stand there smiling at each other awkwardly and then make our way up to the front of the store. Deja's already outside with the hair in a bag. She agrees to give Champion a ride home, and I almost die at the thought of riding in a car with him.

We've only been on the road a few minutes when suddenly Deja jerks the wheel hard to the right and the car jumps a curb and almost rams into a group of girls walking on the sidewalk.

"Deja, what the hell?!" I shout, rubbing a spot on my knee where it slammed up into the dash.

"That bitch Tatyana!" she shouts. Meanwhile, the group of girls she almost ran over start banging on the hood of the car. I recognize them from around the way. We got into it back around Valentine's Day last year because Tatyana's boyfriend had given Deja a necklace. It was a big brawl that ended with us all being banned from the mall.

Before I can stop her, Deja snatches the keys out of the ignition and leaps out of the car like a tiger approaching its kill.

"Oh damn!" Champion says from the back seat, clearly more stunned than I am, because this isn't the first time I've seen Deja start a fight at the drop of a dime.

It's the fire that lives deep inside all us Grady Park girls. Even me. When you see a chick that's disrespected you or your family, it's on sight, meaning you knock her ass out the next time you see her, no matter where it is, what time, or who she's with.

"You stupid ass bitch!" somebody screams.

Deja jumps onto a girl with red jumbo twists, and they fall onto the sidewalk. People hear the shouts and start coming out of a nearby barbershop and hoagie joint to form a circle around the mayhem.

I don't even look back at Champion before I'm out of the car and shoving my way through the circle of spectators. When my bestie needs me, I'm there, no questions asked.

But she doesn't need my help. Deja is straddling the poor girl and backhanding her across the face over and over. Beneath her the girl is shouting something, and a bunch of people with their phones out are screaming "WORLDSTAR!" like they always do.

I start to move away and stand off to the side to let Deja get it all out of her system, but then I remember what the lawyer told Momma and Daddy when they first met with her. If we want a fair trial, we can't give anyone a reason to think less of us. The last thing I need right now is to get arrested.

I try to wrestle Deja off the girl but she's not Deja when she fights. She's like a killing machine, and she doesn't even recognize me.

"Let me do it," Champion says from behind me, and he steps over the tangle of brown limbs and hair with his long legs. He squeezes Deja's arms tight to her sides while she's screaming and guides her back toward the car. If he lets her go, she'll be right back on top of that girl. Finally free, the chick she was pummeling stands up, one eyelash strip on her cheek and her hair looking like it got swept up in a tornado.

"Ahahaha! You mad or nah?! You mad or nah?!" Even though she probably would have died if Champion wasn't there, she has to keep taunting Deja because she's being recorded. We all are. Only my focus is to get us the hell out of here before the cops come.

"Bitch, I'll kill you! I'll slice your fucking head clean off! Stankin' ass bitch!" Deja shouts as Champion tries to force her into the back seat of her car. One of her boobs has popped out of her shirt and I pop it back in before anyone gets a photo of it.

Deja is way too heated to drive, so I take her keys and agree to give Champion a ride since he doesn't live too far. There's nothing romantic about it, though, because the whole time, Rocky Balboa is in the back seat talking shit about the fight.

"Sorry about all this," I say to Champion while Deja is going off in the background.

"It's okay. It gets real out here, I know."

Truth is, he doesn't know the half of it. I don't want him to.

Ten minutes of awkward silence later, I drop Champion off at his house in Purple Hills. It's more like a McMansion with golden gates around the property and huge shrubs cut into the shapes of exotic animals. His dad is a corporate lawyer, and his mom stays home to raise Champion and his sister. I've never met them, but based on conversations with Champion, they do things like vacation in Aspen and visit their second house in Hawaii during the summer.

After he's gone inside, I bang my head against the steering wheel a few times.

"Aye, watch my car," Deja says from the back seat. I want to strangle her.

"What is wrong with you?" I ask, turning around in my seat. We're about to graduate in another year and she's always in some drama. I love her crazy ass to death, but I don't wanna be in my seventies at the retirement home tryna get her to let the poor nurse's hair go.

"Nothing's wrong with me. I'm just not a punk-ass bitch. Tired of people talkin' shit all the time."

"When are girls not talking shit? Today wasn't the place or

the time. You might have just screwed things up with me and Champion!"

"Not even. That boy is sprung off you in the worst way."

"I still don't want him thinking this is what we do every day. Like we're hoodrats or something."

"Girl, we are hoodrats. At least to everybody outside the hood. Here, let's do the hoodrat test. Do you live in the projects?"

"Yeah," I reply.

"Okay then, you a hoodrat," Deja declares.

"Bullshit! You can live in the projects and not be a hoodrat," I say.

"Whatever you say, girl."

I don't feel like arguing with her hardheaded self anymore, so I pull away from the curb and head back to the potholed streets of Grady Park.

Katia never really liked Deja. She said if I kept hanging around her, she'd only drag me down with her. Now I'm starting to see what she meant. Chaos follows Deja like a shadow, and if I'm next to her, I get sucked in right along with her. If I'm gonna stay friends with Deja, she has to make some big changes. And soon.

CHAPTER 5

"YOU SURE YOU WANNA GO ON TV WITH A BASEBALL cap on? At least take one of my old phony ponies so it can look like you got some hair underneath," Deja says, a carton of fries in her hand as I'm getting ready to head back to my building.

"I *do* have hair underneath! It just needs some TLC, that's all," I say, tugging the red-and-white hat down farther on my forehead. "If you hadn't started that fight, maybe we woulda had time for you to do my hair like you were supposed to."

Deja frowns. "Damn, I said I was sorry! Just come by tomorrow, I'll hook you up." She opens the door for me, and I'm halfway down her walkway to the sidewalk when I turn back.

"Hey, y'all are coming tonight, right? To the press conference?" I have this scary thought that it'll just be my family, Ms. Anniston, and a bunch of cameras in the middle of our courtyard. The funeral's over. Maybe everybody else is over Katia, too.

Deja looks at me like I'm crazy. "Duh, we're coming. Everybody in Grady Park is gonna be there. Anybody who doesn't show up is getting a personal ass whooping from me. Stop worrying, okay?"

I sigh. "Okay, yeah. You're right. I'll see you in a couple hours, okay?"

We wave goodbye and I take my time walking back to my unit. The sun dips below the top of Building C. The courtyard where we're holding the press conference is empty, save for a few tricycles and baby toys. An old man is outside flipping meat on his tiny charcoal grill. It smells good and I wish I could eat. The dealers are posted at their corners, as always, like black crows keeping watch over the projects. Orange-and-blue bandanas drape from their back pockets and some of them watch me. Onyx Tigers.

Deja and Sonnet are the only people I've talked to about Jordan. There's no way they know I'm looking for him. Still, I break into a jog, turning around to make sure nobody's tryna sneak me from behind.

I jog the rest of the way to my door, and when I arrive, I'm panting hard. After Deja's WWE match today, I'm exhausted. The bags under my eyes feel like they're filled with stones and I just wanna fall into my bed. *Sleep, I need sleep.* But I can see from the front window that I won't be getting any of that right now.

Inside, my entire family has squished themselves onto couches, stools, chairs, and even some bean bags that someone must have brought with them. There's my mom's sister, Aunt Pepper; her brothers, Uncle Kevin and Uncle Kolby; their wives, Nisha and Rachel; my dad's siblings, Aunt Alice, Aunt Amber, and Aunt

Andrea; at least four people I don't recognize who must know my parents from work or something, and all ten of my little cousins.

I'm dumb enough to try to make a beeline for my bedroom, but then I have to hug and kiss everyone in the room at least five times and assure them I'm doing okay and saying my prayers to the lord every night. I love my cousins and aunts and uncles, but they didn't lose Katia in the same way me and my parents did. Family holiday parties will be different for them. But every morning I wake up for the rest of my life, Katia's not going to be in the bed across from me. There's nothing they can do to make me feel better. There's nothing anyone can do. I just wish I could hide somewhere until this is all over.

"Here, baby, eat you some food," Aunt Nisha says. The kitchen table and counters are covered with foil trays of baby back ribs, French fries, potato salad, gizzards, rib tips, and sweet potato pies. To make everybody happy, I fix myself a big heaping plate of delicious food I know I can't eat. They all stare at me like I'm some interactive art exhibit, and a few people sniffle and whisper to each other.

Momma and Daddy are in the corner of the kitchen whispering angrily, arguing yet again. When they see me with my plate of food, they stop to smile at me. Then the moment passes, and they go back to arguing. I slip out of the kitchen and speed walk to my bedroom where I know I still won't get to be alone.

All the kids have been shoved into me and Katia's bedroom so they can "stay out of grown folks' business." There's toys all over the floor where the younger kids are playing, while the older ones are camped out with their phones and iPads on the beds.

My ten-year-old cousin Elina is sitting at my desk with the lamp on and she's got my sketch of Katia laid out in front of her.

"What the hell are you doing?!" I snap. I tiptoe over the toys on the floor and put my plate of food down on the vanity.

Elina looks up at me with wide doe-brown eyes behind her thick black glasses. I snatch the portrait from out in front of her and instantly feel like an asshole. She hasn't colored or spilled on it; she was just looking.

"Sorry, Beau, I was just trying to see if you had any paper I could draw on. I wasn't gonna mess it up," she says.

"The blank paper is in the top drawer." I pull out a few sheets for her and a pack of colored pencils, the kind I used before I upgraded to the professional ones.

"Thank you," Elina says, smiling up at me with a mouth full of silver braces. I sit down on the edge of my desk and watch her draw a purple-and-green zebra. She needs help with the angles of the legs, so I show her how to make them look realistic.

Elina's little sisters start fighting over a Doc McStuffins coloring book, and they wail like sirens until their mother comes in and glares at them.

"I wish I was an only child," Elina whispers to me with an eye roll.

Then it dawns on me that *I'm* an only child now. It feels scary to think about because there's always been two of us, me and Katia. Even in our home movies when we were babies, any time Katia is in the shot, I am, too. Daddy said I was so obsessed with her as a toddler that I'd follow her around the house all the time. Now that she's gone, it's like I don't know who I'm supposed to be anymore. I don't know where I'm supposed to go.

By the time Ms. Anniston has arrived and finished her pep

talk of dos and don'ts for the press conference, we're all ready to get out of the tiny, cramped space. When we step outside, I breathe a sigh of relief. Not just to be out of the apartment but because there's an enormous crowd gathered in the courtyard of the complex. They're wearing different shades of blue and holding white tea candles, the flames dancing in the wind.

They haven't forgotten about Katia. They haven't forgotten about me and my family. Maybe I do have some people I can count on after all.

Deja waves at me from the crowd. Her momma's here, too. So are the Roblesons, Breon, Mr. Garland, the elderly women who live in Building 7 and pay kids to bring their groceries from their car, our other next-door neighbor Tasha (who we don't really like) and her three kids. There's even some white people in orange fleece pullovers that read "Dave's Pharmacy." Katia's coworkers. My breath catches in my throat when I see Champion's here, too, wearing a baby-blue Tar Heels jersey and matching Jordans. Next to him is Sonnet, in dark blue warm-ups with her hair in a big poofy bun.

Ms. Anniston leads the way through to the front of the crowd, who part to make a path for us. People reach out and grip our shoulders, pat us on the backs, fan some of us who are already in tears. A girl shouts out "WE LOVE YOU, KATIA!" Somebody tells her to hush.

At the front of the courtyard are big lights and at least seven different news station reporters and cameras.

It's surreal to see all of this happening here. The courtyard of the Grady Park projects is where people fight and get arrested. It's usually littered with chip bags, Black 'N Mild butts, and dirty toys, but someone must have came and cleaned it all up.

Me, Momma, and Daddy stand next to Ms. Anniston, and the rest of our family stands behind us. If a reporter asks a question about the case, we have to defer to Ms. Anniston. *Saying too much could come back to bite us in the ass in court*, she'd told us.

Momma tells a funny story about how Katia burned the crescent rolls last Thanksgiving and kept going out to the store to buy more until she got it right. Daddy talks about the time he taught Katia how to drive when she was fifteen.

When it's my turn at the mic, I freeze for a second. There's bright camera lights in my face and I can hardly even make out the crowd. But Daddy nudges me, and I read what I wrote on my index card, keeping my head down so no one can see me crying. I talk about how Katia wanted to be a pharmacist and make enough money to help our parents.

When the press conference ends, there isn't a dry eye in the courtyard. Everybody mills around talking while the news station people gather their things with a quickness to hurry up and get out of here. Ms. Anniston stands off to the side of the makeshift podium with my parents, a worried look on her face as her eyes dart from me to them and back. Daddy looks normal but Momma looks like she's seen a ghost. She's clutching at her chest. When Daddy notices me looking, he leans down close to Momma's ear and suddenly she stops clutching herself and turns away.

Something else bad happened. I don't know what, but the look on Momma's face is almost like how she looked when we walked into the morgue that night, like she doesn't know where she is or why. My parents try to wave me over, but I turn away. I can't handle any more bad news.

I'm squeezing through the crowd, thanking people for coming but really looking for Champion, when I see him. Not Champion but *him*.

Standing across the street in front of the #5 bus shelter. He's wearing a black hoodie, black shorts, and long compression pants. The orange glow of a cigarette illuminates his face. It's not a dream and it's not a hallucination.

It's Jordan.

I start shoving my way through the crowd, ignoring all the weird looks people give me. Sonnet sees me and I don't have to say a word before she's bolting after me. When I finally get free of the crowd and make it to the sidewalk, there's traffic coming in both directions. I wait for a semitruck to pass and then I make a dash for it.

I've got nothing on me but my cell phone, not even pepper spray. This might be dangerous, approaching a dude on the run from the law. Only I don't really care what happens to me now.

But when I get across the street to the bus shelter, there's no one there. Just the smoking end of a lit cigarette.

CHAPTER 6

TWO DAYS AFTER THE PRESS CONFERENCE, MOMMA and Daddy are still going at it. Over stupid little things, like Daddy forgetting to take the trash out for pickup. It's Monday, my first day back at school. Lying in Katia's bed, I can hear Momma and Daddy in the front room start a fresh round of arguing over a bill. Which really isn't too different from our usual Monday mornings.

But everything else today is going to be different, harder. I walk into the small bathroom we share, reach for my toothbrush and stop midway. Katia's blue toothbrush is sitting next to mine in the pink cup beside the sink. She'll never use it again. I pick it up, step on the pedal of our tiny tin trash can. I hold the toothbrush over the can, but then I toss it under the sink instead.

I hop into the shower and Katia's there, too. Her Night Blooming Jasmine bodywash is anyway. The one she told me not to touch because she bought it with her own money. I can use it to clean myself now. I can empty the whole bottle and watch it go down the drain and no one's gonna say anything to me about it. But I reach for the cheap white bar of soap I normally use, instead.

Once I've dried myself off, I slide the closet doors open and start searching for my favorite pair of black leggings, the ones that aren't see through. They're hidden behind Katia's cropped Adidas hoodie, the baby-blue cotton still as bright and wrinkle-free as the day she bought it. Dave's Pharmacy had a uniform, so she didn't get much wear out of her clothes until the weekend.

My fingers trace the white stripes that line the sleeve, the soft billowed cuffs. It's not that weird for me to wear Katia's clothes. Sisters share clothes all the time, so why should it be any different because one of them is dead?

I pull the hoodie over my head, careful not to frizz the shoulder-length crochet curls Deja installed on me last night. At least my hair is one thing I don't have to worry about for a while.

"Good morning," I say, walking through the front room and into the kitchen.

"Baby, do you need a ride to school?" Daddy asks.

I find a single Fruit Roll-Up in the pantry and tear into it. The sugar should keep me awake. All I did last night was toss and turn.

"You never drive me to school," I say.

My parents look at each other and I can tell they've been talking about me. Worrying.

"Today's not a regular day for any of us," Daddy starts. "It's just the three of us now. Maybe we need to change it up so we can spend more time together. I know you don't like riding the bus. And it's dangerous."

"So is Grady Park. I know you're worried about me freaking out at school but I'm fine. I'll be okay," I say, mustering up a weak smile.

Suddenly Momma bursts into tears and collapses onto the floor, her head pressed to the carpet as she hugs herself.

I look at Daddy, who gets down on the floor with her. "What'd I say?" I ask.

Daddy, rubbing small circles on Momma's back, shakes his head at me. "You didn't say anything, Beau. Your Momma and I are just struggling a lil this morning," he says, his own voice cracking.

If I stay in here any longer, I know I'll start crying, too. But I've been doing that nonstop for the past two weeks. I don't wanna cry anymore. I'm tired of it.

"I'm going to school," I say flatly as Daddy slowly helps Momma up and onto the couch. He sits down beside her, and she falls into his arms to sob even louder. I take my chance and escape through the front door.

There's no sun out this morning, just heavy gray clouds waiting to drench me. I love the smell of rain, but today it smells like dirt.

Last night, Ms. Anniston called to talk to us more about the charges being dropped, as if anything else mattered. As if the reason why mattered.

"Every case is different, but I hate to say this isn't uncommon when a case involves a police officer," she'd explained.

"What do we do next?" Daddy asked.

"We move forward with the wrongful death lawsuit against the city. I figured we might end up having to go this route, so I've already started preparing."

The lawyer tells us that we can file a lawsuit because Peter Johnson's actions led to Katia's death, which means he can be held responsible for all of the things we lost when she died. Since he worked for the Chicago Police Department, Ms. Anniston says the city is the one that will have to pay us for the hospital bills, funeral expenses, the money Katia would have made at her job if she was still alive to go to it. Momma and Daddy pulled themselves together enough to hash out some of the details, but we all know that money isn't gonna change anything. Nothing will, except a life sentence for Peter Johnson.

Thinking about him and how he gets to go home to his stupid ass family makes my stomach hurt. If our lives are gonna be fucked up forever, then his should be, too.

On the bus ride to school, I pop in my headphones and let Katie Got Bandz drown out everyone around me. It's my favorite track and my first time listening to it since Katia's service. Somehow it doesn't even sound the same as it did before. Or maybe my ears are damaged from all that hollering Aunt Pepper did at the funeral.

My heart is thumping in its cage when the bus lets me off at my stop. I have to cross the street to get to Millennium Magnet and I try to pump myself up on the way.

I can do this, I can do this.

I told Sonnet I was coming back today, and she promised to wait for me at my locker so I don't have to walk to class alone.

As I make my way through the crowded courtyard full of laughs and happiness and what looks like a fight somewhere over on the far end of the lawn, my thoughts keep running back to Katia. If she's somewhere we just can't see or if she's nowhere now.

A couple people give me strange looks when they see me, but maybe I just look depressed today. There's three thousand kids here. Most of them don't know me from any other Black girl.

I make it to the second floor, and seeing Sonnet leaned up against my locker in her purple tie-dye jumpsuit with her fro loose and draping over her eyes, I almost wanna cry. I told her she didn't have to wait for me because the bus is always late, but I'm glad she didn't listen.

"There you are! I was worried you'd changed your mind." She wraps me in a hug and squeezes me so hard I can feel her heart beating against mine. My throat gets tight, and a hard cry is waiting to burst out of me. Before it can, I pull away, cover my eyes with my forearm to press the tears back where they came from.

Sonnet rubs small slow circles on my back. "Just breathe. In through your nose and out through your mouth."

I know people are probably staring at me like I'm crazy, but it hurts too much for me to care.

When the moment passes, I take my arm away and try to pretend like it didn't happen. The hard part of today is out of the way at least. I made it. I'm here now.

"Here, drink this today." She pulls a purple water bottle out of the side of her backpack and hands it to me. "There was a full moon last night and Ma made a big batch of moon water just for you. I'll bring more tomorrow."

"What's moon water?" I ask, holding the bottle up.

"It's just tap water that's been blessed by the moon. We use it for drinking, cooking, cleaning, bathing. Ma said it'll help."

I take three big gulps. "Thanks. Now catch me up on art

class. What'd I miss? I know I've got two weeks of homework to make up."

"Just a bunch of art history lectures. I don't know why that has to be part of the class. Nobody takes art to read books, we wanna draw!" Sonnet complains.

"Right? But they can't call it school if it's fun, I guess."

"Well, the fun part of the class starts today. Ms. Kubler told me after class last Thursday that we get to paint a mural on the school!"

My ears perk up, and for a moment, I stop thinking about Katia. "Fuhreal? They're gonna let us paint it or just watch Ms. Kubler do it?" I've always wanted to paint a mural. When I was ten I wanted to paint a forest on my bedroom wall, but Momma wouldn't let me.

I grab my books out of my locker and we start toward the stairs to the fourth floor.

"We get to paint it! There's going to be a competition. We all have to present our ideas next week and then whoever gets the most votes wins. I'm already planning a piece entitled *Dick of Corn*."

I snort. "*Dick of Corn*? Like an actual penis?"

"Yes! It's going to be a statement on patriarchy in the Midwest."

"Ohhh." This is why I love having two best friends. Deja always wants to talk about dudes and drama. Sonnet talks about dicks of corn. Together, they make sure I have a healthy balance of hood and high art in my life.

"Well, if the winner of last year's art show doesn't think it's impressive, maybe I should change it," she says.

"Oh, shut up." She likes reminding me of the award I won

last year, as if I could forget. It's the first and only time I've ever won something for my drawings. It was a painting I did from one of Momma's old school photos.

When we walk into the bright art studio, the rest of the class is already seated at the circular tables. Our studio was just remodeled last year. The walls are bright purple with lime-green and orange geometric shapes. There's a big skylight above the area where we do our work so we can get natural light. We have a fully loaded supply station, too. We have pastels, charcoal, oil paint, brushes, easels, you name it. Real top-of-the-line stuff that professional artists use, too.

Ms. Kubler stands at the front of the class writing something on the whiteboard. She looks surprised when me and Sonnet take our usual seats at the back table near the window.

"Ms. Willet, a pleasure to have you back," she says, smiling.

"Thanks, Ms. Kubler," I say, sliding my backpack under the table as I perch on my stool.

Ms. Kubler's one of my favorite teachers, not just because she teaches art but because she's really nice and lets people slide if they turn something in a day or two late. She's a young Black woman but dresses like a seventy-year-old in penny loafers and Cosby sweaters. She probably doesn't think anyone takes her serious because of her age, but we do. We still would even if she didn't dress like somebody's nana.

"Back to the final project. This will be *one* mural to be approved by me and chosen by you. You can choose to work individually or with a partner, although groups of two or more will all receive the same grade, so choose wisely. On Monday, I want to see proposals on my desk. This includes a thorough workup of your idea and a one-page essay on why we should put it on our school."

"Oooh!" This one lacrosse player named Chris shoots his hand up in the air. "Let's do a *Walking Dead* mural! With walkers ripping somebody apart!"

"Your rationale?" Ms. Kubler asks.

"Because it's cool?"

Ms. Kubler raises an eyebrow. "You're going to have to think of something better than that, Chris. This mural will be on the side of Millennium Magnet forever. We need it to be something people will still care about fifty years from now."

"How about a homage to Black singers and artists? Like Nina Chanel Abney and Lauryn Hill," says a girl named Krina.

"Rationale?"

"Well, it *is* a school dedicated to the arts, so we should honor those who came before us."

"I like the way you think. Sounds like you all have some good ideas already. I want you to go home today and really think about it. Now, for today's class, we're going to be talking more about pointillism."

By the end of the period, I haven't come up with any ideas for the mural. My sketchbook is full of sketches of Grady Park, Deja, Sonnet. I think they're cool, but probably not something people will care about in fifty years. Hell, people don't care about us now.

As the class files out for next period, Ms. Kubler asks to speak to me for a minute. I tell Sonnet to go on without me.

"I heard about your sister. Please don't hesitate to let me know if there's anything I can do for you, Beau. I know it can't be easy losing a sibling," she says once the studio has emptied out. She sits on the edge of her desk, and I lean against one of the tables.

"I feel like shi—I mean, I feel like crap all the time. I just want it to be over," I say.

"I can understand that. When my father passed, we'd known for a while that it was coming. We had time to say goodbye, but it still hurt. Unfortunately, grief isn't something you can skip or work your way out of."

I shrug. "So you're basically saying I just have to suffer for the rest of my life?" If I'm going to feel like this forever, I don't know how I'll make it.

"You won't feel like this forever, I promise. But it's important to let yourself feel whatever it is you're feeling. If you bottle it up, you'll still have to deal with it sooner or later."

The door to the room opens and students in the next period start filing in. I say goodbye to Ms. Kubler and slip out into the hall.

As I head down to the first floor, I think of how Ms. Kubler is probably the only teacher who will talk to me about Katia. The rest of my teachers either don't know or don't care. Which is fine by me. I don't need their fake sympathy anyway. I sit through my classes like I would any other day, like I did before I had a dead sister.

After school, Sonnet invites me to her house. I know I should go home and check in with my folks, but I don't feel like being bothered with their arguing and crying.

Once we get off the bus, we cut through a path leading to a huge chunk of forest at the end of a cul-de-sac. A stone path lit by tea lights and surrounded by bright purple-and-blue-painted flower sculptures leads up a steep incline to the top of a hill. The back of my ankles ache as we climb higher and higher. You would think as many times as I've been here, I'd get used to the hike.

At the top of the hill sits a giant log cabin lit up bright yellow and orange from the lanterns inside. Sonnet's house is seriously something out of *Bridge to Terabithia*.

When I finally reach the porch, I'm nearly out of breath.

"Hello, Beau," says a woman's voice from inside. Sonnet's mom sits in the lotus position in the middle of their living room. I can barely see her because the smoke of all the incense and sage is so thick.

"Hi, Ms. Bluefall. How are you today?"

"Lovely, dear. Did Sonnet give you the moon water I sent for you this morning?"

"Yeah, she did. Thanks."

Sonnet and I set our bags near the door and Ms. Bluefall extinguishes the incense because she knows it makes me sneeze.

"I understand what a loss like this can do to a person," she says. "You're looking a little frail. If I send some of my spicy falafel, will you eat it tomorrow at lunch?"

I smile. "Sure, Ms. Bluefall."

Sonnet's mom has treated me like a daughter since the first day I met her at the start of sophomore year. She said I remind her of her family, which I can believe since me and her have the same enormous smile and skinny neck and arms. My own mother doesn't ask after me as much as Ms. Bluefall does. Sometimes I act like Sonnet, shrug and groan when she fusses over me, but secretly I always love it. She makes me feel like I'm not invisible.

"How are things at home?" she asks, rising from her meditation cushion like a freshly bloomed flower. Her afro is twice the size of Sonnet's and touches her shoulders. She wears red canvas overalls and no shoes on her feet.

"Things are good," I lie easily.

Ms. Bluefall rests a hand on my shoulder and pulls me softly into her embrace. She smells like patchouli, sunlight, and wet leaves. I hug her back and mean it.

"You know you're welcome to stay here, right? We can set up the spare bedroom for you," she says.

I know Ms. Bluefall just wants to help me, but Grady Park is my home. Besides, there's no way my parents would ever agree to let me stay here. They think Sonnet and her mom are crazy for living the way they do.

"Thank you, but I'm okay. Really."

"Mom, we're gonna be upstairs studying," Sonnet says.

"Okay. I'll let you know when dinner is ready."

Sonnet pulls me up the winding staircase to her room where she slams and locks the door.

"Sorry about that. I'll ask my mom to back off," she says, sitting down at her handmade desk and pulling out her MacBook.

I flop down on her giant bed and rub my hands across the impeccable stitching of her purple quilt, no doubt made by Ms. Bluefall.

"Don't. You know I love your mom," I say.

"She loves you, too. Are you sure you don't wanna stay with us for a while? It'd be so much fun."

"Yeah, it would, but I can't. If I don't keep an eye on my parents they might strangle each other," I say.

"Things are that bad between them?" she asks.

"Yeah. I don't really feel like talking about it though." My parents already had their issues before Katia died, but I thought they'd get back together once Daddy got a job and Momma cooled down. But now? I don't know what's gonna happen with them. I can't even think about that right now.

"Okay. But if you ever do—"

"I'll let you know. Anyway, you said you had something to show me?" I ask.

"Right! I listened to this podcast last night about the unsolved murder of Linda Ann O'Keefe. Linda was eleven when she was murdered in 1973. Then in 2018, a cold case detective made a Twitter account for her where they added all the details of the day of Linda's death. It went viral and they ended up catching the murderer. I was thinking maybe we could use Twitter to find Jordan."

My eyes pop open and I sit up.

"Sonnet . . . ," I say.

She shrugs and closes her laptop. "You're right, it's stupid. Maybe if we take more time to do some research we could—"

"No! It's fucking brilliant!"

I jump up and squish next to her in the chair and open the laptop. "Sonnet, this is perfect! Nobody will know it's us behind it."

I open a new tab for Twitter and start filling out the information for a new account.

"You really think people will be into it?" she asks, unsure.

"Of course. You're obviously not the only murder mystery fan. We can reach people all over the entire world. People who don't know Jordan or live in Grady Park won't care about snitching. They can DM us any tips they have. Sonnet, you're a genius!"

I plant a kiss on her cheek.

She grins, proud of herself. "I told you watching *Pretty Little Liars* and listening to true crime podcasts would pay off one day!"

We spend the next hour choosing the perfect profile picture and banner for our account. I'm almost mad that I didn't come up with the idea myself. I make Sonnet promise not to tell anyone about the Twitter page because blowing our cover makes the whole thing pointless. We want people to think of this Twitter as Katia asking them for their help. No cops, no lawyers, no family, just my sister.

At 8:09 P.M., I send out our first tweet to the world: "My name is Katia Willet. On January 8, 2018, I was murdered."

CHAPTER 7

BY THE SECOND DAY I'M BACK AT SCHOOL, things have started to feel less strange. I only get a couple looks today and Sonnet only fawns over me when she sees I'm not eating my lunch.

By the end of eighth period, I'm beat. I'm at my locker packing my book bag to go home when someone taps me on the shoulder. I'm hoping it's Champion, but when I turn around, it's Madison Garber.

"Hey, Beau! Do you have a minute to chat?"

"Uhh . . . okay. What's up?"

Madison and I have been in the same art and English lit classes for two years, but we've hardly ever spoken two words to each other. Physically, she's every artsy girl in a teen movie: short curly brown hair that she never combs but still looks amazing, paint-covered overalls that don't quite reach her ankles. And she's the only girl in school who can wear Crocs and not look like a jackass.

"I know we haven't talked much this year, but I wanted to say I'm sorry about your sister," she says.

"Thanks," I say, turning back to my locker. I'm so over being pitied by everyone.

"I know now might not be the best time, but I also wanted to say I think you're an amazing artist. The painting you did last fall of those little girls playing outside? It was one of the best I've ever seen."

"You think so?" I shut my locker and look at her.

"Absolutely," Madison says, her eyes beaming. "Don't tell anyone else I said this, but I've always felt like you were too advanced for a high school class. Not just your technique, but the things you draw and paint. They're powerful, and not a lot of people can say that about their work."

My face starts to get warm. I know I'm a good artist, but it means more coming from Madison, someone who knows real art and on more than one occasion has corrected Ms. Kubler during her art history lessons.

"Thanks, Madison. Your work is really good, too. I thought your piece for the art show was definitely going to win."

She shrugs. "Yours was so much better. In fact, I think we could learn a lot from each other."

"Maybe. I gotta catch the bus, though," I say as I sling my backpack over my shoulder.

"Wait! Before you go, I wanted to ask if you might be interested in collabing on the mural project? I think me and you could come up with something really good."

I raise an eyebrow. "Like me and you submitting one

proposal? I don't know." I'm not really in the popular crowd at school, so when people start paying attention to me all of a sudden, I get suspicious.

She pouts. "Oh, I get it. I know I'm not as talented of an artist as you, but I hoped—"

"No, you're great. It's just . . . Sonnet's my best friend," I tell her.

"Oh. I didn't know you were already working with someone."

I eye the front doors and the crowd of kids rushing through them to the waiting buses outside. If I miss the 3:20 bus, I'll have to wait an hour for the next one or walk.

"We're not working together, but she's my best friend. If I'm going to collab with anyone, I think it should be her," I explain.

Madison smiles politely and rests a hand on my shoulder.

"Beau, you have to learn to separate business from friendships. Julie's my best friend, but she can't even tell the difference between a Van Gogh and a Monet. If you want to take your art seriously as a career, you can't be afraid to level up."

"Well, unlike Julie, Sonnet *does* know the difference between Van Gogh and Monet," I fire back.

"Oh, I agree! She's talented and her wardrobe is everything. But I heard her talking about her dick of corn idea. I'm sure you could work with her on it, but I just thought you might want to actually win this thing."

I do want to win. And if I did, maybe it would remind Momma and Daddy that they do still have another kid. I'm not Katia, but I can still make them proud.

"What makes you so sure we'd win if we partnered together?" I ask.

"Because nobody takes art class more serious than us. We're great artists on our own. How could we *not* produce something crazy good if we worked together?"

I can tell she's trying to butter me up. I'm not dumb; obviously she thinks she has a better shot at winning the contest if she works with me. I had planned to start thinking about my own proposal submission, but Madison is my stiffest competition in the class. I beat her once, but I don't even have a clue of what I'd paint on the side of the school. Plus, with everything with Katia going on, and Momma and Daddy fighting, I've hardly had the time to think about it.

"I don't know . . . ," I say. I'm not a diva or anything, but in my fantasy of winning the contest, I get to sign my name at the bottom. Just mine.

"Can I be super honest right now?" Madison looks around to make sure no one's paying attention to us. "Ms. Kubler is probably going to pick me or you as the winner. We know that much at least. Up until this morning, I'd planned to lock myself in my studio at home over the weekend until I came up with a proposal. But instead of the both of us freaking out trying to beat each other, why don't we just do one proposal together? It'll cut the work in half, and we won't have to be under so much pressure to win. You don't have to say yes. I just thought it'd be better to win together."

Can't fight the girl's logic. If she's scared of losing to me the same way I'm scared of losing to her, it's a toss-up who'd end up with the best proposal. But if we're gonna do this, it has to be split down the middle, the work and the credit.

"What if we don't agree on something? Like the mural theme?" I ask.

"We'll compromise."

"What if neither of us wants to go with the other person's idea?"

"Then I'll go with yours. Just think about it, it's a good plan."

I shrug. I'm giving up my solo credit but it's worth it if we're guaranteed to win. "Okay. I'm in. Let's do it," I say.

Madison smiles and bounces on her heels.

"Great! We're so going to win this contest! Let's get together tomorrow after school. You can come over to my place."

We exchange numbers and for the first time in a while, I feel like I'm doing something that's going to turn out right. If we win, they'll probably even write up a piece about us for the school website. I can almost see it now, a big mural unveiling with everyone there, Momma and Daddy bringing the rest of our family and recording everything, cheering me on. We need something good, and I'm gonna be the one to do it.

I rush down the science corridor in a daze, thinking about how long it'll take me and Madison to draft a sketch, when I run into a brick wall.

"My bad, you aight?" Champion asks, grabbing on to my arm to steady me.

The brick wall is his arm. His sexy, strong, bulging arm that's touching me right now and sending electric currents right to my brain.

"I'm okay. It was my fault, shoulda been payin' attention," I say. I flick my curls over my shoulder and I'm so glad that Deja hooked me up the other day. I feel like a whole new person when my hair is done.

"Hey, did you see our video on WorldStar? People have been blowing my phone up all week," he says like he's amazed. Unlike me, he apparently thinks being on WorldStar is an accomplishment. I'm not surprised. The kids who grow up with the most always wanna be in the middle of some hood action. It's hard to blame him, as boring as Purple Hills is. If we'd gotten on there for something good, like making up a viral dance, I'da been geeked, too.

"You didn't get in trouble?"

"Nah," he says, bending down to grab my backpack that fell to the ground during our collision. I move to take it back, but he swings it over his shoulder and we start walking together. "My parents work a lot, so they don't have time to monitor daily hood fights."

"Oh." Champion holds the front door open for me and we walk outside into the cold winter air. It must have stormed earlier because the ground's wet and it smells like rain. A couple of senior girls hanging at the bottom of the stone staircase give me stank looks and I eyeball them right back.

"So your girl, Deja. She's somethin' else," Champion says, choosing his words carefully. I knew this part was coming. *Your friend's a crazy bitch, why did you have me get in that fight? Why do you hang out with a chick like that? Are you a crazy hoodrat, too?*

"Deja's an idiot," I blurt. Mean, but true.

He just laughs as we sit down in front of the fountain. In the center is a bronze ballerina on her tippy toes. Water flows out from her hips and falls in a blanket around her like a tutu.

"Nah, I get it. My cousin Benny's the same way. We went to this party a few weekends ago in Grady Park and this dude walks in. B's all *Aye, you know this dude?* And I'm like, *Nah bro, why wassup?* Then him and, like, three other dudes step to him like they gonna jump his ass."

"It's not personal. Usually, the only strangers who come to Grady Park are tryna jump or rob somebody."

"I guess that does make sense, then," he says, rubbing his chin.

"Sooo . . . you have basketball practice today?" Anything to keep the subject off Grady Park and hood fights. I want him to know that just because I'm from there doesn't mean I'm like everyone else there. Even if sometimes I act like it.

"Not today, Coach finally giving us a break. I was actually on my way to grab some McDonald's. You wanna come?"

"Really? I mean, yeah, sure!" I can't believe he still likes me after I got us posted on WorldStar for the world to see. I was sure he'd ghost me today.

"Cool," he says. "Just promise there won't be any whoopin's handed out today."

"Oh, you got jokes now?"

He stands up and reaches for my hand, and I feel everyone's eyes on us as we walk through the courtyard. Champion doesn't let go of my hand until we reach his matte black BMW M3.

I climb into the front seat and reach over to open the door for Champion.

"You know, I was surprised to see you today," he says as we leave the school parking lot.

"How come?"

"Well, you know, because of your sister. Thought you might take some more time off."

That's the funny thing about grief. It sneaks up on you all the time. Just like that, my eyes start to burn, and I feel my stomach drop.

"Oh man, are you okay? I'm sorry, I shouldn't have said anything," Champion says, looking to the road and back at me.

I shake my head and wipe away the tears.

"No, it's not you, it's me. I just forgot for a little while, that's all."

"Is there anything I can do?"

I shake my head again. I wish he could kiss me and bring that dead part of me back to life like in *Sleeping Beauty*, but I know it can't be fixed that easy. This is a hard pain, one that's rooted so far deep in my soul, I couldn't touch it if I wanted to.

"Forget McDonald's. I have a better idea," Champion says. He holds my hand as we speed through the city.

———

"Don't let me go."

"I promise I won't."

I let Champion lead me out onto the floor, my hands gripping his for dear life.

"You got it, just stand up a lil straighter," he encourages me. A senior couple zips past us, spinning in circles and somehow not even stumbling once. I feel even more mortified.

Champion drove us to Skate-o-Rama, one of the only roller rinks still operating in the state, although probably not for much longer. Besides us and the senior couple, there's maybe six other people here, tops. The rink is surrounded with red and green lights and there's a huge star on the ceiling made up of orange and blue flashing bulbs.

Since it's mostly couples, the DJ is spinning love tracks only.

He's playing one of my favorites now, a soft RnB jam by Meek Mill and Nicki Minaj.

"What made you want to come here?" I ask as we pick up speed. Champion's skating backward without even looking, so I know he's been here more than a few times.

"I knew it'd be empty. I just wanted to get away from everything. Nobody really skates anymore."

"You come here by yourself a lot?" I ask, trying to talk while also simultaneously trying not to bust my behind on the floor.

Champion shakes his head and guides us closer to the wall.

"I did when I was little, but once I started playing basketball for real, my dad said I couldn't risk the injury."

"Damn, that sucks."

"Perks of being a High School All American. We went to Aspen for Christmas vacation last winter and he wouldn't even let me ski. I had to stay in the hotel and watch TV all day."

I stop myself from rolling my eyes. It's not his fault he's rich.

"Aren't you risking injury by skating with me right now?" I ask.

"You're worth it," he says, flashing me his pretty smile. I feel my body ignite.

"What about your future NBA contract? One and done, right? I mean, if you break your ankle or somethin' out here, I don't wanna be responsible for you losing out on a bajillion-dollar contract," I joke.

"I think I'll be okay. Besides, there's things more important than basketball."

"Like what?" I ask as a father and daughter skate by us like pros.

"Like having fun. Hanging with my friends. Being around

you." He stops abruptly on his toes, and I crash into his chest, where he wraps his arms around me and holds me there. I feel his heart beat against mine and look up into his eyes. Even though it's nighttime and we're indoors, I see the sun in them.

When he bends down to kiss me, I want to say I feel the world stop rotating on its axis, that my breath catches and I forget where I am.

But it doesn't and I don't.

His breath is minty and his mouth is warm and soft. All I can think is, *I'll never get to tell Katia about my first kiss.* Every step forward I move with Champion is a step further away from the version of myself Katia knew. It feels like I'm betraying her somehow. I'm not ready to change.

When we unlock our lips, the senior couple is grinning at us as they fly by. The dad glares at us like we're going to give his daughter some ideas she's too young to be thinking about.

"That was . . . um, nice," I say.

"Sorry, I'd just been wanting to do that for a while," he says.

"Me too."

Champion guides us back over to the rest area and we get cheese fries and an extra-large raspberry soda to share.

"Can I tell you something?" I ask.

"You can tell me anything."

I take a deep breath.

"Don't tell anybody, but sometimes it's like I know what happened to Katia was wrong and that she didn't deserve to die. But I wish I didn't care so much. I hate that I can't change what happened to her." To speak the words out loud frees me and traps me at the same time.

"I get that. Nobody wants to feel like this, to lose somebody."

"It's not just that, though. Nobody cares about Katia anymore. Maybe people are seeing something there that I never did. Like she wasn't this good person, you know? But I'm her sister so I'm, like, *biologically* obligated to think like that."

Champion reaches across the table for my hand. "People do care."

"I know, but not in the same way that they care about that man from Georgia who was killed by the police last summer. His name was Mason Greg. I remember they were doing interviews with his family every day. People were shouting his name in cities all over the country, blocking highways, getting arrested. Whether that cop gets convicted or not, nobody's ever going to forget Mason's name."

Champion pops another cheese fry into his mouth and looks out at the skaters spinning around the rink.

"Yeah, I see what you mean. But I don't think it's on purpose. There's lots of Black women who've had marches held in their honor, freeways blocked off, too. Like that one lady, Denisia Morrow."

"I guess. Or maybe it's that Katia's just not the right type of Black girl," I say.

Last year, there was this one Black girl and boy who spearheaded a whole Black Lives Matter movement in their town after their friend got killed. They went to some super ritzy private school with a bunch of rich white kids. I heard an anonymous donor offered to pay for their college tuition to this Ivy League school that was giving them both full rides anyway. Maybe if I was smarter or my family had more money or I was some type of damn fucking child prodigy, I could have been better at this social justice thing.

"What do you mean?" Champion asks.

"Nothing. I'm just . . . a mess sometimes," I say. I don't want to spend our date talking about Katia because then I'll cry.

"You're not a mess. I always thought you were cool as hell. The way you're handling everything, you're built tough, and I like that."

"I guess you could say that." Tough is for beef jerky and Tonka trucks and Deja. It's not how I feel at all.

Champion reaches across the table and takes my hand. "Can I tell you something?"

"Sure." In my mind I'm praying he doesn't launch into a sermon about what a strong Black woman I am.

"I'm glad you let me take you out today."

"Oh . . . I'm glad you asked me. I'm having a good time with you," I say, trying to hide my disappointment. How stupid am I? Of course he's not going to ask me to be his girlfriend after that WorldStar fight.

"Anyway," he says, standing up. "You ready to get back out there?" He flashes that brilliant white smile, incisors sharp, gleaming, and perfect.

"Let's do it," I say, standing up and taking his hand.

We skate to two more songs, and even though I have a million other things to be worried about, right now I'm not the sister of the murdered girl. I'm just a regular girl on a date with a regular guy. For ten whole minutes, I pretend I'm someone else. But then the music stops and I'm back to being me.

CHAPTER 8

BEFORE

AS SOON AS MY ONE DIRECTION CLOCK ON THE WALL struck 9:00 A.M. on the dot, I showered, brushed my teeth, and put on the coolest outfit I owned: light-blue skinny jeans, brown Uggs, and a hot-pink, sparkly Southpole tee.

My hair was a wild mess, and I'd learned it was better just to leave it how it was. The more I messed with it, the bigger and angrier it got. I didn't put it in a ponytail either, because then it'd just have a dent in it when I took the elastic out.

That day, I was gonna get to hang out with Katia.

"Fix me some eggs, Beau," she said when she finally rolled out of bed, her tank top and shorts twisted from her wild sleeping.

"Okay!" I hopped to it. Deja and Breon were going with us, so I knew it was gonna be a good day.

Katia wasn't letting us tag along because she wanted to.

Momma and Daddy said I was too young to be left alone, so if Katia wanted to go somewhere while they were at work, she had to take me, too.

I fried four eggs and broke up a slice of Kraft to throw on top. When I brought our plates into the bedroom, Katia was sitting at her white vanity putting makeup on.

She didn't even need it. Lots of girls had to work hard to look cute, but Katia was naturally stunning. Big brown lips, deep midnight skin, curly eyelashes, and a perfectly sculpted face that made her look like a model. Aunt Pepper always called her "Naomi."

"Don't forget your money," Katia suddenly said, not taking her eyes off the mirror as she used a toothbrush to slick down her baby hairs. She always wore the same hairstyle, middle part, bone straight #1B hair down to her shoulders.

I got down on the floor and pulled our secret shoebox from out under my bed. It held our savings, which we kept in two separate envelopes (mine full and Katia's empty), my birthstone necklace, Katia's silver charm bracelet from Grandma Willet, a bunch of tiny purple pebbles I'd found outside last summer, and our spare house key.

I put some money in my pocket and pushed the box back under the bed.

"When we get there, don't act stupid and don't touch anything unless you're about to buy it."

"Same for you. I know Monica didn't *give* you that blue Victoria's Secret bra," I said, rolling my eyes.

"She did, and how she got it ain't nobody's business but hers. Come on, let's go and catch this bus," Katia said as she slipped on her swap meet hoop earrings.

As usual, when we got outside, three different dudes tried to holla at her.

"Aye, Miss Thang," Mark from next door said, staring at my sister's ass. His wife worked at the same nursing home as Momma.

A bald dude in a black T-shirt and Girbauds came swaggering up to us from the corner, but Katia didn't even stop to look at him.

When we got to the bus stop at the end of the block, Deja and Breon were sitting on the rusted bench, arguing about something as usual.

Katia clucked her tongue.

"Hey y'all," I said, squeezing between them. Katia stood a few feet away, pretending like she wasn't with us.

"Hey, Beau," Deja said, flipping one of her long, honey-blond ponytails over her shoulder. She was wearing a lime-green halter and skintight black jeans. I always felt plain as hell next to her. "Would you tell Breon that just because a guy offers me something and I take it doesn't make me a gold digger?"

"What guy? Aren't you still with Jeff?"

Breon shook her head. "Nope. She dumped him. With a text."

"Because Jeff is broke. But this new guy, Kareem, I met him at the Wing Joint last night. I was up at the counter looking cute or whatever and I was about to pay for me and Momma's gizzards. Then this fine dude with long dreads comes up and hands the cashier money to pay for my order. Isn't that sweet?"

"How old is he?" I asked.

"He's a sophomore at Grady Park High. And my man has a car, so you know our summer is 'bout to be fun as hell. No more riding on this raggedy piece of shit."

The 408 bus rumbled to a stop in front of us and let out a thick cloud of black smoke from the back. Katia got on first and paid our fare, while Deja paid for herself and Breon. We squished together into the seat behind my sister. We were starting to get a little too big for this since one of my butt cheeks was hanging off the seat, but we always sat next to each other on the city bus so none of us would have to sit next to a stranger.

"Aye, you heard Nicki Minaj's new song?" Deja asked, handing me one of her earbuds. Nicki Minaj was like God to us even though Momma always said she cussed too much. But I liked that she got it out the mud, started off at the bottom and made it to the top all on her own.

"While y'all listening to that, I'm gettin' ready to ace our math test on Monday." Breon opened her backpack and pulled out a thick textbook.

"You could ace that test in your sleep, Bre. It's the weekend; we're supposed to be kickin' it!" I grabbed the book out of her lap, but she snatched it back and swatted at me.

"Not takin' any chances. Every grade counts if I wanna beat Kenyatta for valedictorian."

"Girl, you're a trip," Deja said.

Getting As and knowing everything there was to know in the world was Breon's thing. Nobody expected girls like us to be smart, so I knew she got a kick out of proving people wrong. But she didn't look like the nerd she was on the inside. She always had on a fresh pair of Air Force 1s or Nike Dunks. If the toe even bent up a lil bit, they went in the trash. Her clothes she was less picky about: baggy joggers and graphic T-shirts from Hot Topic and Foot Locker. Today, her oversize black tee said "Korn" in white letters.

When we got to the Purple Hills Mall, Katia's friends, Monica and Clarice, were talking to two white boys they'd just met in the food court. Katia sat down with them while we ordered pizza slices and Cokes from Sbarro. I made sure we sat close enough for my sister to keep an eye on us but far enough that we weren't cramping her style.

The boy that had been talking to Clarice changed his mind when he saw Katia. It was quick and barely noticeable, but suddenly he was talking to her, and Clarice was the fifth wheel. She looked pissed.

"Damn," Deja started. "Your sister be pullin' dudes without even trying! If she wasn't such a bitch maybe she could show us how a pro does it."

I smacked her arm. "Stop callin' my sister a bitch!"

"Why? You said it in the group chat last night. Breon, what'd Beau say?"

Breon looked up from her textbook. "Something like 'This bitch ate the last strawberry Pop-Tart."

"Ha! It was wild berry. But bump all that, she's my sister so I can call her a bitch. *You* can't," I explain.

"Fine, whatever, hoe," Deja said, rolling her eyes. She was an only child and sometimes I thought she was jealous that I had a sister and she didn't.

Deja and I watched Katia and her friends like stalkers while Breon studied. After a while, the white boys had to go and they left their phone numbers with the girls, except for Clarice, who got nobody's number. I always felt bad for her.

"So who's taking you to prom?" Katia's friend Monica asked, swinging her long weave back and forth and smacking on a wad of gum.

"It ain't happenin' for another two months," Clarice said. She probably didn't have a date.

"You already know I'm goin' with my man," Katia said, smiling.

"Speaking of your man, I heard he's applying to Princeton. Only dude from Grady High with the balls to do it."

"More like only dude with the brains to get in. Y'all always chasing after these bum niggas who can't even do two plus two, but you need to get you a man like mine."

Monica busted out laughing.

"Uhhh nah, I can't be booed up with a dude named Medgar."

"He's named after Medgar Evers, who you'd know about if your dumbass opened a book as often as you open your legs," Katia snapped. She and her friends always cracked on each other like that but never got mad.

"Girl, gone, you wanna talk about opening legs? What's Medgar gonna think about you taking that dude's number just now?" Clarice asked.

"Oh that?" Katia took the slip of paper, balled it up, and flicked it off the table. "That was just for fun."

Clarice looked like she wanted to go over and pick it up, but she didn't. That would have just been too desperate.

"See, what me and my man have is serious. The end of senior year is about to be lit. Then I'll go down to FAMU, Medgar will be up at Princeton, and we'll meet up on breaks. Then after we graduate, marriage, a house, kids, maybe a dog, too."

"Sounds like you got it all planned out," said Monica.

"Yeah . . . yeah, I do. If y'all heifers get some act right, I *might* let y'all be in the wedding," Katia said.

Clarice threw a balled-up napkin at her, and they all started laughing. I wanted to laugh, too, but I got this sinking feeling whenever I thought about Katia leaving home. I'd be all alone. Yeah, Momma and Daddy would still be there, but it wasn't like I could talk to them about real stuff, like boys or how to blend my kinky hair with silky straight tracks.

"Okay, I'm tired of listening to these hyenas cackling all day. Go over there and tell your sister we're gonna go to Icing to look at earrings," Deja said, standing up at our table and straightening her top.

"Oooh, Foot Locker, too. I wanna try on the new LeBrons," Breon said.

Later when we stopped at Auntie Anne's for pretzels, Deja and Breon started arguing about which flavor pretzel we were going to split three ways. The girl at the register rolled her eyes at them, but I could have listened to those two all day.

"Beau!" Deja snapped at me. "Tell Breon we're getting a cinnamon pretzel."

"You know I don't like cinnamon. What's wrong with the pepperoni pretzel?" Breon asked.

"Why don't y'all just do rock, paper, scissors?" I said.

"Hell nah, we not leaving this shit up to chance. Cinnamon, or I'm taking back my dollar fifty," Deja said.

"Here you go again," Breon said with a groan as they started the next round of arguing.

Later, when the bus took us back to Grady Park, the

sun was just starting to dip below the horizon and the sky had turned a hazy purplish blue. I hugged Deja and Breon goodbye. Katia waited with me while we made sure they got into their units. Breon lived in Building A, Deja lived next door in Building B, and I lived next door to that in Building C.

"You gonna live around here? When you and Medgar get married?" I asked Katia as we passed a couple arguing on the second-floor balcony of Deja's building.

Katia looked at me like I was crazy.

"Hell naw, we're gonna live somewhere nice. With palm trees and Walmarts that don't check your receipt before you leave the store."

"But what about me?"

She licked the icing from her baby-blue-painted fingernail. "You can come visit us, Bozo."

"Don't call me Bozo," I said.

"Bozo."

I glared at her.

"Oh, come *ooonnn*," she said, wrapping her arm around me as we walked through the littered courtyard. "You can come and visit whenever you want. It's not like I'm dying."

"But it won't be the same," I complained.

"I know. That's the whole point of me leaving."

When we got close to our building, we saw our front door hanging off its hinges a huge dent near the doorknob where it'd been kicked in. Katia rushed up the walkway.

"No fucking way!" Inside, our apartment had been trashed. The TV was gone and the cushions from the couch were spread out over the floor between the glass of our broken picture frames. Even the fridge door was open, like the robbers had made themselves a sandwich.

"Momma and Daddy are gonna go off when they see this!" Katia said, running her hands through her hair over and over and pacing back and forth.

We never called the cops because Daddy said they're not there to protect Black people. In Grady Park, you were pretty much your own police officer. This was the third time we'd been robbed in the last year though. Each time it happened, Daddy said whoever it was probably wouldn't come back. But then they always did.

Suddenly Katia looked up at me, her eyes wide. Then I remembered.

"The box!" we both shouted at the same time.

I tore down the hallway and into the bedroom after her, but we already knew our stuff was gone. Of course the assholes left the empty box there, like we'd use it again.

Katia sat on the floor rocking back and forth with her face in her hands, the empty box in her lap.

"It's okay," I said, putting a hand on her shoulder, "I have more birthdays. I'll get more money."

But she shook her head, tears rolling down her cheeks.

"It's not the money, Beau; my charm bracelet was in there. The one Grandma Willet gave me before she died! Fuck!" She ripped the shoebox up into big chunks and then sat down on her bed, her whole body shaking.

I didn't understand why she was so upset. Everybody in Grady Park got robbed so often that it was like a holiday when you *didn't* get robbed. We weren't okay with the shit, but it wasn't like we could do anything about it.

"See? This is why I have to leave, Beau. Shit like this is why I'm getting the fuck out of here after graduation. You can't have shit in Grady Park. You can't even have a good day without somebody tryna fuck it up for you!"

I sat down next to her as she squeezed a pillow tight to her chest and cried.

"Watch. Momma and Daddy gonna get home and blame me cuz I wasn't here. I'mma get in trouble because some dumbass decided to break into our house again."

"I'll tell them I wanted to go to the mall, too. Then maybe it won't be so bad," I offered.

"It doesn't matter. We should be able to go out to the mall without worrying about shit like this. You know there's places where everybody leaves their front door open at night because nobody steals? Everybody works for their shit, so they don't have time to be takin' somebody else's. Nobody gets arrested, no shootings, no drug dealers."

"What place is like that?" I asked.

"I dunno, somewhere in the country, I think. The point is I'm getting out of here, and I'm never coming back," Katia said.

I was only twelve then. I didn't understand why she hated Grady Park so much. Our lives weren't that bad. I had my room, my sketchbook, my girls, both parents, and my big sister. But I liked the sound of this other place, leaving the front door unlocked. I wondered what that would feel like.

"Take me with you?" I asked her.

Katia considered it for a minute.

"You have to finish school first, cuz I can't shelter no dummies. But after that? Yeah, I'll take you with me."

I laid my hand on top of hers, and she laid her other hand on top of mine. A promise.

CHAPTER 9

I'VE BEEN TO MUSEUMS THAT AREN'T AS NICE AS MADison's house. For one, it's big as hell. The ceilings are high enough for a family of giants to jump around on pogo sticks. The halls are wide enough to walk through with your arms outstretched and there'd still be plenty of space for other people to walk by.

And the art. The *art*. Her dad's paintings are everywhere. Splashes of blues, greens, magentas. Some art portraits of random things, like a water bottle or a garbage can. Others are of people: himself, his family. A gigantic watercolor painting of Madison hangs in the foyer. She even has one hallway just dedicated to her own art. Besides the paintings, everything is pristine, white, and new. The floors, the tables, the couches, the lamps.

This is the family I should have been born into if the universe ever played fair.

"Do you have any ideas for the mural yet?" Madison asks as

we sit in her studio. She has her own freaking studio with more art supplies than our entire school and a big white square table for us to work at.

"I did, but it's stupid," I say. The best I could come up with was the school's name in bubble letters with a bunch of flowers behind it. Nowhere near creative enough to win the contest. "What about you? Do you have something in mind?"

She tucks her hair behind her ear.

"I do. Now, feel free to say no if it makes you uncomfortable, but I think it's something really important that'll have meaning for the school even when we're gone."

"Okay. What is it?"

Madison bites her lip and looks down at her hands.

"I was thinking maybe we could propose to paint a mural to honor your sister?"

My smile fades. "My sister?"

"Well, yeah. Police brutality in Chicago needs to be addressed. What happened to your sister has happened to too many people. A mural of Katia for everyone in the city to see is a way to bring attention to the issue."

I haven't drawn much of anything since I designed the hoodies for Katia's funeral. And even that was draining for me, having to look at her picture for hours on end, her warm brown eyes seeing right through me. I'm thinking about her all the time anyway; art class is supposed to be "me" time, where I can pretend for a little while that everything's okay even though it's not.

"I don't know if I could do that. Look at her face all the time . . . I'm still coping, you know?"

"I understand. Maybe you just need an emotional release. My dad says artists need to wring their brains every now and then. We absorb so much from the world and if we don't let it out, it takes us over completely. If you let your feelings for your sister out on the page, it might help you feel better."

"How am I supposed to wring my brain?" I ask.

Madison gets up and walks to her supply shelves. She lays a huge piece of white butcher paper in front of me and a charcoal pencil.

"Draw it out. Everything that's in your head right now. Put it on the paper. You'll feel better, trust me."

I hesitate for a moment but take the pencil in my fingers. It feels foreign in my fingertips at first. I draw one line and it's not even straight. But then I close my eyes and picture in my mind what's beating in my heart. I start to draw what I see.

At first, I'm fully aware that Madison's on the other side of the table watching me and probably judging with her fancy art taste and knowledge. But after a few minutes, she and the room around me disappear. There's nothing but white space and me with a black pencil to fill it up and make it mean something. I draw for what feels like a lifetime. I push everything out of my heart and out of my brain. When I'm done, I press my hands to my eyes to stop the tears threatening to spill over. I don't want Madison to see me crying.

Madison comes around the table to take in what I've drawn, and I hear her gasp.

"That's it, Beau," she says. "You did it."

"Yeah. I guess I did. You think it's good enough to win though?"

"Good? It's amazing, Beau! We're gonna win this thing and when we're done, the whole city is going to know who Katia was."

I visualize Katia on the side of the school, bigger than life. Reporters would come, photographers would come. There'd be interviews, talk show appearances, the whole nine. If we pull this off, maybe we won't need Jordan's testimony after all.

———

For the first week after we set up Katia's Twitter, we don't get anything in our inbox except some sketchy links from bots and about a million "Thanks for the follow <3" messages. I'm starting to think this wasn't such a good idea after all when we get a DM from a user named MurderSleuth99.

MURDERSLEUTH99: Parker Samson

I'm not sure what he expects me to do with just a name. But Parker Samson must be one of Jordan's relatives. It's 11:00 P.M. and I'm lying in bed on my back, holding my phone above my face.

ME: Who are you and who is Parker Samson?

I get a reply almost instantly.

MURDERSLEUTH99: He's Jordan Samson's half brother, age 17

Now I'm thinking it's just a troll. Jordan doesn't have any siblings. At least, I don't think he does.

ME: Jordan has a brother? Since when?

The next message is an image. I click on it and sit straight up in bed. It's a picture of a guy in a basketball uniform and he has the same blockhead as Jordan and the same mischievous smirk.

MURDERSLEUTH99: They're half brothers on their father's side. Probably grew up in different households. But he lives in Chicago, too.

ME: Where at? How do you know?

MURDERSLEUTH99: He's a senior at Brookstone High. Start there.

ME: What do you mean "start there"? Who are you?

ME: You still there?

After thirty minutes without a response, I give up and plug my phone's charger into the wall. Whoever this Murdersleuth is, he's probably just playing around. If Jordan had a brother, I think I would have known. Not that I ever asked him or anything.

Still, the guy in that picture looks just like Jordan, only with softer features. If they're not brothers, they have to be related somehow. But there's only one way to find out for sure.

———

"What if he doesn't want to talk to us? Wouldn't he try to protect his own brother?" Sonnet asks.

We're standing at my locker after the bell for eighth period

80

has rung, and the hallways are empty except for a few kids running through the halls to get to their last class of the day.

"Maybe they're not that close. Or it could be his cousin or something. You saw the photo, he looked just like Jordan," I say.

Sonnet blows a purple bubble and pulls it back into her mouth before popping it. "Yeah, but what if that Murdersleuth guy was just messing with you? There's a lot of weirdos on the internet who get off on tormenting families who've lost someone."

She has a point. But it's the first DM we've received that doesn't say "CLICK THIS LINK FOR A FREE IPHONE!" Even if it's a dead lead, I'm itching to get out there and start looking for Jordan. It's better than sitting around waiting for another tip that might never come.

"That's why we're gonna go to Brookstone High and check it out. If he's there, we can ask him about Jordan. If he's not, we'll know Murdersleuth is playing us and we block his ass," I explain.

Sonnet sighs. "Fine. But what are we gonna do about eighth period? They'll call our parents if we don't show up. My mom is cool but not that cool."

I hadn't really considered that. I just know my parents won't care so I didn't stop to think about what Ms. Bluefall might say to Sonnet about it. I think quick on my feet though.

"By the time the school calls, it'll be after school. You'll get home maybe thirty minutes after that. Tell your mom it was a mistake or something. She'll believe you," I say.

Sonnet bites her lip and looks down at her teal-sequined high-tops. Guilt is written all over her face. If I don't say something, she's gonna back out. I can't do this alone.

I close my locker and spin the lock. "Sonnet, you said you wanted to help. How many times did you see the Pretty Little Liars ask permission to go out and hunt down A?"

I sling a protective arm around her shoulders and steer us in the direction of the front doors. But Sonnet still looks unsure.

"But my mom never lies to me," she says quietly. "I don't wanna start lying to her."

"Okay, how about this," I say. "Once we find Jordan and turn him in to the police, we can tell your mom the truth. She'll understand why we had to do it, right?"

Damn, I'm good.

Sonnet's shoulders relax under my arm, and she nods.

"Yeah, I think so. She was really upset about that officer getting off. And she used to protest at her college years ago when they tried to impose a dress code. I've seen the photos and everything."

"Because your mom is a badass! So are we. Can't make change if we don't break at least a couple rules, right?"

We're almost to the door when a voice shouts from behind us.

"Hey! Where y'all going?"

For a second, I think we've been busted by a teacher, but when we turn around, it's just Champion, swinging his school ID lanyard as he strolls over to us.

"Where you finna go?" he asks, looking from me to Sonnet.

"We're just cutting out a lil early to go . . . you know . . . chill and stuff at the park or something," I say, gazing at the spot just above his head.

"Yeah!" Sonnet adds, "We just needed some BFF bonding time." She squeezes me to her and we both grin like idiots.

Champion smirks, a twinkle in his dark brown eyes.

"Lemme roll with y'all. I've got my car."

Sonnet looks at me and I hesitate. He can't know about this, although a ride to Brookstone would save us some time. No, still not worth it.

"You have practice after school. It doesn't make sense to ditch when we'd have to come right back."

He looks away and I'm worried I hurt his feelings. Stupid Beau! This is exactly why you'll never have a boyfriend. You don't know what you're doing!

"But let's meet up after your basketball practice gets out. We could go see a movie or something?" I add.

He flashes us his bright, perfect smile and the butterflies in my heart start their chorus again.

"Aight, I'll hit you up later, then."

Once he's gone, we leave out through the glass side door and step into the cold afternoon.

By the time we make it to Brookstone High, my underarms are sweaty as fuck and my T-shirt is sticking to my back.

"That was actually a nice walk! I feel"—Sonnet takes a deep breath in and blows it out—"rejuvenated and refreshed. We should do this more often!"

I wipe the sweat off my face with the front of my T-shirt.

"Girl, bye, you can go for long ass walks and I'll wave to you from the bus."

The front of the school reminds me of Millennium. There's glass windows from the ground up, and on the side of the building in green letters is the school's name. I've never been inside, but I think Deja used to date a guy who goes here.

"Jokes aside, how are we supposed to find him exactly? Just wait for him to walk out?" Sonnet asks.

I pause, then swing my backpack off my shoulder and pull out a pen and paper.

"Okay, turn around for a second," I say. I press the paper against her back and write Parker's name on it.

"What are you doing?" she asks.

"This." I show her the paper.

"What exactly are you gonna do with that?"

"We're gonna hold it up so he sees us when he comes out."

"Okay, but won't he think that's kinda sketchy?"

"It *is* sketchy. That's the point here, to disrupt the norm. Everyone will be looking at us, including Parker or someone he knows. They'll ask what we're doing and hopefully tell us where to find him."

———

I pull up his Instagram on my phone and we both look at it, committing his face to memory. I know I won't miss him. He looks exactly like Jordan but without facial hair and he has a nose piercing.

Around 3:15 P.M., the front of the school starts to get crowded with parents and kids talking, laughing, joking. A few people give us strange looks, mostly Sonnet because she's holding the sign and wearing those loud ass bright yellow pants with green and blue flowers printed all over. The word *incognito* means nothing to her.

I scan the flood of students exiting the building but there's way more people than I thought. Car horns start to honk, and I worry that we missed him. Or that he's still inside doing an after-school club or something.

Sonnet and I are both craning our necks to see above the crowd when a short girl with her hair braided up into two big buns stops in front of us.

"What do you want with Parker?" she asks, narrowing her eyes. I grab Sonnet's arms to pull the sign down.

"We just needed to ask him about something important. Do you know him?" I ask.

She looks us up and down. "Yeah, I'm his girlfriend. Who are you?"

"We're friends of his older brother," I say. "He's been missing for a few weeks, and we just wanted to see if maybe Parker's seen him."

The girl looks at me like I just spoke gibberish.

"What are you talking about? Parker doesn't have any brothers. Just a couple sisters." She narrows her eyes. "How did you get his name?"

Doesn't have a brother? If she's his girlfriend, she'd probably know. Maybe Sonnet was right about Murdersleuth lying.

But Parker looks just like Jordan in the picture. And they have the same last name. It can't just be a coincidence.

I'm fiddling with my hands and saying, "Well, um," over and over to give myself time to think of a response. Then a pair of arms wraps around the tiny girl's waist and a boy with a sharp fade nuzzles his face into her neck from behind.

"Parker?" Sonnet asks. The guy looks up and sees us.

"Who are they?" he asks his girlfriend.

She turns on him. "That's what I wanna know! She over here tryna lie and say you have a brother. I'm not stupid. How do you know her?"

He looks at me and squints. "Maaan, I've never seen this girl a day in my life. Please don't start this mess again, Kya."

"He's telling the truth," I say. "We've never met, but I know his brother, Jordan."

At the mention of Jordan's name, his eyes widen. But just a tiny bit.

"Whatever he got into, ain't got nothin' to do with me. So I'd appreciate it if you just leave me and my girl out of it," he says.

"Wait, you have a brother?!" Kya asks.

"Please, we just wanna ask a couple questions. Do you know where he might be? Where he usually hangs out?" I ask.

"I don't know shit, now leave us alone!" He grabs Kya's hand and tries to pull her away, but she snatches her hand back.

"You have a brother? And you never told me?"

Parker throws his hands up. "Yeah, because it doesn't fucking matter! We don't even talk anymore."

"But you still lied!"

Sonnet and I watch quietly, wondering when the best time to redirect the convo is.

"Fine! I lied! Now can we go?"

Kya shakes her head. "We been together almost two months and it's been nothing but lies. First it was your ex, then Tina, now you got whole family members I don't know about? Tired of this, Parker. I'm done."

She turns on her heel and walks away, disappearing into the sea of kids still mingling in front of the school.

I expect Parker to run after her, but he just watches her go and sets his mouth into a hard line.

This isn't going the way I had it planned in my head at all. We were just supposed to ditch class and ask him some questions, not make his girlfriend dump him.

"We're really sorry if we—" Before I can finish my sentence, he's pushed past us and starts walking away from the school.

Sonnet and I follow. Now that we know Parker Samson is real, we're not leaving without some answers.

"Parker, wait! Can't you just talk to us for a minute? We'll leave you alone after that, I swear," I say.

But he doesn't even turn around, he just keeps on walking like he doesn't even hear us.

"Beau, this isn't working," Sonnet says.

"I know, I know. It's because he doesn't care about Jordan. He's probably glad he's gone missing," I say. There's a million reasons to hate a bum-ass dude like Jordan but if his whole family hates him, we're screwed.

"So?" Sonnet asks as we follow him across the street. "He still could know something."

"I think we should tell him why we're looking for Jordan. The real reason. Maybe he'll want to help then, if he knows we want to turn Jordan into the police."

Sonnet turns to me. "It's worth a shot."

Truth is, it's better if people don't know who we really are or what we want with Jordan, if we actually want to find him. But maybe Parker is the exception.

"Jordan let my sister die alone!" I shout to Parker's back. "*Your* brother let my sister die alone!"

A few people on the street look at us, but I don't care. I need answers. I need them now.

Suddenly, Parker stops walking and turns around to face us. "The girl that was murdered by the cop? That's your sister?"

I don't like hearing Katia being called "the girl that was murdered." Like the only thing people know her for is being dead.

"Her name is Katia," I say, slowly closing the distance between us. "I just need to know what happened that night. We need Jordan's testimony to prove she didn't do anything wrong. But no one's seen him since that night."

Parker's face softens and he looks like he feels bad.

"I'm sorry about your sister. I heard about it on the news. But I really don't know where Jordan is."

"But you're his brother," Sonnet says. "He hasn't called or texted?"

Parker shakes his head. "We don't talk like that anymore."

"What happened?" I ask.

"Does it matter?"

"Just asking."

He takes a deep breath. "He wanted to recruit me for the OTs. But he wanted me to—basically I would have had to do some things that I wasn't down for, you know what I'm sayin'? So I told him I was good on being an OT. I was never really into that kinda mess anyway. Next day when I was walking home from work, a buncha them niggas cornered me in an alley and jumped me."

Sonnet looks horrified by what she's hearing, but I'm not fazed. The OTs have done way worse than jump a kid.

"Jordan told them where you were?" I ask.

He nods. "So that's when I stopped fuckin' with his lame ass. To me, he just another opp on the street. Blood don't mean shit to him."

Damn, if Jordan would set up his own brother, it makes sense that he'd abandon Katia when she needed him. He doesn't care about anybody but himself.

"When did all this happen?" Sonnet asks.

"Last year. It's old news though. I'm over it. That's why I can't tell you where he is. I don't know and to be honest, I couldn't give less of a fuck."

"Do you know any of his friends? Where he likes to hang out? Anything like that?"

Parker looks up to the sky as he thinks. "I mean, he was always running with the gang. They didn't recruit me long enough for me to actually know anything. But his baby momma Cierra might. Did y'all talk to her?"

My jaw hits the ground. "Jordan has a kid?"

"Ol' girl was pregnant last I saw her before we stopped talking. But she said it was his."

Sonnet takes a notebook out of her backpack and starts scribbling notes. I can't believe this fool had a whole baby and didn't tell Katia! No, no way Katia woulda been with Jordan if he had a baby on the way. She woulda dumped him, definitely.

"A baby? Jordan's baby? You're sure?" It's just not adding up in my head. Katia used to stalk Jordan when they got into arguments, driving around the city looking for him at his hang out spots. Wouldn't she have found out about the baby if it was actually true?

"You didn't know that? You should have talked to her before me; she was always up under his arm. Back then anyway."

"You said her name is Cierra?"

"Yeah. Her and her moms stay in Terror Tower."

My heart starts racing in my chest. "Terror Tower?" Terror Tower is one of the most dangerous project buildings in the city. I've never been inside but Deja said somebody gets shot over there almost every weekend.

"Yeah, sometimes we'd go over there and smoke since her moms didn't care," Parker says.

"Terror Tower though? You're sure?"

He nods. "What? You scared to go over there?"

"Us? Scared? Never!" Sonnet says. That's cuz she doesn't have a clue what Terror Tower is.

"It's just, we never been there before," I say.

"Here," Parker says, handing me his iPhone. "Go head and put your number in there. I'll text you so you have mine."

"What for?" I ask, raising an eyebrow.

"Whenever you decide to go over there, let me know and I'll go with you. They know me in that building so I'm not afraid."

We could definitely use backup on this lead. But Parker is still Jordan's brother. We obviously can't trust him, but we might be able to use him to our advantage and then send him off.

I enter my number in his phone and hand it back.

"Cool, cool. Just holla at me when you need me," he says before heading down the street.

"Wow, he's a father. How did he manage to hide that from Katia?" Sonnet asks as we make our way back to the bus stop.

"He probably lied to her about everything," I say.

"Well, at least we know one thing for sure," Sonnet says.

"What's that?"

"Whoever this Murdersleuth person is, he's legit."

That's true. He still hasn't messaged me back yet, but I'm still stuck on Jordan managing to hide a brother and a baby from Katia. How could she be so stupid? And how could Jordan do that to her in the first place?

"This is bullshit," I say, slumping down onto the bench at the bus stop.

"What?" Sonnet asks.

"That Katia died messing around with Jordan and she probably never even knew about any of this stuff!" If she'd known, she would have dumped him, and this would have never happened.

"Maybe she did know and decided to forgive him?"

I look at Sonnet. "Never. She wouldn't have."

"She might have if she thought she loved him. Either way, what happened to Katia wasn't her fault."

"I know, but still. I just wish she'd done things differently."

I open Twitter on my phone while we wait for the bus. Still no response from Murdersleuth. But there's one from someone called ArithMyTick. It's probably just more spam, but I click on the message anyway.

ARITHMYTICK: Be careful. They're watching you.

CHAPTER 10

BEFORE

MOMMA HELD THE DRESS UP ON ITS HANGER IN front of Katia, the long, baby-blue chiffon blowing in the wind from our air conditioner that rumbled and popped whenever we turned it on.

"Katia, you worked so hard to make the money for this dress. Now you tellin' me you just not gonna go? Because some lil nappy-headed boy doesn't want you?" Momma snapped.

Had she bought the dress, I have no doubt she would have made Katia put it on. But since she didn't buy it, Katia was lying on the couch under a blanket, her hair tied up and her eyes red and puffy from crying.

"Momma, he's not a lil nappy-headed boy. Even *you* said you liked him," Katia said from the couch in a flat monotone. She'd been like this for weeks.

I sat at the kitchen table with the flat irons plugged in and a jar of Let's Jam open and ready for a quick glam-do. The prom wasn't gonna start for another hour. Katia still had time to make it if she wanted to.

"That was before that little bastard did you dirty. Just because he's going to Harvard don't make him no better than you. Probably just wants to mess around with the girls up there. It doesn't mean you need to miss this prom, Katia!"

"Princeton, Momma. He's going to Princeton, not Harvard," Katia said quietly.

Momma tossed the dress on the couch over her and threw her hands up.

"I don't give a goddamn if he's taking his blockheaded ass to Jupiter! You worked hard in school. You deserve this night, baby." Momma leaned down and wiped a tear from Katia's face.

"Momma, what is there to celebrate? We were supposed to get *married* one day. It's cuz I didn't get into FAMU. I messed up the plan."

When the rejection letter came in the mail last week, it was small and flat when the good ones were wide and thick. A week after that, Medgar dumped her. I heard her on the phone asking "why" a million times. Then begging, please please please. Then I guess he hung up on her because she kept saying hello hello hello and she dialed his number over and over for the rest of the night.

"Married?! Girl, you barely knew that boy. Trust me, he didn't break up with you because you didn't get into FAMU. He did it because that's what boys his age *do*. They date around. Try to see what they like. That's what you need to be doin', too," Momma said.

"He dumped me because I'm trash, Momma! Who goes to

Princeton dating some girl from the projects? Now I'm stuck here."

"Is that why you're cryin'? Because that boy didn't rescue you? We might not have much, but you always have food to eat and a place to lay your big ass head. If you don't wanna be here, you go to another school, get your degree, and get *yourself* out. You don't ever need to be pinning your hopes on some man."

Katia sniffled. "*You* did."

Momma was quiet for a moment and then she nodded quickly.

"You right." She spread her arms out wide and spun around in a circle like Maria von Trapp. "Look what it got me. My own palace in the projects. Trust me, you don't want to go down the same road I did with your father."

I was suddenly glad that Daddy had gone out to get us dinner from Billy's Ribs. I knew hearing Momma talk like that would have cut him deep.

"What do you want me to do, Momma?" Katia said.

"I want you to put this gown on and go to your prom! I want you to get your ass up off my couch like you don't have shit to live for!" Momma yelled. I could tell she was near tears herself.

But nothing we said helped. I even offered to give Katia my birthday money for the next ten years if she went, but she still wouldn't get up. All the other senior girls who lived in our complex were outside with their families taking pictures in sparkly gowns and posing with their dates on a red carpet spread through the courtyard. We'd wanted to be able to celebrate Katia, too.

When nighttime came, Momma put on her scrubs and went to work at the nursing home. Daddy brought Katia a small plate of gizzards and set them in front of her on the couch when she wouldn't move to take them from his hand. He wasn't mad, he just kissed her on the forehead. I think he was sort of happy about it because he didn't want either of us dating in the first place. That's how things usually went with Dad though. He was sometimes around when we needed him, but he never knew the right thing to say, so he didn't bother trying.

Then it was just me and my sister on the night of her prom. I imagined Monica and Clarice at the fancy hotel with the sparkling blue pond in the front, dancing with their dates in dresses that were much less classy than the chiffon gown and going, "Where's Katia?"

Maybe Medgar was there dancing with some girl who got into Princeton, too, whose parents had money to buy her any dress she wanted so she didn't have to flip burgers all summer like Katia had. Maybe the whole time she'd been planning her house with the kids and dog, Medgar was thinking she wasn't good enough for him. I hated him for her. And if it could happen to Katia, then it could happen to me, too, one day.

I sat on the floor in front of the couch with a bowl of popcorn. Momma had hung the dress up in front of the window, I guess to make Katia feel guilty for choosing to mope around instead.

"I shoulda known a guy like that would never be serious with me. May as well get with one of these dumbasses out here," she said angrily. I didn't know what to say, so I was silent for a while.

"It *is* a really pretty dress," I said eventually, looking up at it.

"You can wear it to your prom," she said, her eyes closed.

"Nah. I'm not going to prom."

Katia's eyes popped open.

"How come? Cuz I didn't go tonight?"

I nodded my head. To me, having something Katia didn't felt like stealing from her.

"You can still go to your prom, Beau. Just choose the right guy to take you. Don't go with a dude like Medgar."

"You said I shouldn't talk to the guys around here. Now you're saying I shouldn't mess with guys like Medgar. Who am I supposed to go with?"

Katia sighed. "A guy who's nice to you. But not because he wants something from you. He should be nice to you just because he wants to be."

I frowned.

"None of the boys in my class are nice to me. They always make fun of me."

"You're only twelve. All that changes in middle school when you get boobs and ass."

"But what if I don't?"

Katia shrugged and sighed loudly.

"I don't know, then take a dog to prom! Damn, you ask too many questions."

It was easy to irritate Katia when she wasn't in the mood. But I knew one thing that would make her feel better.

"Can I ask a question? Just one more?"

"If it's stupid I'm gonna reach over there and smack you."

I grinned. "You wanna watch *The Cheetah Girls*?"

Katia glared at me for a moment longer, shaking her head.

"Fine, go get it."

That night, we watched *The Cheetah Girls* and ate cold gizzards. After the first few minutes, Katia sat up. After another thirty minutes, I sat on the couch next to her. Every now and then she'd glance up at her gown and look sad, but then something exciting would happen on the TV and she'd be sucked back into the story.

After the movie, we zipped the gown back in its garment bag and stored it in the far back of our closet.

"You'll probably want your own dress when you go to prom. But this one's here. Just in case you want it," she said.

We put on another movie and fell asleep on the sofa under Mom's old quilt.

Back then, I saw a future for Katia even though she couldn't.

It didn't have Medgar in it, a wedding, or FAMU. But it had the big house with a white fence somewhere with palm trees and Walmarts where they didn't check your basket on the way out. Katia was a lawyer or a doctor or a scientist or whatever she wanted to be, and I was there, too.

CHAPTER 11

A WEEK AFTER OUR DATE AT THE ROLLER RINK, Champion asks me to have dinner with his family. I said yes but now that the night of the dinner is actually here, I wanna cancel.

I'm nervous as hell and I'm also still thinking about that creepy DM I got a few days ago. Sonnet said it was a troll, but we thought the same thing about Murdersleuth and we were wrong. It sounded like ArithMyTick knew exactly who they were talking to. But I haven't pinned down who would be watching us. The Onyx Tigers? The police? I haven't noticed anyone following me around but I'm a little paranoid.

"His parents probably already hate me," I say. I'm really not in the right headspace for this but if I want things to work with Champion, I can't avoid his family forever.

"That's ridiculous. They haven't even met you yet," Sonnet says.

"No, but I bet he told them I'm from Grady Park, so they know I'm poor. That's all rich people need to know to hate you."

"You're doing exactly what you're accusing them of."

"What?"

"Stereotyping. Not all rich people are assholes. They raised Champion and he's not an asshole."

"Even if they're nice, I'm sure they don't want him dating a girl from the projects. They'd probably want somebody on his level, somebody rich and somebody from a safe neighborhood like theirs. Like Madison," I say, my mood getting worse by the minute.

"Just because you're not rich doesn't mean you're not on his level. You're pretty, you're smart, and you're talented."

"You're saying that because I'm your best friend."

"No, I'm saying it because it's the truth. You're not lucky to be dating Champion. He's lucky to be dating *you*. Remember that during dinner tonight."

But even Sonnet's pep talk isn't enough to keep me from freaking out on the bus ride to Purple Hills. I open the clip of the fight on my phone, forty thousand views and counting. In all the chaos with the person's phone swinging around, it's hard to see that I'm trying to break it up. It looks like I'm part of the fight with Deja. We haven't talked much since the video went viral, but I need her right now.

ME: Hey are you busy?

DEJA: Um a little. Why wassup?

ME: I'm meeting Champion's family tonight and I'm scared.

DEJA: Of?

ME: What if they don't like me? Or they feel some type of way because I'm from Grady Park?

DEJA: If they feel some typa way, then cut his ass loose and find somebody better.

ME: But I like Champion. I just want his family to like me too. Our video is still blowing up, what if they see it?

DEJA: Girl I know, I saw! You see I got 5k new followers on my ig? Bih we are FAMOUS!

I leave her on read. Shoulda known she wouldn't understand, she lives for this kinda ghetto glory. They'll probably make her student of the month at Grady Park High for it.

But as much as I'm irritated by Deja right now, I'm jealous that she can walk around with this I-don't-give-a-fuck attitude. She doesn't give a damn what anyone thinks of her. Maybe I could be like that, too, but I actually wanna get out of Grady Park. So I have to leave this shit behind.

When the bus lets me off near Purple Hills, I walk the rest of the way to Champion's, trying to smooth my hair down and pick off any lint balls on my black jeans. Sonnet convinced me into wearing this deep orange peasant blouse with bell sleeves that billow just at my fingertips. But one thing I wouldn't negotiate on is my black Chucks high-tops. I don't care how tall they'll make me look, I don't do heels.

When I reach Champion's block, it's like I'm in a movie.

Where I've caught the bad guy and now I'm home under a purple/orange sky waiting to reunite with my family inside one of these lit-up mansions. I like Purple Hills. Instead of trap music bumping in the background, there's the sound of birds chirping and crickets. There's no Impalas or Corollas in these driveways, only Range Rovers, Teslas, and every other fancy car that costs more than a house. There's no chip bags, beer bottles, or cigarette butts on the ground, only perfectly trimmed green lawns and those fancy painted mailboxes that sit at the curb. This is the kind of neighborhood I wanna live in one day.

Jesus, I bet the Woodses are gonna serve sauteed duck and caviar for dinner. Suddenly I remember why I was freaking out. I don't belong here and they're gonna know it as soon as I open my mouth.

I make my way up the walkway slowly, taking in Champion's gorgeous and massive house. It's different from the other houses, more futuristic looking. It's shaped like a bunch of squares on top of one another and the windows are floor to ceiling. I wonder if they close their shades at night like Momma makes me do or if they just leave them wide open so the whole neighborhood can see how they're living.

My finger doesn't make it to the doorbell before the big oak door swings inward and Champion invites me in.

"Wow," he says, taking my sweater and hanging it on a rack behind the door. "You look beautiful."

"Thanks. I'm just so nervous right now."

"You have nothing to be nervous about, Beau."

"You're sure they haven't seen the video?" I whisper. The entrance hall is huge, with fifteen-foot-high ceilings that echo our voices.

"Yes, I'm sure. Even if they did see it, you were trying to help break it up. Just relax, okay?"

"Um . . . okay. Just don't . . . don't leave me by myself, okay?" I can't stand when people do that shit. Invite you somewhere you've never been before with people you've never met and then disappear for a couple hours. I hope it doesn't happen tonight because I have no idea what to even say to his parents.

Champion smiles and grabs on to my hand. We walk through two living rooms and a family game room before we reach the dining room. A little girl with shoulder-length hot-pink box braids is laying silverware on the long white marble table.

When she sees us standing there, her eyes light up and she runs over to me and wraps her arms tight around my waist.

"Beau, this is my little sister, Queenie," Champion says.

Queenie looks up at me with the biggest smile showing her two front teeth have fallen out. "I like your hair!"

"Thanks. Yours is really pretty, too."

"And your shirt! And your pants! I knew you would be pretty." I laugh and hug her back. This was the pep talk I'd been hoping to get from Deja.

"Alright, weirdo, let her breathe. Where's Mom?"

Just as Queenie lets go of me, a short, brown-skinned woman in a black maxi dress enters from the doorway that leads to the kitchen. She sets a big platter of fried catfish in the middle of the table.

"Mom, this is Beau," Champion says.

This is the moment I've been dreading. Everybody knows you can't expect to last long with a guy if his momma doesn't like you. I'm prepared for her to be standoffish, maybe a little cold, but she walks over to me with a big smile and her arms out for a hug.

"Well, aren't you just cute as you wanna be?" she says, looking me up and down. She doesn't even make a face when she sees my sneakers. "Come on over here and have a seat. I'm just gonna run and get the sides. Queenie boo, come help Momma."

Queenie shuffles after her mother while Champion pulls out my chair.

"Where's your dad?" I ask as he sits in the seat next to mine and puts a hand on my knee.

"He's on his way. Had to work some overtime at his office. Still feeling nervous?"

"Not as much as before."

"Alright now, we got 'beans, greens, potatoes, tomatoes,'" Champion's mom sings as she and Queenie lay the side dishes on the table beside the catfish. "Don't be shy, Beau, help yourself."

Everybody sits down and starts piling their plates with food. Champion serves me, but I only want a tiny bit of everything because my stomach is still bubbling from my nerves earlier.

"So," his mom says through bites of fish. "Miss Beau, where are you from?"

Damn. My answer will fuck up the whole evening, I know it.

"Um . . . I'm from Chicago."

"Of course you are. But what neighborhood, I mean?"

"Oh, it's . . . um, over on the east side of the city." If I keep being as vague as possible, maybe she'll let it go. But then Champion turns and gives me a pleading look. He wants me to tell her the truth. Fine. "Actually, I'm from Grady Park."

I look down at my hands, waiting for his mom to grab a

broom and shoo me out of the house like a rodent. But she doesn't.

"Aw okay, my favorite babysitter when I was growing up stayed in Grady Park. Her name was Lynn, but we called her NiNi."

I think I know the woman she's talking about. She lives across the courtyard, two doors down from Breon. She's always giving out bags of chips and candy to the little kids when they knock on her door.

I pick up my fork and use it to push the black-eyed peas around on my plate. "Did she live in the Grady Park projects?"

Champion's mother swallows a mouthful of food and starts nodding. "Actually, yeah, she did! She still stay over there?"

"Yeah, she does." I'm tired of waiting for the other shoe to drop. So I drop the bomb myself. "I live there, too. In a different building but Miss Lynn is right across the courtyard from me."

Champion squeezes my thigh but that's the only reaction I get. Queenie and his mother keep eating as though I haven't said anything unusual.

"Small world! What's your momma's name? I might know her, too. When I was your age, me and my friends used to rip 'n' run all over the city. Can't do that anymore but those were some of the best years of my life."

"My mom's name is Basil. She works at a retirement home."

"Basil . . . Hmm, I don't think I know her. What about your dad?"

The more I tell Mrs. Woods about myself, the more relaxed I feel. When Champion's dad joins us halfway into my story about how Daddy almost made it to the NFL, I don't even miss a beat. I guess Sonnet was right about me stereotyping rich people. If I'd met his family anywhere else, I would have never guessed they lived in a mansion.

"Champion tells us you're an artist. Whose work is your favorite?" his father asks, practically drowning his catfish in Louisiana Hot Sauce, the same way Daddy eats his.

"Well, there's this group of artists I've been following on Instagram for years. They're called the Dark Muse Collective. I love all of their work, but I think Bexley O is my favorite. She's from Chicago, too."

"Her name sounds familiar. Was she in the news for a mural she painted of the Obamas?"

"Yeah. Yeah, she was!" I'm so thrilled that somebody actually knows who I'm talking about. And I can tell Champion's dad is really smart. I bet he wins most of his court cases.

"Are you looking into going to art school when you graduate from Millennium?" he asks.

"Absolutely. I mean, if I get in somewhere."

"Daddy, I wanna be an artist, too!" Queenie says.

"I thought you wanted to be a basketball player like me?" Champion says, holding his heart and pretending to be hurt.

"I do! When I'm not playing basketball, I'll do art," Queenie says matter-of-factly. "Mommy, what's for dessert?"

My phone vibrates in my pocket. I turn away from the table and pull it out.

SONNET: Don't get all worked up, but after dinner when you get a chance, can you call me? We got another DM from ArithMyTick. He used your name.

Suddenly it's like I'm having an out-of-body experience. I start feeling dizzy as my mind runs through what this means. If someone knows it's me behind the page, if they know what we've been doing, we're screwed. What if it's an OT? What if they're waiting outside my house right now for me to come home so they can beat my ass or . . . kill me.

I break out into a cold sweat right there at the dinner table and use a napkin to blot the moisture from my forehead.

"What's wrong?" Champion asks.

"Is it too warm in here, baby?" Mrs. Woods asks. "Thomas, can you turn the A/C on?"

"Of course," Mr. Woods says, pushing back from the table. But I push my chair back and stand up before he can.

"Actually, I'd better get going. I just got a message from . . . my mom. It's important. She said she needs me home. Like right away."

Queenie pouts. "But I was gonna show you my turtle later!"

Mrs. Woods puts a hand on her shoulder. "Queenie, enough. Beau, we understand. Champion will drive you."

Champion stands up but I push him back down in his seat. "No! No, please, that's not necessary. I'll just take the bus—"

"After dark? Absolutely not, there's no reason for that when we can drive you. We insist," Mr. Woods says.

I start inching away toward the front of the house but Champion grabs my hand.

"What's going on? It's okay, you can tell me," he whispers to me, our faces so close our foreheads are almost touching.

I wish I could tell him that there's a strong possibility of me getting my ass whooped and/or shot before the night is over. But I know Champion. He's a good guy, he'll try to help and probably make everything a thousand times worse. I can't drag him into my mess.

"I'm sorry. I just have to go." I pull away from him and run back the way we came, let myself out the front door, and fast walk to the nearest bus stop.

CHAPTER 12

"I TOLD YOU IT COULD WAIT UNTIL AFTER DINNER! I shouldn't have even texted you while you were with Champion's family. Did you at least tell them where you were going?" Sonnet asks.

Two bus rides later, I'm sitting at her desk, rereading every line of the DM.

ARITHMYTICK: They know it's you, Beau Willet. Delete the account NOW.

I click on their profile, but they've never tweeted anything. It's a dummy account, created only two days ago and with no profile picture.

"How do they know it's me? I don't get it. Did you tell someone about this?" I ask Sonnet.

"Of course not! Did you?"

"No. Could they have tracked the IP address on your laptop? Sometimes I use my phone to log in; maybe they tracked us that way."

I start pacing back and forth across Sonnet's bedroom, biting the skin on the tip of my index finger. Using Twitter was supposed to protect us, keep us anonymous while still being able to get information on Jordan.

"That's one theory. But however it happened, our cover's blown. We have to delete the page."

"No! What? We can't just give them what they want!" I say.

"We can't get murdered over this either! What if whoever this is tries to make us stop? Like hunt us down and shoot us or something."

"If anything, this DM means we're on the right track to finding Jordan. If we weren't, whoever this person is wouldn't be trying to scare us."

Sonnet sighs. "You might be right. But what if you're wrong?"

I sit next to Sonnet and put a hand on her shoulder. "Whoever 'they' is, if it was really that important, they'd just say who it was."

Unless it's the Onyx Tigers. But that's a theory I'll keep to myself for now. If talking to Parker put us on the right track to finding Jordan, then I know exactly what we need to do next.

I pull out my phone and open a blank text message.

"Who are you texting?" Sonnet asks, peering at my phone.

"Go ask your mom if you can sleep over at my house tonight."

"Okay. But why?"

"Because we're going out."

————————

Before we've even pulled up to the girl's building, I feel like I'm doing Champion dirty just by riding in a car with another dude. I don't know why, it's not like I'm doing anything wrong. But if the roles were reversed, I know I'd be mad if Champion did it.

Sonnet is in the back with her phone out taking pictures every time we stop at a corner because she's never seen the murals painted on some of the brick buildings out this way. Parker's in the driver's seat with it leaned back so far, he may as well be driving from the damn back seat. He steers with one hand which makes me nervous since we're in a Ford Taurus that looks like it's been on the road since the beginning of time. AND he's riding on two donuts.

Parker turns and catches me looking at him, but I turn away and pretend I was just adjusting myself in my seat. I went from having a good time with Champion's family to sitting here in a raggedy hoopty with *him*.

"Why you sittin' up there lookin' all nervous? Chill out," he says.

"Sorry, I just wanna be ready in case you hit a pothole and one of these tires goes flying off into the night."

He laughs. "You got jokes, huh? What's your car lookin' like? That's right, you ain't even got one!"

I glare at him but let him have that one since I started it. But I don't wanna do anything even close to flirting with him.

"Don't worry about me, just get us to this tower of terror," I say. "You told her we were gonna be with you, right?"

He rolls down the window and spits.

"Yeah, I told her I was bringing a couple folk wit me. But y'all gotta play it cool, aight? Especially you back there, Sza," he looks in the rearview mirror at Sonnet.

"What? I'm cool," she responds, the gold butterfly clips in her afro glittering under the streetlight flooding through the window.

"Did you ask her about Jordan?" I ask.

He shakes his head. "I'm not looking for Jordan, y'all are. I'm just here to play bodyguard if you need me to."

"Okay, fine."

"I'm for real. Listen, I can't stand the nigga either, but I can't get in too deep with this. You're girls, you'll be fine."

I tell him it's fine again and we ride in silence the rest of the way. I can't put my finger on it, but something about Parker makes me feel . . . weird. Why is he helping us if he doesn't want to be involved? From the texts he's been sending me all week about how Kya won't talk to him, I think what he wants has nothing to do with Jordan. I don't have a lot of experience with boys outside of Champion, but it seems like Parker might like me. Like, really like me. Which makes me wanna tell him flat-out it's never gonna happen. But I don't know for sure if he's just being nice.

We pull up in front of a red apartment building three stories high. The small patch of grass in front is overgrown and the white metal fence enclosing it has rusted over in places. There's a group of people across the street, playing music from a car stereo and sitting together on the hood and trunk. They all turn to look at us when we get out, but nobody says anything to us.

"This way," Parker says, opening the rusted gate for us.

Sonnet's standing next to me on the stoop just beaming as she looks around at all the different colored town houses flanking both sides of the building. I pull my Bulls snapback farther down on my head to shield my eyes. Sonnet and I probably wouldn't be a target out here just for the fact that we're girls, but Parker might be considered an affiliate. There's always that small chance someone sees us with him and thinks we're opps just by association. That's what I'm mostly worried about out here, being shot just for being around the wrong people at the wrong time.

But I swallow my fear and bury it deep in my heart. I replace my fear with an image of Katia. I'm gonna do what I came here to do. Period.

Parker presses a button and the door buzzes to let us in. Now I see why they call it Terror Tower. The sour odor of urine burns my nose and dead cockroaches litter the cement floor beneath the staircase that leads to the second and third floors.

The door to the first-floor unit is straight down the hall and hanging off its hinges, nothing but darkness visible on the inside. The lone dust-covered light on the wall flickers and Parker turns his phone's flashlight on before leading us up the concrete staircase.

I feel like we're in some scary ride at Six Flags.

"Come on, she lives at the top," Parker says, reaching behind him for . . . my hand? Sonnet's hand? He ain't about to get either. When we reach the second-floor landing, the door to the apartment busts open, and the smell of loud, frying meat and onions floods out toward us. My stomach rumbles.

A little boy around nine or ten closes the door behind him, a small Yorkie puppy barking in his arms. He looks up at us nervously and smiles before squeezing past and down the staircase.

I let my hunched shoulders drop finally and stop trying to hold my breath.

When we get to the third floor, Parker doesn't even knock, just lets himself, and us, right on in.

"Hey, baby bro!" A girl around our age gets up from the sofa and practically leaps into Parker's arms. So this is Cierra, I think to myself, sizing her up.

She's gotta be less than five two and her long, sleek red ponytail is nearly touching the ground as it waves behind her. She's wearing a tight black tube dress with blue lace at the hem and rainbow flowers printed all over.

I feel like I'm betraying Katia when I look at her face, because she's gorgeous. She's wearing thick Bambi eyelashes and a moondust-colored highlighter on her cheekbones, but I can tell she would still look pretty without it.

"Hey y'all, don't just stand there all shy, come in and sit down," she says to me and Sonnet.

Once inside, we step out of Terror Tower and into some fresh Wakanda rain forest. There are plants everywhere. Big potted ones with leaves the size of my head, delicate purple and blue flowers spilling from a vine that hangs from the ceiling. Succulents and aloe plants on every small surface with space. It's a tiny studio but it feels spacious and like the air is cleaner than it was just a few minutes ago.

"This place is sooo pretty!" Sonnet says, taking in the colorful artwork hanging from the walls.

"My momma likes home decor. She's starting her own business soon."

Cierra walks over to the coffee table and hands us all business cards with her mom's name, phone number, and photo on it.

"She does events, too. Weddings, quinces, baby showers."

Cierra sits down on the couch, crossing her legs so her dress hikes up higher, showing off more thigh. I sit down next to her while Sonnet keeps oohing and ahhing and Parker helps himself to a beer from the fridge.

I scoot over on the couch so Sonnet can sit down on the other side of me. Parker pulls out a bag of weed. I don't even want to think about what could have happened if we were pulled over, especially since the three of us are underage. He's just as stupid as Jordan.

"Y'all go to Brookstone, too?" Cierra asks.

She pulls a huge bong out from the other side of the couch and sets it on the glass table with a soft clink. She's a hardcore stoner.

"You want the first hit?" Cierra asks me, nodding at the bong.

"That's okay, we're actually not—"

"Oh my gosh, that thing is massive! And look at the filtration system on this bad boy," Sonnet says, turning the glass pipe this way and that.

I shrug. It's not like I can tell her "no" in front of Cierra. Then she might start to wonder what we're really doing here. But getting high in Terror Tower was not in my plans for tonight. None of this was in my plans for tonight. I just wanted to get through dinner with Champion's family without saying something stupid.

As Parker starts loading up the bong and Sonnet leans over the table practically drooling, my phone buzzes in my pocket.

When I look at the screen, I'm met with a photo of Champion's face, smiling and holding one hand up to stop me from taking the picture. He's trying to FaceTime me. Guilt dragging my mood down, I press ignore.

The smoke session starts, and the apartment is hazy within ten minutes. Whenever it's my turn to take a hit, I fake it, turn my head away to make it seem like I'm being polite and not exhaling in their faces. Luckily, no one's paying me that close attention.

"How's the baby been doing?" Parker asks, lounging on the black shag rug on the other side of the coffee table.

"You mean your nephew? He's fine. My mom makes sure he has whatever he needs. Especially since your deadbeat ass brother still hasn't even seen his own child."

Parker raises his hands. "Aye, I tried to tell you on the low Jordan wasn't shit."

She nods and leans her head on her elbows. "Yeah, you did. But it is what it is."

Now's a good time to get in. She might know something about Jordan that can help us find him. "Were you guys together for a long time? You and the baby's dad, I mean."

"We were together for almost a year when I found out I was pregnant. Come to find out, he had a whole girlfriend the entire time we was talking!"

She must mean Katia.

"But I caught up to her one day," Cierra goes on. "My girl Britt had to stop me from going to jail because that lil white girl was really tryna test me."

Okay, so not Katia. I'm not surprised to hear he was cheating on my sister with at least two girls, but I'm pissed that he thought he could treat my sister like just another chick.

She passes the bong to me, and I take a small rip. I can get a little high as long as I don't overdo it. And as long as my brain hasn't melted into a puddle. There's no point in asking the questions if I won't remember the answers later.

"Anyway," Cierra goes on, "I'm just glad the situation is through with. Ain't nobody got time for that bullshit."

"True dat," Parker says.

"What was it like dating a gang member? Did you have to get, like, sexed in?" Sonnet asks, her eyes turning bright pink.

What the hell is this idiot thinking? If I'd known there was gonna be weed, I never would have brought her.

"Nah, I wasn't in the gang. The other girls were cool to me because they knew Jordan but they're not doing anything interesting. They don't know it but they really there just to take the fall for the dudes. Or to seduce niggas into alleyways and get them robbed or shot."

Even my eyes go wide at that. She says it so casually, like it's not a big deal. Then I wonder if Katia knew about all this stuff Jordan was doing. She must have. So why didn't she just dump his stupid ass?

"Did Jordan ever make you do anything like that?"

She licks her top lip and leans her head back against the sofa.

"He tried. But that first time he asked me to hold some money for him I let him know right off top I wasn't with that shit. He ain't ask again after that. But we never really went anywhere after that either. He'd always just come over here."

The weed hits me hard as hell, because I can barely feel my legs and suddenly, Cierra's couch is the most comfortable seat I've ever been in. I never wanna leave.

I bite my lip to pull me back to reality. *Focus, bitch, focus!*

I feel a weight hit my shoulder and turn to see Sonnet knocked out. Her fro blocks my view but I pat it down so I can see.

Sonnet and Parker are talking about something and laughing but I missed what she said. Suddenly a baby's cries fill the apartment. Cierra shrugs and stands up.

"I'll be right back, y'all," she says, disappearing into a bedroom and closing the door behind her.

I turn to Parker.

"I thought you said she'd know where Jordan was."

Parker looks up at me with hazy eyes. "I said she might know something. But she might not."

"Well, I need to know for sure. I'll go and talk to her. Come on, Sonnet."

I pull her up off the couch and she staggers after me to the back of the apartment. I knock on the bedroom door.

"Cierra, can I come in? It's Beau and Sonnet."

There's quiet behind the door for a moment and then I hear the click of the door being unlocked.

I step inside and close the door behind us. Cierra's room is just as cool as the rest of the apartment. The walls are painted a dark forest green with plastic plants hanging from each corner of the ceiling. There's a twin bed hidden by a curtain of plastic hanging vines and next to it, a small white bassinet and a changing table packed with open packages of diapers and wipes. She's cradling the baby in her arms.

Cierra's sitting cross-legged on the bed, tears running down her face.

"Are you okay?" I ask, sitting next to her. Sonnet spills herself over the foot of the bed and closes her eyes.

Cierra nods and wipes her cheeks with her hands. "Yeah, girl, I'm cool. It's just . . . I don't know, sometimes when he cries, I feel like I gotta cry, too. And every time I look at him, I see Jordan."

"Do you know where he is?" I ask.

"You been asking a lot of questions about Jordan. How do you know him again?"

I rub my eyes, trying to wipe the fog away. "Through Parker. Sort of. I'm just tryna find Jordan because he . . . he took something from me. Something important. And I need to find him if I wanna get it back."

"What'd he take?"

I think about telling her the truth. But she might flip her shit if she finds out she and the white girl weren't the only ones seeing Jordan.

"A ring. From my older brother. I don't know how he got it, but my brother was killed a few months ago and I just want the ring back. To remember him."

Not the truth but close enough.

"That's fucked up. But I don't think I ever saw him with no ring. Just those fake-ass cubic zirconia studs he be tryna pass off as diamonds."

"Even if he sold it or something, I just need to know what happened to it. I've been looking all over the city for him. Parker said you might know where he is."

"I don't know why he told you that. If I knew where he was, I wouldn't be raising this baby by myself," she says. But her eyes don't meet mine when she says it. She definitely knows something.

Cierra notices me looking at the baby and asks if I want to

hold him. She holds him out to me and for a second, I hesitate. I *know* Katia didn't know Jordan had a baby on her. That's the ultimate offense. But I do sort of wanna see what he looks like. Maybe it's not really Jordan's kid.

I take the bundle of blankets from Cierra, supporting the baby's head in the crook of my arm. I push the blankets back away from his face, prepared to hate this baby for Katia.

But he's beautiful. Little black wispy hairs lay across his head, which is shaped just like Jordan's. His little brown cheeks are flushed, and he looks up at me with these tiny dark eyes. He doesn't know anything about the world yet, that I just lied to his mother, that his father is a deadbeat who doesn't care about him. All he knows is what's happening here and right now, me holding him in a jungle-colored room and his mother watching him.

I really hate Jordan. It's one thing to ruin Katia's life, or Cierra's. But how can he turn his back on his own flesh and blood? How is it that I'm holding his son even before he does?

"I'd help you find your brother's ring, but I swear I don't know nothing about it," Cierra says, gently running her fingertips across the baby's head.

"That's okay. Do you know where he usually hangs out? Or anyone who might know?"

"Well . . . you can't tell him I told you, okay?"

"I won't tell anyone," I promise.

"Okay. Jordan called me last week from a private number."

Jackpot. The world still feels hazy and strange from the weed, but I try to fight it and clear my head.

"He said he needed a place to stay for a lil while. But I told him no because he hasn't sent me a dime for Jordan Jr. My baby's almost eight weeks old"—she starts banging her fist into her palm for emphasis—"and he's never met his father."

"What did Jordan say?"

"Got mad. Started calling me all types of bitches. Then I heard from somebody that this fool was on the news a while back. A cop shot some people and Jordan ran off. So they lookin' for him now I guess."

"Where do you think he'd go to hide? Does he have other family or friends around the area?" I ask.

"He's got a whole harem of hoes across the city. He's probably laid up somewhere with one of them."

I can keep questioning her but I'm not sure she knows any more about where to find Jordan than Parker does.

Cierra takes the baby and lays him down in his bassinet. I open the bedroom door and we step into the haze of smoke. Parker's still on the couch, scrolling through his phone.

My phone.

"Gimme my phone!" I shout, rushing forward to snatch it from him. I turn it over and see a series of stoner selfies he must have taken while we were in the bedroom.

Cierra stands between us, confused. "What's going on?"

Parker just sits there with this smug look on his face like it's a joke. "Nothing, Beau just thought I was on the phone with her boy, that's all." Then he falls into another fit of laughter.

Heat floods my cheeks and rushes down my arms, through my hands, into my knuckles. If he had time to take all those selfies, what else did he see on my phone? Did he open Twitter? If so, then he knows waaay more than he's supposed to.

I force myself to take a few deep breaths and calm down.

We're still in Terror Tower and Parker is still our ride home. I swallow my anger, play it off like I'm in on the joke and sit in between Parker and Sonnet.

Cierra still looks confused, but she sits down and lights the bong.

By the time Parker is sober enough to drive, it's nearly 1:00 A.M. I make sure to exchange numbers with Cierra, in case she hears from Jordan again, and then me and Sonnet pile into the Ford Taurus.

I keep my arms crossed tight across my chest the entire time.

We're almost halfway to Grady Park when Parker builds up the nerve to speak to me.

"Why are you being like that? I ain't even go through your phone. I was just taking pictures."

I don't even turn to look at him. "Don't."

He checks the rearview mirror where Sonnet is fast asleep in the back seat.

"I didn't tell your man about what you were doing. Is that why you're mad? You don't want him to know you're with me?"

I pinch the bridge of my nose. "I'm not *with you*. We just happen to be sitting in the same car right now."

"You know, if he's really your man, he should be the one helping you. Not me. It's a reason you not afraid to tell me what you're doing but you can't tell him."

I turn to him, hatred burning in my eyes. "Can you just shut the hell up and drive?"

"Don't get mad at me for speaking the truth. You had everything you needed to come over here without me, but you didn't. You called *me*, baby, not the other way around."

"For the last time, you psycho, I was scared!"

"Scared of Terror Tower or scared your lil basketball boyfriend would see who you really are?"

I dig my nails into my thigh.

"My boyfriend knows who I am. You don't."

"I know we're both from the hood. Mr. Champion Bankroll ain't. Even if you asked, you know he wouldn't bring his scary ass out here to look for no nigga."

"You don't know that," I say softly, because he's right.

"Front if you want to, you know I'm right."

"Parker, you're the last person who should ever be talking about relationships to anybody. Remember Kya?"

"Forget her, that girl on some bs. That's why I let her go, I was getting tired of her. Then you show up at my school for me . . . looking how you look . . . and you got a dope personality on top of that?"

If he thinks he can run game on me, he's even dumber than I thought.

"Anyway, you should let me take you out next weekend. Dinner, a movie, the museum—"

"Boy, if you don't take your ashy-ass hand off my thigh!" I knock his hand off my leg and scoot as far away from him in my seat as I can.

He pulls his hand back and puts it on the steering wheel. "Why? Your friend back there sleep, she don't care."

"Does it look like I'm playing? I. Do. Not. Want. You. Period! Just drive this old ass car and take us home. PLEASE."

Maybe the please is what does it, because he doesn't touch me again or speak except to ask for directions to Grady Park. I want to tell him that after this night, I want nothing to do with him. But I can't help feeling like he knows something.

I have him drop us off a block away from my building. I shake Sonnet awake in the back seat and let her lean on my shoulder as I help pull her out of the car and onto her feet.

"I don't wanna get up, still tired," she says groggily.

"I know, we're going home."

I lead her across the street and hear Parker call my name.

"What?" I ask, turning back.

"Think about what I said, aight? You don't have to hide with me."

I give him the finger and turn back toward Sonnet. We've barely made it onto the curb before the raggedy Ford Taurus peels out.

CHAPTER 13

ON FRIDAY MORNING, I'M STILL TIRED AS HELL from our trip to Terror Tower. And for some reason I can't get little JJ's cute baby face out of my head. I don't even like babies that much, but it's different when you're holding one.

I lend Sonnet some of my clothes since she didn't pack an overnight bag.

"That was a wild night," she says sleepily as we take our seats on the bus.

"Yeah. Maybe we should ditch first period and go take a nap somewhere," I say, leaning my head against her shoulder.

"No way! Today we're voting on the mural proposals. I really think you and Madison are gonna get it."

I'd almost forgotten about the mural. That's one thing I have to look forward to. We didn't get the info I thought we would from Cierra, but if I win the mural contest and Katia's painted on the side of our school, larger than life, I bet the tips will start pouring into our DMs. I hope so anyway.

In art class, Ms. Kubler has arranged all of the proposals around the room on their own easels. Most people worked in pairs so there's eight murals to choose from, not counting Sonnet's dick of corn, which has been propped up in a corner.

Ms. Kubler has us rotate around the studio in pairs, with one full minute to look at each proposal. The competition is stiff, especially the Lauryn Hill tribute Krina did.

"Okay, class, now that you've had a chance to see your classmates' work, write your vote on a slip of paper, fold it, and place it on my desk," Ms. Kubler says.

I bet most people are voting for themselves. I would, too, but I know Sonnet would be heartbroken if the only vote she got on dick of corn was her own. So I cast my ballot for her.

As if the anticipation isn't enough, Ms. Kubler insists on waiting until the end of the period to actually tell us the results.

"I've tallied the votes and the winner is, by a landslide might I add, *Katia's Butterflies* by Beau Willet and Madison Garber!"

"Oh my god, yes!" Sonnet shrieks, pulling me into a tight hug. I hug her back and start jumping up and down. We did it! No one will ever be able to forget Katia when her face is painted on the side of the school.

The class gives us a round of applause, except a few kids who look annoyed their proposal didn't win. After class, Madison comes up to me as I'm putting my pencils away in my bag.

"See? I told you we couldn't lose with your talent!" she says.

"We both worked on it. What I did was okay, but I think your added touches really took it to a whole 'nother level," I say.

"We are SO going out to celebrate after school. How about the Sugar Factory? Around 4:00 P.M.? Bring Champion and your friends and I'll bring Josh and some of my friends. It'll be a blast!"

"That sounds fun but I really—"

"We'll be there!" Sonnet finishes for me.

"Great! Text you later, k?"

Once Madison has walked away, I turn to Sonnet.

"We don't have time to go out, we have a Jordan to find, remember?" I whisper to her. We leave the art studio and wade into the crush of kids migrating through the halls to their second-period class.

Sonnet claps a hand on my shoulder. "Beau, I think we can take the afternoon off. Katia is going to be painted on the side of Millennium Magnet. For like, ever. If this isn't a good time for a celebration, I don't know what is."

"I guess you're right. But have you seen the prices at that restaurant?"

Once I asked Daddy if we could have my birthday dinner there, but he said we didn't have money to pay for Kool-Aid with suckers and gummy bears on skewers sticking out of the glass when we can get the same stuff at the corner store for less.

"Don't worry about that, it'll be on me."

"Sonnet, you don't have to."

"I know, but I want to."

I muster up a small smile. It's embarrassing to have other people pay for me, but I know Sonnet just wants me to have a good time.

"Okay, thanks, girl. I'm sorry dick of corn didn't win. Are you okay?"

"Totally. I've accepted that the masses of Millennium Magnet aren't ready to deal with the repercussions of patriarchal values in our society," she says.

"Ah. Well, as long as you're okay."

I text Champion during lunch about the Sugar Factory and he invites the whole basketball team, who invites the whole cheerleading squad. After school, Sonnet and I ride with Champion to the restaurant. By the time we get there, there's so many of us, they have to reserve four booths. But since Madison's dad is who he is, all she has to do is drop his name and we're moved to the front of the line.

"Did you really have to invite everyone you've ever met in life?" I whisper to Champion as we scoot into a booth.

"I only invited Dre and Josiah! But you know how it is, if one of us goes, everybody wants to go."

"If you say so . . . ," I say, folding my arms across my chest. There's candy and bright colors and TVs everywhere I turn. This place is like a five-year-old's dream. But there's a lot of people here and it makes me nervous.

Champion kisses me on the cheek.

"Don't worry about them, we're here to celebrate your mural. Do you have a picture of it?"

Suddenly a blond head with a giant blue bow on top leans over from the booth next to us. A cheerleader. "Yeah, let's see it!" she says perkily.

I do have a photo of it, but I'd rather not show it to the entire popular crowd of Millennium Magnet. Because if I do, they'll ask who the girl covered in butterflies is and then I'll have to explain what happened to her. Champion's friends seem nice, but they didn't know Katia and they don't really care. Plus, I don't wanna start crying in front of people I just met.

"Sorry, I don't. Guess you'll just have to wait till we get through painting it," I say.

The cheerleader pouts and dips back into her seat. Across the table, Champion's loudmouth friend Dre flags down a waitress.

"Excuse me, miss, but can you turn one of these TVs to the news? They're supposed to be playing some clips of us shooting in the gym."

The waitress looks like she's about to say no but then Madison chimes in. "Oh wow, I'd love to see that!"

"Sure, just a moment," the waitress says, her attitude doing a full one eighty.

If Dre notices how racist that shit was, he doesn't say anything about it, just goes back to tugging on the ponytail of another wide-eyed cheerleader sitting next to him.

Next to me, Sonnet passes me a menu.

"Here, Beau. Order whatever looks good to you."

Knowing that she's paying makes me want to order the least expensive thing on the menu. I would never order a twenty-dollar soda filled with gummy candy if I was paying for myself.

The waitress turns the nearest TV to the local news and starts taking everybody's order.

"I'll have a basket of fries and a glass of water," I say, handing the menu back.

Sonnet glares at me. "No, she won't. She'll have the Super-Duper Garlic Fried Chicken strips and the Godzilla Triple Threat Sundae."

"Sonnet, I can't eat all that," I say.

"I know, I'm gonna help you," she says with a grin, handing the menu to the waitress.

The sundae turns out to be bigger than either of us thought. It's so huge, we decide to share with the whole table.

"This is too good!" Madison says, shoving a spoonful in her mouth. Her boyfriend takes one of the maraschino cherries and dangles it just above her nose while she bats it away.

It *is* pretty good, a huge bowl of every flavor ice cream they have, covered in chocolate sauce, sprinkles, pop rocks, sugar cubes, and rainbow twister lollipops. I take another bite and close my eyes to enjoy the sweetness.

"Hey, you got a lil chocolate right there," Champion says. He rubs a spot on my chin and then licks his finger.

After a while, I start to relax and have fun. Being Champion's date means this is my crew, too, now. Yeah, so maybe none of these kids even said hi to me before today but if they're willing to look past it, so am I.

"Hey, Beau! Come over here, we're about to do that new challenge on TikTok," a cheerleader with curly black hair calls out to me.

Champion scoots over to let me out of the booth and I grab Sonnet's hand. She catches onto the moves of the challenge really quick, and Josiah records us.

The music starts playing and me and the rest of the girls stand together in a line before weaving in and out of one another like a snake. For the second part, we put our hands on our knees and pop our butts out three times. I know we must look stupid as hell to the waitress and the other diners but it's been so long since I've had fun that I don't give a damn what anybody thinks.

After we dance until our arms and legs get tired, I sit next to Champion and lean my head against his shoulder. This is what

I always wanted. To fit in somewhere outside of Grady Park. Here, I fit perfectly.

"Hey, y'all, look, the news is on!" Dre yells, turning up the TV that hangs behind our booth.

The news channel logo flashes across the screen with a red breaking news banner at the bottom.

A white reporter wearing way too much blush pops up on the screen. "Good afternoon, I'm Carol Dawson and this is CNTV News at Five. Chicago Police have just released new information related to the death of Katia Willet, the twenty-two-year-old woman who died of a single gunshot wound to the head by an off-duty police officer this past January. We'll now join our correspondent Tim Ashton live outside the Chicago Police Department precinct downtown."

Sonnet and Madison turn to look at me, but my eyes are glued to the screen. I can't believe this is happening. Prosecutors must have finally decided to file charges against Peter Johnson! I knew they'd figure out that piece of shit was lying and arrest him! If they've got him, then we don't need to bother finding Jordan.

The TV cuts to a young white guy standing outside the police station alone. "Thank you, Carol. I'm here at the Chicago Police Department where just moments ago, police chief Roger Jem issued a statement regarding the investigation of the death of Katia Willet by off-duty Chicago officer, Peter Johnson. Here's what he had to tell us earlier about their findings."

The TV cuts again to the police chief, an older Black man with a thick mustache and cold dark eyes.

"After an internal investigation, we have deemed that Officer Johnson did indeed breach officer protocol by using his city-issued weapon. However, we also just received tests back from the lab and can confirm that a significant amount of cocaine was discovered in the back seat of Ms. Willet's vehicle."

My heart sinks. Cocaine? In Katia's car? The two phrases don't even connect in my mind. Yeah, she smoked a lot of weed, but Katia would NEVER do cocaine or heroin or any of those hard drugs that stay fucking people up in Grady Park.

"Holy shit, that was your sister?" Dre asks in shock.

Suddenly I remember where I am, and that the entire popular group at Millennium Magnet has just heard that my dead sister had cocaine in her car.

Sonnet squeezes my hand. "Hey, Champion, maybe we should, uh, get Beau home?" she says across me.

Champion, who had his eyes glued to the screen like everyone else, snaps to life and nods his head.

The three of us slip out of the booth and leave through the restaurant's back door. Maybe I should have said goodbye first, I think to myself as Champion opens the car door for me. Maybe we should have stayed, laughed and played it off like no big deal. Now that we left without saying a word to anyone, it makes it seem like she's guilty.

"Beau? Are you okay? You haven't said anything," Sonnet asks as Champion pulls away from the curb.

"I just don't get it. If they found drugs in her car, why are they waiting until now to say something?" I ask.

Champion looks stressed at the wheel. "They probably didn't know what it was at the time. But didn't you say your parents were filing a wrongful death lawsuit against the city?"

"Yeah, so?"

"Sooo if the city loses, they're gonna have to pay your family

131

that money. But if they try to make it seem like your sister was in the wrong . . ."

"Then they don't have to pay us anything," I finish.

"Basically. The city is taking the cops' side. No surprise there," he says bitterly.

I'm already knowing my parents will be on ten whenever I get home. Getting knocked up and using drugs are my parents' major house rules for me and Katia. And they're not gonna be able to yell at her so they'll probably chew me out instead, thinking I knew something about it when I honestly had no idea.

Champion puts a hand on my knee. "Why don't you come over to my house? You can come, too, Sonnet."

But I shake my head. "No, that's okay, my parents are gonna wanna talk to me. The longer I wait, the worse it's gonna be. I'd rather just get it over with."

As we ride through the city streets to Grady Park, I can't figure out why my boyfriend and best friend haven't asked me if the drugs were Katia's. They could be afraid to ask. If they did, I'd tell them the truth: I don't know if Katia was using cocaine or not. Just like I didn't know her boyfriend was expecting a baby with someone else. I'm starting to feel like I never really knew Katia at all.

When I get home, Momma is sitting at the kitchen table in her baby-blue scrubs, a lit cigarette in one hand. I haven't seen her smoke a cigarette since I was, like, eight so I just stand there in the doorway, confused.

When she finally notices me, she gets up, drops the cigarette in a dirty mug that's been soaking for the past four days.

"You're smoking again?" I ask, stepping inside and locking the door behind me.

"No, no, nothing like that. Shirlen had a spare and I thought it might help me relax a little. This stress on me is too much."

She sits back down at the table, and I sit across from her.

"You're not working the late shift tonight?" I ask.

She shakes her head. "I was going to, but I'm just too tired. Where you coming from?"

She doesn't even get on me about not telling her I was staying out after school. This is so unlike Momma, to just not care.

"Studying with Sonnet. Did you watch the news yet?"

"No. Why? Somebody get killed?" Her voice doesn't sound concerned, just exhausted.

"Not exactly. The police chief did an interview earlier. They said they found drugs in the back seat of Katia's car."

I expect my momma to get up and start cussing and going off. Or even say it's a lie and the entire thing is one big conspiracy, but she doesn't. Her face doesn't even change.

"You should stop watching so much TV, Beau. Nothing good ever comes from watching the news out here."

"Shouldn't we do something about it? Like call the lawyer? Or you could call the news station and give a statement over the phone or something." Not just for Katia but for me. I get short of breath just thinking about the dirty looks I'm gonna be getting all day at school on Monday. It's hard enough shaking my reputation as a girl from the projects. I don't want even more people looking down on me for something that's not even true.

"To say what? That I know it wasn't hers? Nobody ever believes the mother."

She's got a point there. Everyone would expect us to be defending her, even if we knew the drugs were hers. Our words wouldn't mean a thing. The only way to set this straight is for Jordan to admit the drugs are his.

"Okay, Momma, but we can't just let the news say stuff like this about her."

She looks up at me with bloodshot eyes. "She's dead, Beau." I flinch at the word *dead*. "What the world thinks about her doesn't matter to Katia anymore."

"But it matters to me! I still have to live in this world, don't I? It's bad enough being the girl whose sister died but now I'm gonna be the girl whose sister was using or selling drugs!"

I don't know what the hell is happening to Momma, but I'm tired of it. I want her to snap out of it and stop acting like she doesn't care about anything anymore.

There's a knock at the door. Daddy. As soon as I let him in, he starts going off.

"Cocaine, Basil?! Motherfucking cocaine?!" He drops a bag of McDonald's on the kitchen table while Momma starts massaging her temples.

"Arlen, calm down."

But Daddy's huffin' and puffin' like the big bad wolf. "Calm down?! You knew she was seeing that lil gangbangin' boy and you let her get hooked on drugs?!"

I was wrong when I said Momma didn't care about anything. One thing she does care about is annihilating Daddy whenever he gets out of pocket with her.

"Excuse me? I didn't get her hooked on anything! Katia was a grown woman. I couldn't tell her who not to date. Don't forget she has *two* parents!" Momma stands up and gets right in Daddy's face. They never get physical with each other, but they still hurt each other.

Daddy puts a finger in her face. "Oh, no you don't! You're not blaming this shit on me. I wasn't even here! YOU were the one living in the house with her! Maybe you just weren't paying enough attention because you was too busy on your phone with that damn janitor from ya job."

My parents have completely forgotten I'm in the room. I don't get how they can argue like this over Katia, but when it comes to me, they don't even care where I'm at half the time anymore.

"Lord Jesus, Arlen, don't pretend like I kicked you out for some other man. I kicked your trifling ass out because you not leading this family like a man should! You don't work, you don't clean, you don't do shit but try to criticize my parenting!"

I know I shouldn't butt in, but they're forgetting the big picture here.

"Hey! Can y'all stop arguing for a minute?! Don't you think we should be figuring out how to defend Katia? It was on the news. Everybody and their gramma has probably heard about it by now."

Daddy steps away from Momma and sits down at the table next to me.

"Beau's right. We need to call up Al Sharpton, Jesse Jackson, one of them. Tell them to get down here and help us sort this mess out."

Momma starts laughing coldly. "No one's going to come, Arlen. If they were, they would have done it weeks ago! The reason why is because to them, Katia was guilty. Especially with Jordan fleeing the scene, and now we know they had cocaine in the car?"

"But Momma, I think it was Jordan's because—"

"That don't matter! It was her car; she'd still be an accomplice. Your sister made some stupid, STUPID choices, and this is what happens."

Daddy stands up again. "Basil, what the hell does that have to do with a police officer shooting our daughter in the face?!"

"It happened. No matter what we do or say now, we can't change that. Whatever people think about Katia, good or bad, she'll still be gone. I can't tell y'all what to do, but I'm not fighting no more pointless battles. I'm not." She shakes her head at us and disappears into her bedroom at the back of the hall.

"Don't listen to her, Bobo, she's not right in her head. Now here, you want a chicken sandwich or a burger?" Daddy passes me the greasy McDonald's bag and then goes to find paper plates for us to eat on.

I don't know whose side I should be on. Daddy wants to prove Katia's innocent, like I do, but I can't depend on him to follow through on anything. I don't like how Momma just wants to act like this isn't happening and forget it, but she's the one who's been here with me and Katia our whole lives. But maybe she's right about this being a pointless battle.

Either way, I know one thing for sure. School on Monday is going to be hell.

CHAPTER 14

MONDAY MORNING AT SCHOOL, I'M CALLED INTO the principal's office before the bell for homeroom has even rang.

As I sit in the stained red fabric chair in front of the school secretary's desk, I already know I'm in trouble. I've gotten detention for ditching a few times before, but I haven't done that in a while. Some kids probably get called to the principal's office when they do something good, like score really high on those standardized tests, but that never happens to me.

"Beau Willet?" Principal Marcos's voice calls through the crack of his office door.

I step into his office and plop down in the chair in front of his cluttered desk. He's not smiling so I know it's something bad.

"Hello, Ms. Willet. How are you doing today?" he asks, moving a stack of papers to his right so we can see each other.

"Good," I say.

He nods and steeples his hands, like he's getting ready to give me some terrible news.

"Are my parents okay?" I ask, gripping the wooden armrests of my chair.

"Oh yes! Yes, they're fine—I'm so sorry, I didn't mean to make you worry—"

I exhale and loosen my grip. As long as they're okay, I can handle whatever news he has next.

"Oh, okay. What did I do, then?"

He takes a deep breath. "The administration has some concerns . . ."

"About me? Thanks, but I'm okay, really."

". . . about the mural you and Madison Garber proposed. We've received complaints about the subject of the mural—"

"Katia."

"I'm sorry, what?"

"You said the subject of the mural. Her name is Katia. She's my sister."

"You're absolutely right, my apologies," he says, his face turning red. "However, in light of these complaints, the administration—"

"Who complained? Everybody in the class voted and our idea got the most votes."

"I'm not at liberty to discuss the identities of those who reached out to the school district. But I will say that some of these individuals have expressed credible threats against the school should this specific mural move forward."

Threats? Nobody even knows about the mural except the art kids, so it had to be one of their racist ass parents.

"So some parents called and threatened the school and now

138

you're saying we have to do what they want? That's not fair!" I bet if my parents called and threatened the school about something, it'd stay the same. They wouldn't care.

Principal Marcos sighs and pulls his glasses off his face. He doesn't really look sympathetic, just tired.

"I probably shouldn't be telling you this, but we suspect many of these calls are coming from a local Blue Lives Matter group. And given the . . . ah . . . new information that's come to light about the murder, the superintendent, among others, feels a mural of Katia could create a hostile and divisive environment for learning."

There's people who don't even know Katia that hate her. And if they know I proposed the mural, they hate me, too. They can't do anything to her, but they could probably find me if they really wanted to. I've seen what those kinda people are capable of on the news all the time. But I didn't think Katia would ever pop up on their radar, especially since Peter Johnson is walking around a free man. What's there for them to even be mad about if they've technically won this one?

"I don't get a say in any of this?" I ask, already knowing the answer.

"Unfortunately not. I know this wasn't the outcome you were expecting, but it would be best if a different mural was created in place of the one you and Madison proposed."

I sit there for a moment in silence, trying to figure out if I should play nice or start flipping shit over.

"I just wanna make sure I got it right. You're saying even though everybody already voted on it, we're not allowed to paint my sister on the school?"

"Beau, I know it might not make sense to you. But as principal of this school, it's my job to protect you and every other student at Millennium Magnet. Going forward with this mural poses too great of a risk. Ms. Kubler has already been informed of the decision, but I wanted to be the one to tell you."

I sit back in my chair, the air sucked out of me as I realize what I already knew: as bad as things are, they can *always* get worse.

"This is bullshit! They weren't her drugs. Katia didn't even do anything!"

"Language, Ms. Willet! I understand there's two sides to every story, but we have to be on the safe side. I know you and Madison will come up with another idea."

Principal Marcos stands up and ushers me out of the office. When I step out into the hall, it's quiet and empty. First period must have just started.

I walk as slow as I can, not wanting to walk into art class and have everyone know I was basically defeated. All because Jordan thought it was a good idea to use Katia's car as a drug storage center apparently. Nobody's saying anything about him, trying to figure out where he's hiding or anything. But they've got all day to talk about Katia being the one who was killed, the car being in Katia's name, the drugs being on the back seat on the floor behind her.

Losing the mural is nothing next to losing Katia, but that painting was gonna make things easier. It was gonna make people care, and if they cared, maybe I could get some real help finding Jordan. But now that's gone, too.

I round the corner of the arts wing on the fourth floor and run smack right into Madison. The books in her hands fall to the floor and I bend down to help her pick them up.

"I was just about to go looking for you. I'd been waiting outside the art class doors for you. You talked to Principal Marcos?" she asks softly.

"Yeah, I did. I can't believe he's serious! We worked hard on that mural and nobody's gonna get to see it."

I hand her the chemistry book and we both stand up.

"He did say we can propose another mural. We don't even have to do a vote this time as long as the school board approves it."

She says it like it's supposed to mean something.

"What's the point? The school board is never gonna approve anything about BLM if they're worried about racists bombing the school over it."

"Then we pick a topic we know they'll agree on. I'm sure no one would object to a Dr. King or Rosa Parks mural," she replies.

"I don't want that."

"Um, okay. What *do* you want?"

I step over to a window and bite my nail as I try to think of a solution.

"We could do like a mini protest! Tell Principal Marcos and the administration that if we can't paint Katia, then we won't paint anything," I say. Maybe I can't get people to fight for Katia, but I bet I can get them to fight for art. The more attention we bring to Katia, the more likely it is someone will see and want to help.

Madison's mouth makes an O shape. "You think that will change his mind?"

"Maybe. But even if it doesn't, at least we can say we did something about it, right?"

Madison runs a hand through her brown curls.

"You're sure about this?" she asks.

"Absolutely. We're not supposed to start the mural until next week so let's talk before then and come up with some ideas."

She gives me a tight smile and we head down the hall toward the art studio. Madison obviously doesn't think the protest will work, but it doesn't matter what she thinks. We just need most of the art class to back us up.

At the end of the class period, I linger behind to talk to Ms. Kubler alone. Her whole mood was off today. Usually she's cheerful and fun, but today she's been sort of sad looking.

"I take it you had the conversation about the mural with Principal Marcos?" she asks as the last student leaves the room and she closes the door behind them.

I nod. "I guess I shouldn't waste my time asking if there's anything you can do about it, right?"

I wish I could tell Ms. Kubler about the protest but I don't think she can say yes to things like that since she's a teacher.

"Believe me, I tried to change his mind, but the school board wouldn't budge on this."

I do believe her. I know Ms. Kubler would fight for me, not just because she knows me, but because she really loved the mural, too.

"Thanks for trying," I say.

"Have you got any new ideas that you might want to run by the school board?"

I have to play along like I'm really doing this. "Not yet, but I'm gonna meet up with Madison and come up with something for Monday."

"Excellent, let me know if you need any help. I'm so sorry some narrow-minded individuals ruined what would have been a beautiful mural. But I hope you'll include the sketch in your portfolio. It really is one of your best pieces so far this year, Beau."

I smile. "Thanks, Ms. Kubler."

I spend the rest of the school day coming up with ideas for the protest, including some crazy ones, like chaining ourselves in a line around the building we were supposed to paint the mural on. Or sneaking in early in the morning and painting the mural anyway. But I doubt I could get the rest of the class to go along with that. No, it has to be something low stakes, where the most trouble we can get into is a detention or something. I'm not going to let a bunch of racist parents say my sister isn't good enough to be on a mural.

Then I come up with a perfect idea. A sit-in. In the art studio. It'd be a peaceful protest, I think. Plus, Principal Marcos doesn't care that much about the arts program. As long as we weren't occupying the gym or his office, we might be able to get away with it. During government class, I sneak my phone out under the desk and text Madison.

What do you think about doing a sit-in? Like the kind they did during the civil rights movement. We could do it in the art studio.

After school, she still hasn't responded. I figure she's busy with other homework. Then around 8:00 P.M., I call her. It goes to voice mail.

It's not that weird for someone to be busy, but when she first asked to work with me, Madison was responding to my texts lightning fast. She's one of those people who has her phone glued to her hand 24/7. She could be ignoring me but why would she? I decide to give her a break until I know for sure what's up.

But I can't wait to hear what she thinks. The mural was just the beginning. We're about to change things. For real.

CHAPTER 15

I'M ON THE BEDROOM FLOOR, FRANTICALLY looking for anything that can double as a brain model for my psychology class.

How could I forget about the project worth 30 percent of my grade? I might be able to skate by missing homework assignments here and there but this project could be the difference between me chillin' this summer and spending it in summer school hell.

I'm about to call Sonnet for emergency help when my cell rings. It's Champion.

"Hey. What you doin'?"

I stop biting the skin off my thumb and sit down on the edge of the bed, my leg jumping with anxiety.

"Freaking the fuck out. My brain model project is due tomorrow and I completely forgot!"

"Relax. You're going through a lot. Don't you get a grace period?"

"Yeah, and it ended once I came back to school. I can't keep using Katia as an excuse if I ever wanna graduate."

"Okay, let's figure this out, then. Will your mom let you out tonight?"

I snort. "She's been in her room with the door shut all day. She doesn't even know I'm here probably. But I can't go out. Didn't you hear me just say I'm about to flunk junior year?"

"No, you're not, Beau. I'm on my way over. Give me twenty minutes."

"What?!" Champion has seen the outside of my complex before, but never the inside. His closet is probably bigger than our entire apartment. Not to mention the place isn't exactly viewer ready since Momma stopped cleaning. My white socks are black as tar from the floor and there's a sour smell coming from the back of the refrigerator.

"I'll stop and get some supplies," Champion goes on, ignoring me, "and we'll have it finished and ready for tomorrow. I did the same project last semester so we can just copy that idea."

"You really don't have to do that; I'm the one that forgot. It's my problem to fix, not yours."

He sighs on the other end. "I want to help, Beau. It'll be fun, and I've never been inside your house before."

"But my mom—"

"You just said she doesn't even know you're there. Just let me help, okay?"

I shrug. I do need the help. And it definitely beats being alone.

I tell Champion okay and then do my best to make our filthy home at least smell okay. I light some of my mom's Bath and Body Works candles in the living room and douse the hall and kitchen with linen-scented air freshener. Then I open the living room windows to let it air out.

The whole time I'm cleaning, Momma doesn't make a sound in her room. Boys aren't supposed to be in the house when I'm alone, but technically she's here, so I convince myself that it doesn't matter.

At seven thirty, Champion knocks at the door. He's holding a bag of markers and construction paper in one hand and a white Styrofoam wig head in the other.

"Uh, are we building a brain model or making a lace wig?" I say, stepping aside to let him in. He dumps the supplies on the living room floor, and I instantly remember I forgot to run a vacuum over it.

But Champion doesn't seem to mind the dust bunnies rolling around in the corner or the crumbs of Cheez-Its on the coffee table. He's probably just trying to make me feel better by not saying anything.

"We're making a brain. This is one of my mom's old wig heads. We can map out each part of the brain on construction paper and then glue it to the top of the head. Like a three-D effect."

I sit down beside him on the floor, resting on the back of my heels.

"That's actually a really cool idea. Oooh, and we can paint the head so it looks like a real person, with eyes and brows and stuff!"

"I'll leave that part to you since I'm not the best with a brush. Let me see your textbook. I'll trace the brain sections onto the head."

I tiptoe past Momma's room, even though I don't need to, and come back with a ton of art supplies that I spill onto the dirty living room floor, on top of the old fruit punch stain.

Champion's laser focused on sketching, so I pour myself into it, too. He can say or think whatever he wants about my house later. But for now, we need to finish this project.

"Thanks for letting me come over," Champion says after a while, his mahogany eyes gazing into mine. After a couple seconds, it's too much for me and I look up at a spot on the wall just above his head. I don't know why, but it makes me feel scared looking him in the eye for too long. But the spot on the wall? Safe.

"Boy, you basically invited yourself. But . . . I'm glad you came."

I smile at him and he's still staring at me with those sexy bedroom eyes that I know I can't resist. But I have to.

I go back to painting the irises on the Styrofoam's eyes, but I can still feel him staring at me. His eyes traveling down to my lips, my chest, my thighs, and back up to my eyes.

"Can you not?" I say playfully.

"What?" he asks innocently, leaning back to rest on his elbows.

"Tryna be cute or whatever and staring at me."

"I can't help it. I like watching an artist work."

"Well, I don't, it's creeping me out."

"Why?" he asks coyly, completely abandoning his job to write out the labels for the parts of the brain.

"Because . . . I dunno, it makes me nervous and I don't—"

I feel him take my hand in his, remove the paintbrush from

my fingers, and lay it on the square of newspaper we put down to prevent any mess.

Champion scoots closer to me, stroking my hand with his thumb. This is the moment I'm supposed to do something sexy, like lick my lips or let down my hair.

My hair's up in a messy bun so with my free hand, I lightly tug at the purple scrunchie. It doesn't come loose.

I swear shit like this can only happen to me.

The scrunchie gives way a little bit but then the messy bun flops in front of my eyes and the scrunchie gets tangled in my curls.

I feel like such an idiot, but Champion just laughs. "Let me help you," he says.

Normally I don't like people touching my hair, especially boys who might find out what weavical secret I have. He's not supposed to see the tiny knots or feel the roughness of four-week-old synthetic hair. He's supposed to think this is all me.

But I let him gently work the scrunchie out of my hair. Once it's out, I try to shake my hair loose like a white girl, but the crochet hair is still knotted within itself.

I try to laugh the embarrassment off but then, suddenly we're kissing, his hand caressing the side of my neck and my hand holding on to his forearm. His mouth is minty cool from an Altoid he just ate, and I pray he doesn't taste the Hot Cheetos I had for dinner earlier.

Before I'm ready for it to end, Champion pulls away slowly, his eyelids lowered as he gazes at my mouth.

"Your lips are so soft," he whispers, nuzzling against my neck.

I don't know how to act. I've never done anything like this with a dude before. Even though we're already dating, I'm still scared of looking stupid in front of Champion.

As he plants light moist kisses against my throat, I think of all the girls he's probably gone further than this with. He knows how to move his hands, his body, his lips, his tongue, like he's been doing this forever.

Suddenly, the kisses on my neck stop and Champion backs away from me, taking his warmth with him.

"What's wrong?" I ask him, my body still tickling with fire.

"Nothing, I just thought maybe you weren't in the mood."

"I-I am. I'm in the mood. Why would you say that?"

"I don't know, you just seem really tensed up. And you weren't really touching me either, so I thought—"

"I'm sorry, it's me being stupid. I have no idea what I'm doing."

He laughs and his white teeth melt me even more.

"Just be you. You don't have to do anything special. There's no instruction manual, you know."

I playfully flick his shoulder.

"I know that."

Champion grabs his piece of paper and starts tracing again. *Great, I messed up the moment.*

I'm not ready to stop kissing. I want more. But what do I say? *Kiss me?* No, that sounds like some cheesy old-timey film.

I go back to painting the Styrofoam head a deep shade of brown but I'm really staring at Champion, willing his luscious pink lips to make their way back to mine. But he's acting like he doesn't notice.

Half an hour later, the Styrofoam brain is complete and

drying on the kitchen table. Not my best work, but it damn sure doesn't look like it was done in two hours.

"See?" Champion says, his arm around me as we lounge on the sofa. "All that freaking out earlier was for nothing. If you don't get an A on that brain model, I wanna talk to the teacher myself."

We both laugh, stop, stare at each other, then burst into nervous laughter again. It's almost 10:00 P.M. but I don't want him to go. Not yet.

Once our laughter fades away, I lightly trace the line of his jaw with my finger, turning his head to face mine.

I expect him to lean in the rest of the way, but he's not making it easy for me. Maybe he just wants to see that I want him as much as he wants me.

Leaning forward, I press my lips against his, feel his hands holding my waist, his deep breaths in between each kiss. He leans back and pulls me with him, so I'm lying on top of him.

I debate whether or not to try putting my hand underneath his T-shirt.

Then I hear a sound that stops my heart dead. The annoying SCRRREEEEEEEECH of our screen door. Then, two loud knocks.

"Basil, it's me, let me in," Daddy shouts from outside the door.

I jump off Champion so fast I nearly twist my ankle.

"It's my dad!" I whisper shout as he jumps up, too.

"Aw, hell naw, you got a back door?"

The doorknob twists but I know Daddy doesn't have a key. But he could still wake Momma up and she might get up and answer.

"My bedroom's at the end of the hall. Go out the window!"

I start pushing him away from the front door, but he stops in the middle of the hallway.

"Beau! Basil! Come on now, let me in!"

The knocking doesn't stop, and I know it's just a matter of time before my dad gets worried and tries to break the door down.

"Champion, you need to get out now unless if you wanna die!"

I push him back toward the bedroom.

When I hear the sound of my window opening, I run back to the front door and unlock it.

Daddy walks in and narrows his eyes in suspicion. It's like daddy radar; they can smell when a boy has been in the house.

"Whose head is that on the table?" He gestures toward my drying brain model.

"It's just a project for school. I've been up trying to make sure it's perfect when I turn it in tomorrow." I smile and try to even out my breaths so he doesn't know I was just running around at warp speed.

"That's my girl, time to get back on the grind," he says, walking over to the fridge. "Gahd-dayum! What the hell is in this refrigerator smelling like doodoo?"

"I think it's that casserole Aunt Nisha brought over a few weeks ago."

"You said a few weeks ago? Well, what the hell it's still doin' in here? Paying rent? Hand me a trash bag from out under the sink."

We both scream when he unwraps the furry green-and-gray

casserole and it slides into the trash bag in one giant solid slimy piece.

"I just wanted to come by and make sure you and your momma are alright. How is she?"

I look toward the closed door and back to Daddy.

"Yeah, I figured. But Beau, you need to help out, too. I know your only chore was windows before, but now, you gotta step up and pick up your momma's slack. No more casseroles stanking up the place, okay?"

"Okay, Daddy." He kisses me on the forehead and lugs the fur casserole out into the dark night behind him.

Through the peephole I watch him walk out of the complex. My mind is racing. Did I really just get away with having a boy in the living room *with* my momma still in her room? Deja is gonna flip when I tell her I've finally crossed over to the dark side.

I turn out the kitchen and living room lights and walk into my bedroom. I take my phone off the charger and lie back on Katia's bed.

Before I gossip with Deja, I wanna make sure Champion got home okay.

ME: Didn't get caught. U on the way home?

I hit send and two seconds later there's a *BING!* sound. Not from my phone but from the closet. The door slowly slides open and Champion peeks his head out.

"Miss me?" he asks with a grin.

I nearly explode with joy.

"What the hell? You were supposed to leave out the window!" Even as I'm scolding him, I'm wrapping my arms tight around his waist and looking up at his beautiful face.

"Aye, you can't kiss a man like you did and expect him to have the balance to jump out a window. I can barely see straight after you put it on me." He crosses his eyes and makes a silly face.

"Boy, stop. You're lucky my daddy didn't walk in here and find you."

"I'm not scared of your daddy."

I tilt my head at him. "You sure about that?"

"Okay, I am," he says, "but I'd step to him over you if I had to. You're worth it."

I'm worth it. Not Deja, not Katia, not Madison. Me. If this is what it feels like to be loved, I'm starting to get why it drives people crazy. My room doesn't feel as empty or sad with Champion standing in it.

We lie down next to each other on top of the covers of my bed, our hands interlocked.

"My dad's a trip, man. He came over here talking about I need to help clean when he doesn't even have a job and I know he doesn't help clean Uncle Kolby's house."

"He should give you a break, you have school all day. You can't be your own parent."

I snort. "Yeah, well, that's what I've been doing since—since you know what happened."

"I know. But you still shouldn't have to do it. How 'bout I come over again tomorrow and help you clean? I have basketball practice but afterward—"

"No, Champion, that's okay, really. I'm working on getting my family back on track. I just need more time."

"How are you gonna do that?"

No. Nope, no, never. I don't care how close we get, I'm not telling him about me and Sonnet's search for Jordan. He already knows my parents are falling apart. I don't want him to think I'm in the middle of some gang war or that Katia was into that kinda stuff either.

He might be giving me a break on our sour-smelling house in the projects, but if he knows just how fucked my life really is, there'll be no reason for him to stick around. I'm not losing him over something that's not even my fault really.

"I'm gonna convince my parents to go to counseling," I lie. It's only a half lie because I did mention it once a couple months back to Daddy. He said therapy was for crazy white people, so I didn't push it any further.

"That's a great idea. Therapy really helped me when I was in middle school."

I sit up in surprise. "You went to therapy? Why?"

"I went to a private school and had to deal with a lot of bullying, racist white boys. I would be so angry about it when I got home because I couldn't fix anything at school. Anyway, therapy helped me calm down a lot. You ever been?" He talks about it so casually, too, like it's not a big deal or embarrassing.

I bite my lip. "No."

"If you can get your parents to go, you should try it with them. It's not as awkward as they make it look on TV."

"Yeah . . . maybe."

He squeezes my hand. "I should get going. Not because I'm

scared, but in case your dad comes back," he says, standing up and stretching his arms over his head.

"Riiight. You should still go out the window. Just in case."

"Got it."

We walk over to the window and I pull the curtains aside and open it for him, pulling the screen inward.

"I'll see you tomorrow," he says, snaking his arm around my waist.

After one last kiss, I watch him clamber out the window, and he waves before jogging into the darkness of the parking lot behind the complex. Then, I lie in bed with my phone next to me on the pillow, the ringtone volume set all the way up.

CHAPTER 16

IT TURNS OUT THE SIDE OF THE GYMNASIUM WE'RE working on faces the heating plant building, not the football field. Meaning it's not a wall anyone would be able to see unless they specifically walked all the way around the gymnasium to this dead-end corner that goes nowhere. But there's a faculty parking lot back here and it's better than not being allowed to paint on the school at all.

Ms. Kubler is dressed in her "art" clothes today, paint-splattered overalls and an oversize black tee. Everybody else is wearing old clothes they don't care about. I made sure not to put on anything of Katia's today, just an old ratty long sleeve and some black sweatpants.

Beaming with glee, Madison walks around the empty parking lot, passing out papers with a grid layout of where the mural will be painted on the wall.

She holds a paper out to me, and I snatch it from her hand with the dirtiest look.

Sonnet elbows me in the side. "Beau, calm down. Don't let her get to you," she warns me.

But I'm already fuming. Everything in my life just feels like shit right now. Like I've been given all these broken things without the toolbox to fix them. Then I see people like Madison who don't have dead siblings or know drug addicts or gang members or go home to the projects every night and they *still* get everything they want. Everything I want.

"Madison, why don't you tell everyone how you tricked me out of the mural," I snap.

Heads immediately turn in our direction, ready to see a show.

Madison turns to me and frowns. "What are you talking about, Beau? I never tricked you."

"Yes, you did! We said we weren't going to propose a new mural. Then you go ahead and turn one in behind my back."

Madison looks to Ms. Kubler for help, but she waits for her to answer. Ms. Kubler looks confused and concerned.

"You said you weren't going to turn in a new proposal. I never said I wasn't," Madison says. "You wanted to stage a protest and I didn't think that was a smart idea. I know you wanted your sister on the mural, but I felt like we should still paint something since Ms. Kubler went through all the trouble of getting the project approved."

I think back to that conversation we had outside the art studio last week. Maybe Madison didn't say it exactly, but she knows she made it seem like she was on my side. She was the one who asked me what I wanted to do, like she cared.

"If that's how you felt then why didn't you say so? You just wanted to take all the credit for the mural!"

"*Ooooohhhh*," the rest of the class goes.

"Now, ladies—" Ms. Kubler starts.

"Real classy, Beau. Don't blame me because you decided to throw your opportunity away. If you really wanted to, you would have submitted a new proposal on your own. I see an opportunity, I take it. Maybe you should try it next time," Madison fires at me.

All the anger I've been feeling lately starts to bubble inside me like acid and I know there's no stopping it. I'm mad. About everything. About Katia, Momma, the Onyx Tigers, losing the mural to Madison's lying ass. She probably sketched her idea in her snug little Purple Hills home near her Olympic-size swimming pool.

"Or maybe I should try kicking your skinny ass," I say, getting right up in her face.

"Beau, you should really stop. You're just making yourself look crazy now."

She knows I won't hit her. Not in front of Ms. Kubler. Probably not anywhere, unless I want her rich daddy's lawyers to put me in juvie. If I was just a little more cutthroat like Deja, I'd do it anyway. Smash my fist right into her jaw because that's the only way you can get your point across to some people.

Instead, I take my copy of the mural grid, hold it up right in front of her and rip it into a million tiny pieces. Then I throw them in her pretty, stupid, perfect face.

"I'm outta here," I say, grabbing my backpack and heading back inside, twenty pairs of eyes watching me in shock as I go.

ME: hey where r u

DEJA: busy

ME: r u ok?

DEJA: im fine

ME: ok. Can I come over?

After five minutes go by without a response, I know Deja is ignoring me. I want to know what's going on but all she's told me is that she'll handle the Onyx Tiger situation. It's not my place to bug her about it when the whole situation is my fault.

Once I'm back home, I grab the remote and change the channel from NBC to cartoons. I'm not in the mood to hear about any more robberies or shootings. It feels strange being at home now, which is why I've been trying to avoid it as much as possible except for sleeping.

Momma is in her bedroom with the door closed. Sometimes I hear her snoring; other times I hear her sobbing uncontrollably. It's been days since we've talked but I don't dare knock on her door now.

I pick up my phone and start a text message to Sonnet. I kinda wanna know what people said after I stormed out of class. More importantly, I have to tell her we can't look for Jordan anymore. But doing that feels so final. I close the draft of the text without pressing send. Outside the sun is just starting to set and an orange glow dips through the slats in the blinds. I zone out on the couch for a while until there's a knock at the door. I let Daddy in. He's got a big pizza from Nicky's down the street, and I open the box and take a slice before he even has a chance to set it down.

"How was school?" he asks, taking off his Bulls hat and running his hands over his bald head.

"It was fine," I lie. Like I'd actually tell him I flipped out on a white girl in front of everyone.

"How's your mother?" He nods toward her closed bedroom door.

"Same as yesterday. Crying all day. But we're outta Pop-Tarts so I guess she ate while I was at school."

"Aight, that's good, that's good. You keeping your grades up?"

"No."

"Why not? Don't you want to go to college?"

I laugh. "Is that really what you care about right now, Daddy? Momma's a zombie, Peter Johnson's not going to prison, and Katia's gone. But you wanna know if I'm keeping my grades up?"

Daddy looks flustered and rubs his beard. "I'm hurting, too, baby, but the fastest way we gon' get back to normal is if we start acting like we normal. We still need to live our lives!"

I drop my slice of pizza on my plate and push it away. "You want normal? Fine. Then I'm gonna go to my room and shut the door because *normally*, you wouldn't be here."

I leave my father sitting alone at our kitchen table and slam my bedroom door behind me. Who is he to tell me I need to act normal? If my parents weren't such a hot mess, I wouldn't have to be taking care of everything for Katia.

I'm lying facedown on my bed when my phone buzzes in my back pocket.

It's Sonnet.

SONNET: hey, r u ok? Everybody was asking about you after you stormed out of class

I don't feel like talking anymore though. I hook my phone up to the charger and place it on Katia's nightstand. I pull her covers up over my head and pretend this is my world, this dark warm space underneath her gray blankets.

Katia, now would be a good time to come back to life.

CHAPTER 17

PRINCIPAL MARCOS IS FINISHING UP A CALL WHEN THE secretary guides me to the mauve plush chair in front of his desk again on Friday morning. I put my backpack between my feet on the floor and try to make myself look as pleasant as possible without grinning like an idiot. There's framed photos of his wife and two daughters on the desk facing me. It's always the people with strange-looking families trying to shove them down everyone's throat all the time.

When he hangs up the phone, Principal Marcos leans back in his chair and folds his hands over his belly with this smug look on his face like he's not surprised to see me back here.

"Ms. Willet. Back again. How are you today?" he asks.

I'm trying to look as polite as I can because people see girls like me and automatically think we have an attitude or that we're being disrespectful just because of the way we look or speak.

"I'm doing great, Principal Marcos," I say with a smile.

He doesn't smile back.

"I just had a meeting with Ms. Kubler, Madison Garber, and her father this morning. Can you tell me what you think it may have been about?"

"I left class early without asking yesterday," I say, looking down in mock shame. Now I'm about to get in trouble for something Madison started! The sneaky ass bitch was probably plotting on me before she even asked me to partner with her. All that shit about my art being amazing was just a cover. She never liked me or my art, she just wanted to win, even if it meant screwing me over. I can't believe I was stupid enough to trust her.

Principal Marcos isn't buying my innocent act. He shakes his head like he's tired of me already and takes a long drink of coffee from his "World's Best Principal" mug.

"You did a little more than just leaving early, according to Ms. Garber. She says you verbally assaulted her and destroyed her drawing."

My jaw drops open and damn near hits the floor. *Verbally assaulted?!*

"I did not verbally assault Madison! We were having a conversation about the art project, and I asked her a question—"

"Ms. Willet, you're verbally assaulting your classmates and destroying property. I know you lost your sister this past winter and that may explain some of your more recent behavior, but the grace period has ended. We can't make exceptions for one student who chooses to break the rules."

But my sister died, I want to say. I know I'm not acting normal, but I'm *not* normal. I'm *not* okay.

"Principal Marcos, I don't know what Madison said but—"

"If I were to walk into that class right now and ask your classmates what happened, Beau, what would they tell me?"

Sonnet would have my back, I know, but I'm not so sure about the rest of the class. Maybe the three other Black students but that's still fifteen against five. I can't win this one, which doesn't surprise me.

"I didn't mean for it to happen," I say, my voice cracking. I'm not crying because I'm sad, I'm crying because I'm angry as hell and there's nothing I can do about it. I have to sit in this chair and just take it because he's the principal and I'm a student. This will be my whole life, sitting and letting people shit all over me because they can.

"Well, it did happen. I've discussed it with the guidance counselor, and we think it's best for you to start going to study hall instead. You'll complete your final project by turning in a—"

"What?! You're kicking me out of class?!" I shout. *Unfuckingbelievable!* The only reason I wanted to get into Millennium Magnet was to become a better artist. Art class is literally the one thing I'm good at. It's the only thing I have and now that's gone, too.

As if things can't get any worse, Principal Marcos tacks on a one-week suspension. Which is overkill, but I bet Madison's father told him he'd sue the school district if he didn't suspend me. Poor Ms. Kubler probably couldn't do anything about it either. She saw what I did.

On my way out of the office, I see my art class loaded with paint cans and brushes headed out toward the back of the school to start work on the mural. Sonnet is there waving at me to come on with a paintbrush in her hand. I mouth to her that I can't.

Then I see Ms. Kubler in her splattered overalls and holding a folder full of Madison's stupid sketches. She stands in the hallway looking at me sadly as the class files past her and out the doors to the faculty parking lot. She looks like she wants to say something, to help me, but I know she can't. It's not her job to clean up my messes.

I'm not gonna lie, I want to rip all those sketches up in Madison's face and line everybody in that class up for the *verbal assault* of their lifetime. The way they're walking past and sneaking looks back at me, like, *hey, there goes the crazy girl*. The way Ms. Kubler follows the last person down the hall and out of sight, leaving me standing alone like I'm not good enough to be in the same space as them.

Like I don't matter.

I walk home from school with a letter explaining my suspension that I'm supposed to give to a guardian. Too bad I don't have one who gives a shit. But I'm still fuming. I want to beat Madison's ass but then I'd just go to jail. Besides, I know this is my fault. I should have never let her talk me into working with her on the proposal.

When I get to Grady Park, I stop at the corner store for a blue Fanta. The old man at the counter asks me why I'm not in school. I tell him I got suspended. He narrows his eyes and shakes his head at me, and I have to bite my tongue to keep myself from telling him to mind his own elderly business.

I take a sip of pop, try to calm the tight ball of anger that's forming in my stomach. If Katia were here, she'd tell me not to worry about it, that nobody cares about high school after it's over and Principal Marcos is a dickhead. But she's not here to tell me that. Even if she was, it wouldn't be good enough. Not this time.

I need to *do* something.

Anybody on the street might see me dressed in all black with a hoodie on and think I'm up to something criminal. On most days, they'd be wrong, but tonight, they'd be right.

When I call Sonnet after she gets out of school, I tell her about my suspension and Principal Marcos looking down his nose at me like I was a thug. She's mad. She's even madder than I am.

I think I've turned her into a rebel, because she's the one who comes up with the idea to wreck the mural. My original plan was to just storm back into school despite my suspension and hold a one-person protest, but Sonnet's idea is more exciting.

"If they're going to deny you your right to an education over ripping up a picture and telling some stupid girl off, then you may as well do something worth a one-week suspension!" she yells after she picks me up from my house in her mom's Fiat. For once, she doesn't have anything glittery or colorful in her afro. She's braided it into two long pigtails that hang by her ears. She's even dressed the part, wearing black sweats and a black hoodie.

"How'd you get your mom to let you borrow her car?" I ask as I buckle myself in the front seat. Sonnet's mom only has the car for emergencies, and she's never let Sonnet even sit in it before, let alone drive it. I'm pretty sure Sonnet doesn't even have a driver's license either but I don't bother to ask since we're about to do some hoodrat shit anyway.

"She doesn't know and as long as I have it back before she wakes up, everything should be fine."

We drive straight to the twenty-four-hour Walmart and pick up three big cans of baby-blue paint. We were going to do red at first, but that seems like blood, like we're mocking Dr. King. We want to destroy the mural because Madison went behind my back to steal the mural from me, not because we have a problem with Dr. King.

At half past midnight, Sonnet parks the coupe a few blocks away from Millennium Magnet, and we creep with our buckets of paint to the back of the gymnasium. We move quickly so we have less chance of getting caught, although if I'm being honest, I don't even care anymore. If they want to arrest me for doing the right thing, then so be it. I ain't scared.

When we get to the wall of the mural, it's only halfway done. They've only gotten as far as painting Dr. King's shoulders and chin, but all that work was for nothing.

I pop the lid off a can of paint and hurl it at the wall.

"Yes! It'll take them forever to paint over all this!" Sonnet pops open her can and douses the wall with it.

We splash blue paint everywhere until you can barely see the mural underneath anymore. Just several thick coats of Katia's favorite color. I've snuck out late at night to hit up parties with Deja, but this is better. Me and Sonnet sneaking in the dark, the wet sound of the paint hitting the wall and dripping down onto the concrete. We get it on our hands and a little on our shoes. But it feels like we're doing something *right*. Like Angela Davis and Assata Shakur and all them.

Once we're finished, we toss the empty cans in a dumpster on the next block and casually walk back to the car like we were just out for a midnight stroll.

"That was so damn cool," I say, buckling my seat belt while Sonnet throws her black skully into the back seat.

"Hell yeah, it was! We're vigilantes now, you know that, right?!" she says with a big smile.

"Yeah. I just wish I was gonna be there to see their faces tomorrow. You think they'll know we did it?"

She shakes her head. "I doubt it. But even if they do, it's not like they have any proof."

I sink down in my seat and smile, really smile, for the first time in a long time. I had a problem, and I did something about it. I'm proud of me and I know Katia would be, too. I want people to stop thinking they can do whatever they want to us and get away with it. I want them to know, we fight back.

We sit in silence in the dark for a few minutes letting the euphoria of being bad fully sink in. The street we're parked on is silent. This is a neighborhood where people are asleep at midnight. I lean my head against the window and watch a white cat slink across someone's lawn.

Suddenly, I see a figure appear across the street. He's walking with a backpack on and a basketball in his hands. There's something familiar about that walk, the way he sways from side to side like he's listening to music. The shape of his block head.

I rub my eyes to make sure I'm not seeing things.

"What is it?" Sonnet asks, alert, turning to look behind her out of the window.

"That dude over there across the street. I think it's Jordan!"

"What?! Are you sure?! Here, I'll call the police, what street are we on?" she says, pressing numbers on her cell phone screen.

"There's no time. I have to catch him," I say, jumping out of the car and racing down the block. I don't think about Deja or the Onyx Tigers. I don't think at all, I just do. I'm not running after Jordan, I'm chasing down the memory of that night, of what happened to Katia.

I hear Sonnet call after me to stop, but I'm not letting Jordan get away again. I'm running full speed a block behind the figure when he hears my sneakers pounding the pavement and turns around.

When he sees it's me, he bolts.

I'm a fast runner thanks to Momma's genes, but he dips into a side alley and cuts through a backyard. I trip over my own feet and go careening into a dumpster. I think I skinned my knee, because it's stinging, but I get up and keep hauling ass. By the time I get into the yard, Jordan has already hopped the fence on the other side, and I've set off the motion sensor lights.

I'm standing in a backyard dressed in all black in an upper-class white neighborhood with a spotlight shining on me.

I already know what's going to happen next.

CHAPTER 18

SONNET COULD HAVE GOT IN HER MOM'S CAR AND drove off, snuck back into her room, and went to sleep like she had nothing to do with it. I wouldn't have blamed her if she had.

But she didn't.

She chased after me when I ran after Jordan, and when the cops arrive, they cuff us both. I try to tell them about Jordan, but they won't listen to me. They mirandize us as they drag us both from the yard, falling a few times to our knees before they wrench us back up hard. On the street, their berries are flashing and all the white people on the block have come outside in their night robes and slippers to see what's going on.

A female officer pushes Sonnet into a squad car, and she bangs her head hard on the side and starts crying. I don't know if the cop did it on purpose or not, but I don't care. We shouldn't be getting arrested in the first place.

"Aye, don't do her like that!" I shout, stomping on the cop's foot so he'll let me go and I can get to Sonnet. It's a stupid move, but I'm not thinking straight. All I know is I have to protect my friend. The big dude officer holding me hauls back and socks me in the stomach, real slick so the people standing outside don't see what he just did.

"Shut up and stay down!" he bellows at me.

The wind rushes out of me and I fall to the ground, my knees in something cold and wet, my cheek pressed to the grass as I struggle to breathe. But even then, I tilt my head up to watch Sonnet, to make sure they're not hurting her even though I couldn't do anything if they were.

"We didn't do anything!" Sonnet cries, a slow trickle of blood running from a cut on her forehead.

She doesn't deserve this. I know she's scared out of her mind. But I've seen plenty of people get arrested in Grady Park. Like when Uncle Kolby came over tryna hide and the cops came and he ended up getting hit with the taser. He froze and fell flat on his face like a cartoon character. I was nine years old and I knew then that these cops just don't give a fuck.

When the cop jerks me to my feet, I'm not even surprised this grown man just sucker punched me. I see the black gun in his holster and almost wish he would use it on me. I wouldn't have to worry about shit like this happening to me again. At least I would see it coming out here. At least I would get to see Katia again.

"Just fucking do it!" I scream.

But the cop doesn't reach for his gun.

He doesn't shoot me.

He opens the door to the squad car and slams me inside just right so I hit my head on the opposite window. I ignore the pounding in my skull and stomach and scoot over so I can sit up.

There's a black grate that separates me from the cop and the seat in the back is made of plastic, hard and uncomfortable. I can't sit right because my hands are cuffed tight behind my back. The squad car with Sonnet in front pulls off and then we follow it.

I'm terrified and I know she is, too. *What are they going to do to us?*

———

When we get to the station, they treat us like real criminals even though we're only in high school. We get fingerprinted and photographed. They take our phones and purses and even the laces from our shoes.

While we're being processed, we see them bring in a tall man dressed in all black who they call Ed. Most of the officers seem to know him so he must get picked up often. He looked so much like Jordan from behind. I could have sworn it was him.

The police ask for my name and I consider giving a fake one, but that only works for so long.

"Beau Willet," I tell the officer quietly, hoping no one else in the area hears. But they do. Before, we were just getting the regular Black person treatment; now they up the ante. They yank us around this way and that, snap at us when we look at each other and tighten cuffs around our ankles even though we haven't tried to run.

Eventually, the arresting officers stick us in what looks like an interrogation room together and handcuff us to our chairs, which I know has to be illegal somehow.

Sonnet's stopped crying and they give her a bandage for the cut on her head. I should have never let her go along with this. Her mom will probably never let her see me again after tonight.

The lady officer leaves us alone in the room but we both know why she's doing it. They want us to think we're alone and say something incriminating to each other. I heard some of them whispering while I was being fingerprinted, and apparently they think we were working with Ed.

So Sonnet and I don't talk. We don't even look at each other. If they wanna charge us, they're gonna have to do the legwork and prove we did something illegal.

After what feels like a million years, a detective with a gun in his waistband walks into the room and shuts the door. He's a white man with jet-black hair and blue eyes.

"Ladies," he says in a booming voice before he sits on a chair in front of us. "What were you doing out there tonight, huh?"

Neither one of us speak. I know it's illegal to question minors without a parent present, but he thinks we're stupid.

"Looks suspicious, you sneaking through backyards at midnight. In a neighborhood you don't even live in."

Never mind the fact that these fools *saw* my school ID when they went through my bag. Maybe it doesn't fully explain why we were out there in the dead of night, but it's not like we're some seasoned criminals out here robbing people.

"We've been waiting for you," he says, turning to me. "What do you think they'll say about this on the morning news, huh? Maybe you wanna give a jailhouse interview? Should I call up channel five?"

He's taunting me, but I still don't say anything. I pretend I'm a statue, like those freedom fighters who sat in diners and were trained not to move or react while people poured milkshakes and mustard on them. I try to be like them but it's hard. Real hard.

"Your family caused a lot of trouble for one of my brothers. Now here you are, taking up where your sister left off, huh?"

Still I say nothing. My hands grip the arms of the chair so tight I'm afraid it's going to break. Suddenly the officer pulls my chair toward him and slams it down so we're knee to knee, nose to nose. Sonnet whimpers but I don't make a sound. I just look him dead in his eyes, the smell of his coffee breath and cologne turning my stomach.

"What'll you say about me? Brought you in alive, didn't I? Not a mark on you." He pushes my chair back next to Sonnet and I struggle to keep the tears from falling.

"We've called both your parents. They'll be here soon." I can tell by the nasty way he says it that they have not called our parents and they will not be here soon.

He gets up from his chair and slams the door behind him.

Sonnet looks at me, panicked, but I shake my head. We're still being recorded. No talking.

I don't know how long they keep us chained up. There's no clock on the wall so I try counting seconds in my head. *One Mississippi, two Mississippi, three Mississippi.* I don't know how many seconds I count before I fall asleep. I wake up with drool on my chin and see Sonnet with her head leaning forward and snoring. I have to pee. Bad.

"Hey! I need to use the bathroom!" I shout at the door. This wakes Sonnet up with a start. We both try calling out for someone, but the door stays shut and we stay chained to our chairs. The natural instinct when trapped is to do whatever you can to escape, but even if we could get ourselves out of these chairs, that'd just be an excuse for them to come in and do something worse to us. So we sit.

I hold my pee for as long as I can, but my vision is starting to go blurry and my teeth are starting to hurt. "Fuck," I whisper as pee trickles down the leg of my joggers.

I sit there, itchy and pissy, until eventually I hear a man out in the lobby of the police station yelling and hollering at somebody.

"Daddy!" I scream. But still, no one comes.

We wait for what feels like another hour before an officer comes in and unchains Sonnet.

"But what about my fri—"

"Worry about yourself," the young blond officer says tersely, leading her out of the room.

Thirty minutes later, they let me go. I know we've been locked up for hours because there's daylight streaming through the front windows when I get out into the lobby.

I also know Daddy is pissed. He's always disliked cops, but after Katia, he hates them. When I see him in the lobby, he's pacing back and forth holding a plastic bag full of the stuff they took from me earlier. He's in sweatpants and a white tee with holes in it. He's even still got his raggedy house slippers on that show the backs of his ashy ankles. They must have woken him up out of his sleep when they called.

"Daddy," I croak, because they wouldn't give us anything to drink and my throat is dry.

My father stops pacing when he hears my voice. He sees me standing there and bursts into tears.

The only time I've seen him cry before was at Katia's funeral.

I run into his arms, and he squeezes me tight and kisses the top of my head over and over. *I'm safe now, I'm okay now.* When he got that call in the middle of the night, I know he must have thought I was dead, too. I hate myself for putting him through this.

The cops behind the counter watch us like they wish they could have kept me back there longer, shipped me off to prison with all the rest of the girls like me.

I hate them for doing this to me and Sonnet. I hate them for doing this to my family.

On the car ride home, Daddy goes off, which is mainly a mix of him yelling and crying, then yelling a little more but mostly just crying.

"What were you *thinking*?!"

I tell him that me and Sonnet were just talking in her mom's car when the police rolled up on us. I don't tell him about the mural, how I thought I saw Jordan but it was really Ed, or what that cop did to me. He'd lose his mind if he knew they'd hurt me, and Daddy getting arrested isn't going to fix anything.

The door's unlocked and the shades are drawn when we get home. I see the red scarf from behind on the couch and I know it's Momma.

"Basil, let's not start in on her now. It's early as hell; we're all tired. Let's just go to sleep," Daddy says.

Momma gets up and comes around to stand in front of me. She's wearing nothing but a silk nightie and tears down her face. Bones poke out of her chest from not eating much these past few weeks. She looks broken.

"You got arrested," she says breathlessly.

I don't respond.

"After everything . . . how could you let them get you? How could you do this?!"

She starts crying and grabs my shoulders, jerking me back and forth. I feel my brain smacking around in my skull.

"Basil!" Daddy yells, but she's already stopped.

"Beau, you're my last baby. You the only thing I got left that's *mine*. If they kill you, too, I'll *die*. I will DIE! Do you want me to die?!"

"No, Momma," I say, tears streaming down my face. Not because I'm scared or ashamed, but because I'm happy. Momma's up and screaming at me, asking stupid rhetorical questions again. This is the version of my momma I've been needing. *Momma's back.*

She pulls me against her, and her face is wet against my neck as she cries softly.

Even though I'm crying on the outside, inside, I'm smiling, because this time . . .

I made it back home.

CHAPTER 19

BEFORE

"BUT HE CHEATED ON YOU. I SAW HIM."

I stood near the frosted window of the restroom, my arms wrapped tight around myself so I wouldn't accidentally touch anything.

Katia was standing in front of the dull mirror applying a thick coat of maroon lipstick.

"Beau, please. I'm not even thinkin' about that boy. We're just here to have a good time and chill."

"Oh, whatever, in the whole city of Chicago, he just happens to be at the same beach at the same time and day as us?"

"What does it matter anyway? You was whinin' about being bored at home. I got you out the house. I could have left you and came alone, if I only came for Jordan."

"You might as well have! You're gonna be all over him anyway," I snap.

"Me? All over a nigga? Fuck outta here, you must have me confused with Clarice."

"You're acting just like Clarice, putting all that makeup on and stalking Jordan."

Katia replaced the cap on her tube of lipstick and cut her eyes at me.

"You'll never get it. You're too young."

"Try me," I say.

"Not everything is black and white, Beau. It might seem like it to you now but when you're grown, you start to understand why you have to learn how to forgive people."

I rolled my eyes. "When did Jordan ever apologize for what he did?"

"He was probably too scared I'd reject him. Dudes are sensitive like that. How would anyone ever change if nobody gave them a shot?"

"Momma and Daddy can't stand him."

"They won't be able to stand anyone you date either. They just wanna be in control of our lives till we're seventy. They only met him the one time anyway. They don't know him like I do. Neither do you."

"Whatever you say, Katia," I reply, rolling my eyes.

"What's with this family? Do y'all think I'm stupid or something? I know what I'm getting myself into and I can take care of myself."

"But Jordan—"

"I said I can handle it, Beau. But thanks for the advice. Especially since you've never even had a boyfriend."

Her words sliced through my chest like a razor. I stood there, my cheeks burning red because it was true. I had never had a boyfriend. Maybe that was why I hated Jordan so much. I wanted Katia to myself and maybe without realizing it, I was jealous that boys liked her and not me.

But then I remembered Jordan's hand on that girl's butt, Katia's face when I told her.

Nope, I was definitely not jealous of that.

When Katia realized I wasn't going to return fire on her, she told me to meet in the parking lot at 8:00 P.M. Then she left me standing there in the bathroom, feeling ugly and stupid.

Breon and I spent most of that outing walking up and down the beach while Katia and her group drank beer out of soda bottles before chucking them into the lake.

"Hey, isn't that Triana?" Breon pointed to a group of kids posing for selfies near the big boulders flanking the lake.

I liked Breon's older cousin okay, but I'd mostly been cool off her since she and Deja got into it over something stupid last year. But I figured it was better than the nothing we were already doing.

But as soon as I saw the Styrofoam cups and bags of Jolly Ranchers, I turned right back around.

"Beau, where you going?" Breon called out to me.

I motioned to her to follow.

"What is it?" she asked.

"You know I don't like being around that kind of stuff."

"Oh okay, I gotcha. We don't have to hang with Tri. I'm supposed to go over there tomorrow anyway," Breon said.

"Well, how about I hang out here and draw? That's what I really wanted to do anyway."

"You sure?"

"Yeah, go ahead. We gotta meet Katia at eight though, remember."

Drawing was how I got my anger out and I was definitely still pissed at what Katia had said to me earlier.

I drew a little girl I saw with two big poofs on both sides of her head. Drawing happy things made me feel a little better. I was deep into my work when I felt a hand on my shoulder.

I screamed and my sketchbook went flying in the air.

"Oh, my bad, my bad, I didn't mean to scare you."

I watched Jordan pick up my sketchbook where it had landed a few feet away. Then he started looking through it.

Who did he think he was? I jumped up and snatched it back from him.

"This is private," I said, giving him the death stare.

"My bad, my bad. I just thought a good artist would wanna show her work off."

He licked his lips and I understood why girls wanted him so bad. The brother was smooth as cream and cold as ice. His skin was a deep caramel and his face looked like it'd been constructed by one of those ancient Greek artists. It was perfect in every way, how his cheekbones sat high up, how long and curled his eyelashes were, the soft roundness of his nose, his full pouty lips, and bright brown eyes. He was slim, with just the right amount of muscles. His white tank top was slung around his neck, and I tried so hard to keep my eyes away from his abs.

"Yeah, well, I'm not a real artist yet. I'm still learning." I held my sketches tight to my chest.

Still, Jordan only moved closer.

"If you want something, you gotta act like you already got it. Otherwise you won't know what to do when you finally do get it."

"Whatever. Don't you have to get back to your friends?" I asked.

"Beau, how come you don't like me?"

Was he serious right now?

"Uh, I don't know, probably because you cheated on my sister."

He dug his foot into the soft sand.

"But I didn't cheat on her. Not really. Your sister didn't tell you the full story. Now I ain't gon' lie, I was hanging out with Ashley. But that's because I saw Katia hanging with some dude the day before."

"Yeah right. What dude?"

"I don't know who he was, some tall nigga with dreads. But he was all up in her face, and she wasn't even trying to stop him."

I had to admit, that did sort of sound like something Katia would do. Boys liked her. Even if she didn't like them back, she ate the attention up.

"He was probably just one of her friends. Anyway, it's not my business."

He raised an eyebrow. "You thought it was your business when you ran and told her I had my hands on that girl's ass."

"Because you did!"

He put his hands up. "I know, I'm just saying. But me and Katia are good now. She wants me and you to be friends."

"We all want things. Doesn't mean we're gonna get them."

I started to turn away, but he grabbed my hand gently. Even though I couldn't stand him, wanted to rip his lying tongue out his mouth, his touch made me turn around.

"From what I saw, your sketchbook is nearly full." He pulled a crisp one-hundred-dollar bill from his worn brown leather wallet and held it out to me. "Take it. Get yourself a bigger and better one."

I'm not ashamed to say I didn't hesitate before taking the bill. I didn't like the asshole, but I wasn't stupid.

"I'll do that. But my friendship's not for sale," I told him.

"That's cool. Just wanted you to know that I'm not the kinda guy you think I am. I'm from a different breed than most of these niggas. I'll see you."

I watched him walk back to his group before pulling the bill out of my pocket and holding it up to the setting sun. It was legit. Damn, maybe he really did like Katia. There were plenty of other girls he could have on this beach without bribing their little sisters. Giving somebody money for nothing in Grady Park meant you really cared about them.

At 8:00 P.M. sharp, I was already sitting on the hood of Katia's white Toyota Corolla. The beach was closing soon so the parking lot was crowded with people trying to get to their cars and then out into the street.

Katia practically floated to the car.

"I heard you and Jordan had a good talk today," she said, unlocking the doors.

I climbed inside the passenger seat and put my feet on the dashboard.

"He told me YOU told him to do it."

"All I said was I wanted y'all to get to like each other. It was his idea to talk to you. I know he's done his shit in the past, but there's a sweet side to him, too."

I wondered if she knew about the money. But I sure as hell wasn't about to risk her trying to take it back so I didn't say anything.

"Yeah, he's okay, I guess," I said. I knew he was a dog, but I also knew Katia wasn't about to let him go. If I wanted things between me and her to be okay, I'd have to start faking nice with Jordan. It felt like a steep price to pay just so Katia wouldn't hate me, but I didn't have much choice. Besides, it wasn't like he hit her or slept with someone else. He just rubbed a booty. If Katia was okay with it, then I'd pretend to be okay with it, too.

CHAPTER 20

IT ONLY TAKES FOUR DAYS AFTER MY ARREST FOR
Momma and Daddy to go back to how they were before. Me
being hauled off to jail by the same police department that killed
Katia suddenly made me visible to my parents again. The morning after my arrest, a Saturday, Momma cooked me breakfast
for the first time in months. The bacon was burned to a crisp
and the eggs were runny as snot but I was so happy she was up
and doing normal things again that I cleaned my plate and asked
for seconds.

Even Daddy started coming around more. On Sunday, he
spent the whole afternoon watching ESPN on the couch. He
played a couple games of checkers with me but just having him
home made me feel safer. But on Monday, he went back to Uncle
Kolby's, said he had to get back to his job hunting. Momma
didn't come out of her room that morning either. I knocked and

asked if she was still going to make breakfast, but she threw something at the door and yelled for me to leave her alone. So I did.

I know my parents are grateful that I'm okay after being arrested, but there's only so much happiness they can feel about me being alive before they start to remember that Katia isn't.

On Tuesday morning, the second day of my suspension from school, I'm sitting at the kitchen table holding a letter from the nursing home where Momma works at. It'd been sitting in our mailbox along with a stack of collection notices for at least a few days. I opened the letter, thinking maybe it was a check or something, but the letter says Momma's been fired for violating some code.

I read the letter through two more times, hoping that maybe I just read it wrong. Momma's been working at the nursing home for the past four years. They can't just fire her for being depressed and missing a few days! Don't they know we're going through enough already?

I get up and knock on her bedroom door. Momma has to work a certain number of hours to qualify for housing assistance so if she's really fired for real, we could be out on the streets by next month.

I knock on her door again, but she still doesn't answer. The TV inside is on. Sounds like a *Living Single* rerun, her favorite show.

I let myself in and the warm, stuffy air sticks to my skin. The comforter has been taped over the window to block the sunlight from getting in. Clothes, tissues, and empty food cartons litter the floor. Momma lies in bed, curled into a ball, eyes staring at me but not really seeing me.

My heart stops but she blinks slowly, and I know she's alive.

I sit on the edge of the bed and hold the letter out to her.

"It's a letter from work. Did something happen? Is that why you were home early that one day?"

She doesn't look at the letter. "One of my clients fell and bumped his head on a railing."

"Oh. But it was an accident though, right? Old people fall over all the time, don't they?" I ask eagerly. I know Momma likes most of her clients, so I don't understand why she's talking about one of them getting hurt like it's no big deal.

"I don't know. I wasn't there," she says like she's bored.

"What do you mean? You stepped out of the room?"

"I was at home. I told Betty I needed to leave early. But Tammy was running late as usual. Why I gotta be responsible for covering my shift and part of somebody else's? My child is dead!"

Now I think I understand what happened. She left before her relief got there, so the clients were all by themselves. If he really did get hurt before Tammy got there, then it probably is Momma's fault.

"Momma, you gotta do something! Can you call them and ask for your job back? How are we gonna pay the bills?" Before Katia died, Momma handled everything. Whatever we needed, if she didn't have the money, she'd get it somehow, every time. She was the one who fixed everything and made sure we were good.

Now, she stretches and rolls over to face the wall. "Why are you asking me that? How 'bout you ask your daddy why he's not working? I told y'all one day you would learn. I can't do everything!" she snaps at me.

I want to cry but that wouldn't have any effect on her the way she is now. And since she can't be strong, I have to be. So I fold the letter up and put it back inside the envelope.

I leave Momma to mope alone and make myself a peanut butter sandwich with the crusty ends of the loaf, which everyone knows you only eat when there's literally nothing else. We don't even have any emergency packs of ramen.

I need to talk to somebody. But not Sonnet and not Champion. I need somebody who understands poor people problems.

"Hey girl, wassup?" Deja says when I call her cell.

I take my dry ass sandwich into my room and close the door.

"My momma let some old guy bump his head and the nursing home fired her."

"Oh my god, for real?! Damn, why she do that?"

"I dunno, I guess she was sad about Katia. So she left before the next shift came in," I explain. "Anyway, she's acting like she doesn't even care! There's barely any food in the house now."

It's scary because I've seen my mother happy, excited, pissed off, but never like this. Even when Grandma died, she still got up every day and made sure our family kept running smoothly.

"What did your dad say about it?" Deja asks.

"Nothing yet. I'm gonna tell him when he gets here. But he's been looking for a job since, like, January. I doubt he's gonna find one anytime soon. And there's nothing in the fridge but mustard and relish. We were already poor; we can't afford to be extra poor."

"Girl, I feel you." She pauses. "Don't you have some birthday money saved up?"

"Yeah, a little, but I think I'd better save it in case they try to evict us." My savings probably wouldn't cover more than a week's worth of rent anyway.

"This ain't right! You shouldn't have to worry about this kind of stuff when you have two parents," Deja replies.

I take a bite of my sandwich. "Right? Not like my parents were perfect before, but now, it's like they don't even remember I'm alive. I feel like I can't even have a chance to be sad the right way because—"

"You have to look out for them," Deja finishes for me.

"Yeah. That's exactly it." I knew she'd get it. She always does.

I hear the front door open and tell Deja I'll call her back later.

Daddy's standing at the kitchen table, sorting through three big greasy bags of Chinese food.

"Hey, Bobo! I got your favorite, shrimp egg foo young. Grab them paper plates off the top of the fridge."

I hand him the plates and then set the letter on the table.

"What's this?" he asks.

"It's from Momma's job. She got fired because one of her clients hit his head."

Daddy doesn't even look surprised. He keeps opening cartons of food and piling two plates with a heap of every dish.

He hands me my plate and we both sit down.

"Beau, your mother's job called me a few days ago," he says.

"You already knew? Why didn't you tell me? Why didn't you tell *her*?" I can't believe he knew and didn't tell me! This is exactly what I was telling Deja about. At least Momma gets things done when she's not in mourning, but Daddy is always too little and too late. I'm starting to see why Momma kicked him out in the first place. Most of the time, he's useless.

"Watch your tone," he warns, pointing a chopstick at me. "Your mother's got a lot going on. She doesn't need to be working right now. If she didn't have such a good rapport with the nursing home, she could have been thrown in jail."

"But we need money. She can't just not work!" It's like I'm the only person in this house who gives a damn about anything.

"Beau, you know it's been a hassle just getting her to lift her arm so I can rub a little deodorant on her," Daddy says, his mouth full of fried rice. I don't like the way he says the word *hassle*, as if taking care of Momma isn't his job.

"Maybe we can try talking to her again, together?" I suggest.

But Daddy just shoves another bite of greasy food into his mouth.

"Beau, your momma needs something we can't give her. That's why she's going to stay with your Aunt Pepper in New York for a lil while. Give me and you a break, you know?"

A break from what? YOU haven't done shit! I want to scream. But I know I pushed my luck as far as it's gonna go when I got arrested.

"I don't need a break, though," I say simply.

Daddy sighs. "Well, your mother does. It'll do her some good, trust me."

"If Momma's gone, what happens to me?"

"That's the other thing I wanted to talk to you about. You know I've been staying at Uncle Kolby's place. I told him what was going on and he thinks it might be a good idea for us to let this place go. You'll live with me in the living room till we get back on our feet. It won't be that long, two, three, five months tops."

My stomach drops to my feet because I can tell he actually thinks this is a good idea. He really thinks I'm about to spend half a year in somebody else's living room.

"You mean . . . leave Grady Park? For good?" It takes forever to get approved for public housing in Chicago, and there's been a wait list for people to get into our complex and every other building like it since before I was born probably. If we give up our place, we won't be able to come back.

"Yeah, I know a living room isn't the best place for us to be staying, but it's real big. We can even put a sheet up to divide the room so you can have your privacy," Daddy says.

A million thoughts race through my mind. My life is here, has always been here. Me and Katia's room, the courtyard where I first met Deja and Breon when we were five. And most importantly, Jordan is still here. Somewhere.

"We can't just move! What about my friends?!" I shout.

"You can still see them on the weekends. Green Oaks ain't that far."

"Daddy, I've never even heard of that neighborhood."

"That's because it's on the West Side. I don't see why you getting upset. You've always talked about leaving Grady Park one day," he says.

"Yeah, Daddy, for college or California or somewhere better! Not to move across town. Where's Momma gonna live when she comes back from New York? She's not gonna stay in somebody else's living room," I say. The fact that Daddy even brought this stupid idea up shows just how much he doesn't know or care about me and Momma. Now I understand why she was always arguing with him. He's not a father, he's like an obnoxious uncle who keeps coming by because he can't get his shit together. It's crazy how Momma was so good at being a mom that I never noticed Daddy wasn't helping out at all. All he does is bring us takeout food and then go back to Uncle Kolby's to drink beer and sit on his ass. What kinda father is that? A real father, the kind I need right now, would have never moved out in the first place. He'd wanna stay with us, take care of us, protect us. I don't get why Daddy can never just do what he's supposed to do.

"This is just temporary, Beau. Once I find a job, we'll have our own place again. Maybe somewhere closer to the North Side," he says with a smile. How can this baldheaded fool smile in my face knowing he's feeding me a bunch of bull? Maybe Momma used to fall for it, but not me. Not anymore.

"But you've been looking for a job for months. If you couldn't get one then, what makes you think you'll find one now?" He probably doesn't even wanna work. His life is so easy. I bet he sits on Uncle Kolby's couch watching TV and drinking Old Milwaukee all day.

Daddy opens his mouth for a rebuttal but then closes it. He looks down at his plate and then gets up to grab a beer from the fridge.

"I try. You know I do," he says. "You and your momma know that all I do is try. They don't make it easy out here for Black brothers. I've been turned away from interviews on the spot because they thought I was a white man over the phone! But I still try. Everyday."

He pours the beer into a plastic tumbler and takes a big gulp.

Trying isn't good enough. If Momma "tried" the way he does, we'd have starved to death on the streets a long time ago!

"Maybe you have to try harder. Because you always say you're gonna do this and you're gonna do that, but you never do! You never do what you're supposed to do!" I shout. I know better than to get loud with an adult but why should I have to stay in a child's place when I'm handling things like I'm the adult?

Daddy finishes his beer and tosses the cup into the sink full of dirty dishes. He sits back down in his chair and looks at me with dark eyes.

"I don't have to explain myself to a child. You are not in charge in here, do you understand me? I am! Don't you ever forget that!"

"But I—"

"Shut up!" he roars over me. "I'm the man of this house, I make the decisions. You don't like it, you can hit the door any-time. I said we're moving. That's what's gonna happen. Do you understand me, little girl?"

My nostrils flare like a bull and my vision blurs from the hot tears I'm trying to hold back. I can't fucking stand him. But right now, I don't have a choice.

"Yes, sir," I say roughly.

We eat the rest of our Chinese in silence. I'm not even hungry but I feel like leaving the table means admitting I was wrong and I'm not gonna do that when I know I'm right. After dinner, Daddy leaves to go play poker with his friends and I leave a plate of plain white rice in Momma's room in case she wants it.

Mopping and straightening up the kitchen was always Katia's chore, but it looks like I have to do it if it's ever going to get done again. I can take care of everything by myself. Because unlike my daddy, I'm not a lazy piece of shit.

I'm running warm water in a bucket in the tub when I hear knocking at the front door.

When I open it, it's Deja, her arms filled with overflowing bags of groceries.

"Special delivery for the Willet family!" she says with a smile.

I feel my eyes start to well up with fresh tears.

"Bitch, don't you start crying because then I'ma start crying, and my face is too beat to be streaked right now."

But I can't help it. As alone and helpless as I feel, I know I have at least one person who will always have my back.

Deja puts the groceries down and we wipe each other's tears, smiling the whole time.

"Daddy says we have to move out of Grady Park since Momma's not working. Talkin' about movin' into Uncle Kolby's fucking living room."

Deja wraps her arms around me tight. "No offense, but your daddy can go to hell because nobody's gonna take my best friend from me. Ever. I promise." I wanna believe her but I know this is a problem too big for her to solve. Deja only stays for half an hour though. Her new boyfriend is taking her out to eat. I wish she would have stayed longer but she's already done way more than a best friend should have to.

I'm putting the rest of the groceries away that night when my phone buzzes in my back pocket. Another DM. Two of them. I click on the one from ArithMyTick first.

ARITHMYTICK: You're getting colder.

ME: Wtf are you talking about?? Who is this?

Then I open the next one. Finally, Murdersleuth has sent us another tip.

MURDERSLEUTH99: Sorry about that, been busy with my job. Did you ever find Parker?

ME: Yeah, we did. We found out Jordan has a kid, too. But nobody knows where he is.

MURDERSLEUTH99: There's one person who might. There's a rumor that Katia and Jordan weren't the only passengers in the car the night of the murder.

ME: What? There was someone else in there with them? Who??

MURDERSLEUTH99: Keep in mind, it's just a rumor. She's just a kid, a sixteen-year-old who lives in the Grady Park Complex. First name Briana. Last name Jefferson.

I drop my phone and it clatters to the floor, a long crack running across its screen. There's no Briana Jefferson in the projects, just Breon Jefferson. Breon. My Breon? In the car with Katia and Jordan the night she was murdered? My heart starts to pound and I place my hand over it, trying to catch my breath. I don't wanna believe it. I can't believe it. But why would someone make up a rumor like that if there wasn't at least a little truth to it somewhere? I pick up my cell phone and text Sonnet.

CHAPTER 21

"WHOA. 'BREON' AS IN YOUR OLD BEST FRIEND Breon?" Sonnet asks.

"It's gotta be. Her last name is Jefferson. But I've talked to her since the funeral. Breon would have told me if she'd been in the car," I say, exiting the app.

"Not if she was scared! You said she tried to talk to you at the funeral, right?"

"Yeah, but Deja interrupted us. Still, I've seen her a few times since then. She would have told me."

Sonnet blows a raspberry with her mouth. "Orrr, maybe she's the one hiding Jordan."

I stand up and walk over to the open window. Ms. Bluefall is down in the backyard sitting in an orange beach chair and holding a stick with a cube of tofu on the end over their firepit.

I know Sonnet's coming up with theories to try to help, but sometimes she doesn't know what she's talking about. She definitely doesn't know Breon, or she'd know that we don't play about life or death things. We fell off, but I know Breon doesn't hate me. She would never keep that kind of info from me, and she'd never protect Jordan.

"Sonnet, we don't have time to chase down every single rumor. Breon would have told me if she knew anything," I say.

"You're right, we can't follow up on every rumor. But we should at least try to follow up on the ones that seem possible," Sonnet says.

"Do I have to write it on my forehead? I said no," I tell her.

Sonnet pulls at her tight curls and the periwinkle turtle clips in her hair sparkle. "Fine, then I'm overruling you on this one."

I turn around to face her. "You're what?"

"I'm overruling you on this decision. I know I said this was your case and you're the boss, but I think we should make sure Breon doesn't know anything."

"Did you forget what this entire investigation is for? My sister. You can't overrule me," I counter.

Sonnet stands up and points to the two stitches in her head. "You see this on my forehead? That happened because you thought you saw Jordan and I chased after you."

"It looked just like him from behind! What was I supposed to do, let him get away again?"

"If you had stopped for a second and thought like a real detective, we could have caught up to him in the car. Then we would have seen he wasn't Jordan, and we wouldn't have been running through people's yards in the middle of the night," Sonnet asserts.

"Wait, now you're blaming me for what those racist white cops did to both of us? I got hurt, too, Sonnet!"

"I'm not blaming you, I'm saying you're not always right about everything. But I've still been going along with it. I think I should be able to make at least one choice, don't you?"

I do still feel guilty for getting us caught up with the police. We're lucky things didn't end up way worse. As much as I hate to admit it, Sonnet is right.

I go to the bed and pick up my phone.

"What are you doing?" she asks.

"Calling Deja. She might know where we can find Breon."

Sonnet smiles at me and I nod in return.

"Hey, girl, I was just about to call you," Deja says when she answers.

"I gotta talk to Breon about something important. Have you seen her at all today?" I ask.

"Who the hell knows and who the fuck cares?"

"D, I'm for real. I have to ask her about some stuff," I explain.

"Like what? How much cough syrup to mix with Sprite? Forget about her triflin' ass and tell me what you're wearing tonight?"

"What I'm wearing tonight? For what?" I ask, confused.

"Jacques is havin' another kickback tonight! This is gonna be a big one, too. They already getting the DJ booth set up in his momma's room. So what are you gonna wear?" Deja repeats.

I'm about to tell her I'm not in the mood for any parties but then I remember that Breon loves parties. Especially the ones Jacques throws because there's always plenty of free drugs and drinks.

"I haven't picked an outfit yet but meet me at my house in an hour, k?"

"Cool, bye."

"Welp," Sonnet says, flopping back onto her bed. "That went well."

I tug her upright by the arm. "It did. Jacques's parties are wild as hell, and I think we might be able to find Breon there if we go."

Sonnet's eyes light up and she claps her hands like a little kid. "Oh my gosh, I haven't been to a party in forever! Quick, help me pick out an outfit."

She walks over to her wooden wardrobe and flings the doors open wide. There's so many colors and patterns. It's like the '70s and the '90s had a baby and it threw up everywhere.

"Okay, you're not wearing anything in that closet," I state.

"What? I just got these crocheted joggers from the thrift store last week. They're so cute!"

I start playing with the string of my hoodie. "Um, Sonnet, maybe it's better if I go to the party with Deja alone? Jacques's kickbacks can get a little intense."

Truth is, I'd need more than a few hours' notice to get Sonnet briefed and prepared to enter a Grady Park party and not get herself into trouble. Hanging out with Parker and Cierra is one thing but there's too many things that can go wrong if I bring Sonnet with me.

"No way," she says, "it was my idea. I'm going. Besides, my interview skills are rivaled by none."

"Whether you go or not, *you're* not going to talk to Breon, I am. She won't talk with a stranger around," I tell her.

"Beau, it's a house party. There'll be tons of strangers there, right?"

I bite my lip. There's no polite way to tell her that she sticks out too much. Even without the gold bangles and hot-pink velvet bell-bottoms, they'd still be able to tell she was an outsider after talking to her for two seconds. But I owe her one after getting us arrested so I agree to let her come along, under the condition that *I* choose her outfit and hairstyle.

Forty-five minutes later, we're in my bedroom and I'm brushing Sonnet's hair up into a high puff.

"Let me get the edge control and toothbrush real quick," I say.

"Ugh, I haven't slicked down my baby hairs since I was, like, a baby. Do you even know what kinda chemicals are in this gel?"

"Ask me if I care." I dip my finger into the open jar and put a few dabs of brown gel on her hairline. "This is how we wear our hair out here. Baby hairs are a way of life."

I pull out the shortest tendrils of hair with the toothbrush and use my fingertip to smooth them into half crescents. When I get to her sideburns, I dab more gel on and wrap them around my fingers a few times until they curl up.

"Okay, go look in the mirror."

Sonnet goes over to the vanity and starts putting her hands in her hair.

"Don't!" I say, slapping at her hand. "You'll mess it up."

"Oh! Sorry. You know what? I actually kinda like it . . . minus all the sticky gloop. There's gotta be an all-natural vegan edge control right?"

"If you manage to find one that can actually slick 4C hair, let me know. Now that your hair's done, let's go over the rules we talked about."

Sonnet sits down on the vanity bench and clears her throat. "Rule one, don't initiate conversation and if anyone asks, I'm a junior transfer at Julian High School. Rule two, no partaking in any drugs." She pauses. "That doesn't include weed, right?"

I stare at her. "Yes, it does. I'm not carrying your high ass home again like last time."

"Ugh, fine. But if I get a contact high, that shouldn't count."

I shrug. "Moving on. What's rule number three?"

She rolls her eyes up to the ceiling. "Rule three, no dancing. What kind of party doesn't have dancing?"

"Oh, there's gonna be dancing there," I say, slipping a pair of Katia's gold hoops in my ears. "You're just not going to be doing it. The moves can get a lil freaky and since you can barely clap on beat—"

"Hey! Just because I'm rhythmically challenged doesn't mean I can't dance," she says.

"You do realize we're not actually going to the party to have fun, right? We're only going so I can talk to Breon. Let's stay focused tonight, okay?"

Sonnet pouts but nods in agreement.

We both do a final once-over in the full-length mirror on the back of the door. I let Sonnet borrow Katia's all white Air Forces and my white biker shorts and cropped hoodie. Seeing her in something not so colorful is strange, but she looks like one of us now. An authentic Grady Park girl.

I'm wearing my black Chucks, black high-rise leggings, and a matching black sports bra that says "FILA" across the front. Of course, my baby hairs are slayed and laid. It's the first time I've gotten dressed up like this since Katia died. I wasn't really in the partying mood, but now that the sun is down and I got on this fly outfit, I'm a little excited. One thing about Grady Park is we know how to turn up. I missed this.

We put on two giant hoodies, just in case Momma happens to come out of her room and see us, but as usual her door is closed.

Deja's waiting for us at the end of the walkway in a pair of tight ripped blue jeans, crystal stiletto heels, and an emerald lace teddy. She even brought out the green thirty-inch lace wig to tie the look together. One thing about my bestie, she does *not* play when it's time to turn up.

"Okay, body! Deja, you look amazing!" I say.

"Thanks. Who is this?" She turns her attention to Sonnet who's standing there smiling all goofy-like.

"This is Sonnet, my friend from school I told you about." There's no point in lying to Deja. She knows I only have two friends, even though they've never met until tonight.

Deja laughs and tosses her long hair behind her shoulder. "Hol' up, this is Sonnet? The one who lives in the Keebler elf tree house in the woods?"

Here we go. Barely a minute in and Deja's already throwing shots. But Sonnet's not petty like her. She doesn't insult her back, just smiles politely.

"It's not a tree house, it's a log cabin," Sonnet says.

Deja looks at me with her WTF face and I signal to her to play nice for once in her life. She can't stand me having friends other than her, but she needs to get over it already.

"Ah, okay. So, Lyric."

"It's Sonnet," I remind her.

"Uh-huh, sure. What you tryna go to a party in the projects for anyway?"

"I invited her," I say. "Deja, can we just go to Jacques's?"

I can already hear the drill music banging from across the

courtyard. There's a few groups of kids milling around in the courtyard, smoking joints and laughing on their way to the kick-back.

Deja sucks her teeth. "Okay, whatever, but I'm not holding nobody's hand tonight. I came out here to have fun."

"Fine, let's just go," I say.

A few boys try to grab onto our hands as we walk to the party, but we brush them off. We're on a mission.

"Ladies, ladies, ladies, got *damn* y'all lookin' too good tonight," Jacques says when we walk up to his door. He's wearing a Hornets snapback and holding a coffee can in his hand. He holds it out to us, and I put six singles in it to cover our fee.

Inside, the apartment is dim, lit only by a single red light bulb hanging from the ceiling. It smells like ass, weed, and sweat but I'm used to it. I grab on to Deja's hand as she snakes Sonnet and me through the crowd to a couch covered in plastic.

"I'll get us some jungle juice," she says, slipping back into the throng of people sweating and dancing. I hear the opening line of Juvenile's "Back That Ass Up" and I thank the universe for finally being on my side. This is our chance to look for Breon.

Pulling Sonnet behind me, I search the middle of the living room and see where the crowd has parted to make a circle around Deja. She's bouncing up and down in a split while everybody cheers her on and some dude starts throwing singles at her. This is her song, so we've got at least five minutes before she comes looking for me.

We move to the back of the unit where the line for the bathroom wraps in a twisted circle.

"Girl, don't you see we in line?!" some chick shouts from behind us.

"Bitch, shut up before I clock your silly ass," I say, daring her to try me. I don't normally talk like this, but this is Grady Park protocol. People will start messing with you just to get into a fight for fun. You gotta know how to hold your own if you want them to back off.

"Uh, Beau, what's happening?" Sonnet whispers in my ear, digging her nails into my hand.

The girl steps forward and she might have fifty pounds on me but the bigger they are, the harder they fall. I push Sonnet behind me and step right up to the girl.

"Yo, Beau!"

Suddenly Breon squeezes between me and the girl. "Aye, Yolanda, this is my girl, Beau and uh . . . her friend. Y'all ain't having issues or nothin', are you?"

Yolanda narrows her eyes at me but shakes her head.

"Nah, it's all good. How you been, girl?" They kiss on the cheek two times.

"I'm good, I'm good. Look, I'ma see you later, okay?"

"Aight, cool," the girl says, giving me one last glare.

Breon takes my hand as she leads us to one of the bedrooms in the back of the unit.

Once we're inside, she flips on the light, closes the door, and locks it. This must be Jacques's room because it smells like dude all up in here. Poor brother is still sleeping on faded Batman sheets at thirty years old.

"Thanks for that, ol' girl was trippin'," I say.

"You know how these girls be. It's not a Friday night unless they beefin' wit somebody," Breon says.

"True dat. Anyway, I was looking for you. I wanted to ask you about something."

Breon moves to sit on Jacques's bed but nearly misses. She's on something. Which might work in our favor.

"What'd you wanna ask?"

Since she's pretty far gone, I cut to the chase.

"Breon, think back to the night Katia was shot. Did you get a ride from her and Jordan that day? Because there's a rumor that you saw what happened."

She blinks a few times and her sober self peeks out from behind the curtain of lean.

"Who told you that?" she asks, suddenly serious.

"Is it true? Were you there?"

"No! Hell no!" Breon shouts.

Sonnet steps forward. "You sure? Because if you were, it'd be in your best interest to tell us now before we get the police involved. Leaving the scene of a crime is punishable by law."

Breon turns on Sonnet with hatred in her eyes.

"Who is this bitch?" she asks me.

"Just a friend. Sonnet, why don't you go and find Deja. *Now*." I open the door and push her out of the room before she can say anything else. I can't believe her dumbass. And I can't believe my dumbass thought it'd be okay to bring her behind along. Threatening Breon was never part of the plan.

Breon's standing up now, watching me warily and swaying side to side.

"That's what you replaced me with? Some private school bitch?" Breon sneers.

"Millennium Magnet is a public school, Breon. And I've never tried to replace you." Not that Deja would have let me if I wanted to. She's got drama with so many different chicks, we'd probably have to go to Egypt to find a girl she hasn't fought yet.

"Then why you got chicks in here accusing me of shit I didn't even do?!" Breon asks.

"I'm sorry, okay? She was outta line. But forget her, this is about us. I know things haven't been great between us the past few years, but I still have love for you. You know that."

The tensed muscles in her face relax. "Pssh. So you say. But I wasn't there that night! Somebody out here is tryna set me up!"

"Did you see her or Jordan at all that day? Did they give you a ride or anything?" I ask.

"On God, I swear I didn't see them that day or night, Beau."

I believe her. Her hands hang loose at her sides. Back when we were younger, I could always tell when she was lying because she'd stuff her hands in her pockets.

"Breon, I'm sorry, I was only trying to—"

"Aye! What y'all doin' up in here?" Jacques bursts into the room with a joint between his lips and a red Solo cup sloshing purple liquid onto his carpet.

"Nothing, sorry, we'll leave," I say standing up and heading for the door. I turn around for Breon to follow, but her gaze is fixed on Jacques's cup.

"I'll see you later, aight?" she says, dismissing me.

"Yeah, aight."

In the living room, the party is all the way turnt up. A Megan Thee Stallion song is playing and girls are on the floor showing out, twerking like there's no tomorrow. The old me would have been on that floor backing it up on somebody's son, but now's not the time.

I scan the room for Sonnet but through the haze of kush and cigarette smoke, I can't see anything but shaking butts, braids, and gold hoops.

"'Scuse me, 'scuse me, please." I try squeezing through the group but somehow end up getting shuffled back to the hallway where I started.

I stand on a plastic chair and try to get a bird's-eye view. Still, I can't see Sonnet. But in the kitchen, backed up against the sink is Deja. I can only tell it's her because of her green hair.

She's talking to some guy, definitely not her type, but he's pressed up on her close, saying something.

Deja tries to push him away, but he grabs her by the wrists. Nobody around her seems to notice or maybe they just don't care. But nobody touches my best friend, period.

I swoop down off the chair and start elbowing people to get through to her. I don't care if I start a fight, I have to get to my girl.

When I make it to the kitchen, the dude is gone and Deja looks rattled. Before I can say anything, she grabs my hand and starts pulling me toward the front door.

"Wait! We gotta get Sonnet!" I shout over the music. We're standing in the middle of the living room getting jostled around when I spot her. She's in the corner with some guy, waving her arms in a circle over her head and struggle twerking.

"Hold on," I say to Deja. I grab Sonnet's hand and then Deja's and we form a chain until we're back outside in the cool night air.

"Hey, what happened?" Sonnet asks as we head to the bus stop. Deja gives me a look and I nod.

"Nothing, we always leave early in case the cops shut it down."

Sonnet pouts. "Okay, well, next time there's a party, you have to let me come again! That guy I was dancing with said he goes to Fenger and he's on the varsity baseball team!"

"That's great," I say flatly. I really want to talk to Deja, but I can't in front of Sonnet because if she knew Deja was threatened, she might get too scared to keep trying to look for Jordan with me.

"So . . . what did your friend say after I left?" Sonnet asks.

And I can't talk about what Breon said in front of Deja or she'll know I still haven't stopped looking for Jordan. Everything is too complicated.

"Nothing important, I'll tell you later," I say.

The three of us wait for the bus and try to ignore all the cat-calling dudes that drive by. Once Sonnet is on the bus safe and headed back to her house, I turn to Deja.

"What happened? Who was that guy?"

"Just an old boyfriend," she says.

"Bullshit. I know every guy you've ever dated so tell me the truth."

She shrugs. "Fine. It was an OT."

"Onyx Tiger? What does he want with you?"

"He was warning me. Because *you* keep interfering with their search for Jordan. I told him you haven't been because you promised me you would stop. That's when he grabbed me."

Now it's my turn to look away and fiddle my fingers. "Why didn't they come and threaten me?"

"Because everybody knows you're soft or whatever. You don't run the streets like I do. I'm your people so I'm responsible for you."

"What are they gonna do?"

"No, it's about what you're *not* going to do anymore. Don't you get you're not just putting yourself at risk running around asking questions? If I hadn't played it cool, things could have went way left tonight. I coulda got shot!"

"But I haven't been talking to anyone in Grady Park about Jordan!" Not in person anyway.

"The streets got eyes and ears everywhere. I don't know what you've been out here doing but whatever it is, stop it! I'm not asking you."

She stands up and walks back across the street to the complex. I sit on the bench, alone and scared. I can't lose Deja.

But I can't give up on Katia either.

CHAPTER 22

I'M STILL WORRIED ABOUT DEJA BY THE TIME I make it to school after the weekend. She keeps telling me she's fine and that she's got it under control. But she doesn't know what me and Sonnet have been doing. If anything happens to Deja, I'll never forgive myself. But if I just give up and let the world think all these awful things about Katia are true, I won't be able to live with myself.

When I get to my locker, I'd hoped to see Sonnet waiting for me, but Champion's there instead.

I start to smile but then I see that he isn't smiling. And I remember we had a date planned for Friday night. A date that I completely forgot about. I didn't even text him to say I wasn't gonna be able to make it.

"I'm really sorry I missed our date. I had to deal with some family stuff at home," I say, trying to look apologetic by staring at my feet.

"Family stuff like what?" he asks with his arms crossed.

"Um . . . we were just going through Katia's old things and figuring out what we should keep and what we should donate. My mom got really upset looking at it all and . . . it was just a really heavy night for us." It *was* a heavy night. Up until that night, I thought our biggest problem was trying to find Jordan. Now, I've put people's lives in danger. The last thing on my mind was eating a damn scone with Champion.

"Is that really what happened?" he asks me with an eyebrow raised.

"Yes," I lie. As far as he knows, that IS what happened. As long as I stick to my story, we'll be okay.

"Really. Because I heard you went to a house party with Sonnet Friday night. In Grady Park."

Shit, shit shit shit!

"Where did you hear that?"

"Is it true?"

"Champion, there's a lot you don't understand about—"

"Is it true?" he asks again, his eyes narrowing. People in the hall turn to look at us. Great, now we have an audience to our drama.

"Okay, fine, it's true, okay? But it's not what you think. We weren't there to have fun."

"Whatever you were doing was clearly more important to you than I am," he says, looking away from me.

"No! No, it's not, it's just that . . . Champion, believe me, I'd rather hang out with you over a house party any day. It's just I had to find an old friend and—" I'm scrambling to make up a lie that's good enough to convince him. I don't want to lose him. I can't.

"I'm not tryna hear it, Beau," he interrupts.

He's looking at me with those same honey eyes, only now, I don't feel butterflies, just his hurt.

"But I didn't blow you off on purpose! If you'd just listen to me—"

He laughs. "Why should I? You just lied to my face about being at that party! How do I know you're not lying now?"

"God, can't you just accept that there's some things in my life I can't tell you about?"

Maybe I have been lying but I have a lot on my plate right now. I'm probably stupid for even thinking he'd understand. How could he? His family has everything and mine has nothing. As much as I try to pretend, we're not the same.

"Beau, I think I deserve at least some explanation. This isn't the first time you've stood me up. If this is what it's gonna be like to be with you, then I don't know, man. Maybe we should just forget the whole thing."

I can practically hear my heart shatter. He's over me. The thing I've been trying to prevent from the jump is finally happening.

"Are you saying you don't wanna see me anymore?" I ask. I try to sound strong, but my voice comes out small and squeaky.

"Not if you're going to keep lying to me. You act like you don't wanna be bothered with me."

"That's not true!"

"But it feels like it. You're hiding something from me. Why won't you just tell me?"

"I can't tell you because I'm trying to protect you. That's the truth, I swear." Please let it be enough for him. It has to be.

But he shakes his head slowly and I know that it's not.

"Then I should just remove myself from the situation, I guess. I'll, uh . . . see you around," he says, turning to walk away.

"Wait, that's it? You're just gonna walk away like that?" I call after him.

He turns around. "Yeah, Beau. I am."

I start to panic. Champion's been like the one good thing that's happened to me since Katia died. I can't lose him, too. Not now.

"I can't believe you're doing this! Why, so you can date some other girl?"

"If I do, that's my business now, not yours."

He doesn't wait for a reply, just disappears down the hall and out of my life.

———

I've had enough of Deja's excuses. Even though she didn't answer my twenty texts over the weekend, I show up at her door after school, ready to force my way in if I have to. I need support, the kind you can only get from a friend who's had a man do her dirty before.

"Girl, why are you out here knocking like the police?!" Deja asks when she swings the door open.

"Bih, you won't believe what happened today. Champion dumped me! He fucking dumped me," I say, the tears I've held in all day starting to spill down my cheeks.

"He did? Oh my god, I'm sorry, come in, come in!"

We sit on the sofa, and I run down the whole story to her, minus the part about me ditching the dates to look for Jordan.

"He had no right talkin' to you sideways like that. Do I need to call some of my niggas? Because they'll get on his ass if they need to," Deja says.

I groan and lean back on the couch. "No, I don't wanna hurt him. I just wish he was different. Y'all got anything to drink?"

"Yeah, hol' on, lemme see."

Deja gets up to go to the kitchen and while she's gone, I finally notice the living room around me. It's a mess. There's pizza boxes on the coffee table, ashtrays full of Black 'N Mild butts, and there's candy wrappers and chip bags all over the floor. Deja's place was always a little filthy, but this is more than usual.

"Did you have a party here or something?" I ask when she comes back with a can of soda.

"Nah, I've just been really busy. I'm gonna clean up later today. But forget about that, we need to work on hooking you up with Jamar. I told you he was asking about you awhile back."

Sometimes I can't tell if Deja is joking or if she really just doesn't get me anymore.

"I don't want Jamar, I want Champion. That's why I came here. I figured you'd know how to help me fix it."

Deja sighs and flips her long white hair over one shoulder.

"I don't get why you want him back if he played you like that. Believe a nigga when he tells you who he really is!"

"But this was my fault, sort of. I did forget about our dates. And I did lie to him."

Deja waves the thought away with her hand. "Please, this is not your fault. He was gon' find some reason to drop you eventually. Black dudes like that end up with white girls all the time. So unless you was planning to wake up as Ariana Grande, it was never going to work."

I wanna tell her that's bull, but maybe it's not. Deja's got way more dating experience than I do. But Champion never came off as one of those kinda Black guys. The kind that make fun of us for wearing weaves or having too-dark skin, as if their own momma don't look just like us.

"Champion's not like that, though. His family is cool, too. They act regular and they didn't care when I told them I was from the projects."

"Yeah, because they probably figured you wouldn't be around too long anyway. I told you this would happen that day we saw him at the beauty supply."

"If you knew it was doomed, why did you keep telling me to talk to him 'n' shit? You sound like you're happy about it!"

Suddenly we hear a voice from the back of the apartment. "Cut all that yelling out! Damn!"

I lower my voice. "Sorry, I didn't know your momma was home."

"Shit, me either. But I don't like seeing my bestie get her feelings hurt, if that's what you tryna say."

"Coulda fooled me," I say, crossing my arms.

"Babe, stop. You know you're my girl always and forever. I just wanna see you with a guy that's more on your level, that's all."

"And that would be Jamar from Building A with his two baby mamas?"

Deja opens her mouth to reply but there's a knock at the front door. When she opens it, I'm surprised to see Breon standing there.

"What do you want?" Deja asks angrily.

"What are you talking about? I—Oh! Hey, Beau." Breon

waves at me over Deja's shoulder. "I just wanted to see if I could borrow some . . . mustard. We're out."

"So are we. Goodbye." Deja slams the door in her face so hard I get a lil offended.

"Damn, D, was that really necessary?" Although I'm more confused by Breon having the guts to come over here after what went down with those two after the necklace.

"Who cares, it's just Breon. Anyway, you want me to hook you up with Jamar or not?"

"Not. Anyway, did the OTs say anything else to you after Friday night?"

"Nope. I'm minding my business and they're minding theirs. Why? Did they say something to you?"

"No. But that was scary as hell. He walked up on you like he was gonna do something to you."

"I know, but he didn't. I'm okay, you're okay, everything's fine now. We just gotta keep our heads down for a lil bit."

"But I—"

"Beau, you don't have to worry about me. I can take care of myself. And watch out for you. I've been doing it since we was babies. This is nothing new."

I came to Deja's house because I've always felt safe around her. She always knows what to do and she can handle any situation, like the time I tried to relax my hair after bleaching it and it started falling out in clumps. Deja whipped out her scissors and cut it into the cutest pixie.

But Champion dumping me and the Onyx Tigers putting us on their hit list are problems she can't fix.

Because it's all my fault.

CHAPTER 23

A WEEK AFTER CHAMPION DUMPS ME, IT STILL DOESN'T feel real. Even when we pass each other in the halls and he does everything he can not to look at me.

I haven't said anything to him since the breakup. It's stupid, but I've been waiting for him to come to his senses, to change his mind and ask for me back. The only other option is for me to ask him to take me back and there's no way I'm doing that. I'm not gonna give him the chance to reject me two times in a row.

On Saturday morning, I'm lying awake in Katia's bed, scrolling through Instagram and trying to keep my mind off my life for a change. I double-tap a clip of Deja twerking to some Drake song, scroll past a photo of Madison with her parents at a museum. Not exactly prime time stuff.

But there's one person who I'm curious about. I tap Bexley's name into the Instagram search bar and click on her profile. It's mostly just photos of her work and dog, but her most recent photo catches my eye. It's of a yellow wooden tabletop with a small lantern in the center and Bexley's laptop, sketch pad, and pens arranged neatly around it. The initials RJ are carved into the corner.

She's at Elena's Coffee House on Michigan! It's been a long time since Katia took me there, but I recognize the table and the initials carved into it.

I check the time stamp, ten minutes ago. Which means there's a good chance Bexley's still there right now.

I throw the covers off and start rushing into the sweatpants and T-shirt I left on the floor last night. I can't do anything about the Onyx Tigers threatening Deja or Champion hating me, but maybe it's not too late to fix this mural situation. If I can just explain to Bexley what happened and how Madison's two-faced self tricked me, I know she'd understand. She might even ask Principal Marcos to let me back into art class!

I brush my teeth and tuck my matted crochet hair into a Bulls cap. There's no time to worry about being cute.

With my sketch pad tucked into my backpack, I tiptoe out of my bedroom. I grab my momma's car keys off the kitchen table and make my escape.

———

It only takes me ten minutes to drive to Elena's, but then I have to circle the block for another five minutes before someone leaves and I can get a parking spot. I cut the engine and take the key out of the ignition. Now that I'm actually here, this feels like a horrible idea. She's a working artist who came to a coffee shop to get her work done in peace and quiet. She's not gonna wanna be bothered with some random high schooler.

I stick the key back in the ignition.

Although if Bexley really wanted complete privacy, she probably wouldn't have posted where she was. Maybe this is stupid, but she's here, I'm here. It's now or never if I want her help getting back on the mural.

When I step inside the dimly lit coffee shop, it's not as crowded as it seems from outside. There's navy velvet sofas, old-fashioned armchairs, and a long bar with yellow cushioned stools.

It's mostly college kids, doing group projects on their laptops or studying next to giant piles of books. I scan the crowd and see Bexley's long, neon green, purple, and blue braids. She's in a corner sitting on a sofa next to a tall green plant.

"Here we go," I say to myself. The worst that can happen is she ignores me. Then I'd just drive back home and cry for the rest of my life or something. It soothes my nerves a little to know I have a plan.

"Excuse me," I say, standing across from Bexley, "I don't mean to bother you, but my name is Beau Willet and I'm an artist, or I want to be an artist one day, like you, and I was in the art class you're helping fix their mural at Millennium and I was supposed to be there but—"

"Whoa, slow down!" Bexley says with a laugh. "All I caught was mural, Millennium, and . . . your name?"

"Sorry, I'm just a little nervous. I'm an art student at Millennium Magnet. My name is Beau."

She motions for me to have a seat next to her on the sofa and I nearly leap over the table.

"Please, call me Bexley. You're an art student at Millennium? Why haven't we met before?"

"Yeah, but in a different class than the one that's painting the mural." I throw my plans of getting back on the mural away. I don't want Bexley to think I'm a troublemaker. And she seems too cool to deserve to be put in the middle of my drama with Madison.

"It's terrible what happened to the original mural. I've had more than a couple of my own defaced over the years," she says sadly.

"Really? By who?" Anything to take the discussion away from Millennium Magnet's mural. She'd think I was a complete jerk if she knew I'm the one who wrecked it.

"Bigots, racists, fascists, etc. It's never stopped me from painting, but as artists, we put so much work into each and every piece that we do. Having one destroyed in just a few seconds hurts. Especially if the mural was something important to you."

Pssh. Well, I guess I know Madison isn't hurt over what I did. That girl didn't give a rat's ass about who we put up on that wall, as long as she got to say it was her idea.

"Some people are just cold-blooded," I say, heat rushing to my face. "How did you become a professional artist though? I mean, like getting paid to do murals and shows and stuff."

"Everyone's path is different, so I don't want you to think there's only one way. But for me? It started with my sister, Pam."

"She's an artist, too?"

"Of a different medium. See, when we were growing up, we'd get bored during the summers and one day Pam decided she was going to write a book that we could make copies of and try to sell to people in the neighborhood. So Pam wrote this story about a little girl who goes off in search of a butterfly. And I drew the pictures. Nobody ended up buying the book but our parents, but I was so proud of my work that I started drawing all the time after that. After high school, I went to art school, but I dropped out after a year."

Whoa. Bexley O is a college dropout? I don't know why, but she always seemed so put together and perfect. Not the type of person to drop out of anything.

"Why did you drop out? I'm worried I won't even be able to get into an art school."

"That's a longer story for another time. But let's just say I encountered some racist classmates and didn't like how the school handled it."

"What happened after you dropped out?"

"Got a job at a coffee shop and did my artwork on the side. One of my murals ended up going viral and that's when the commissions started coming in. Two years later, here I am."

"Wow. That's amazing. So, you don't think I have to go to college to be an artist?"

"You have to find the right path for you. Just because college wasn't for me doesn't mean you won't have a better experience. And, as Pam always likes to remind me, there's some doors that only open if you have the right credentials."

She sees my backpack and points to my sketchbook sticking out the top.

"Is this yours? Can I see?"

"Um . . . yeah, sure! It's just some stuff I do on the side. They're super rough and everything."

I watch silently as Bexley flips through my book. There are sketches of Momma and Daddy, the rib shack up the street from my house, Deja with a sucker in her mouth and her edges swirled over her forehead, and then toward the end, the sketch

223

of Katia I used for our hoodies at the funeral. Bexley stops on that one.

"This girl, she looks so familiar. Who is she?"

My stomach starts to twist itself into a coil.

"My sister. Her name is Katia."

Realization suddenly dawns over Bexley's face. "I remember hearing about her murder on the news some months back. I'm so sorry for your loss."

I turn away and pretend like I'm stretching when I'm really just trying to will the tears not to come. I'm not gonna fall apart in front of my idol. Not today!

"Thanks. I'm okay, though," I lie.

"I just can't imagine that kind of pain. Especially at such a young age. Have they arrested the police officer yet?"

I shrug. "No. Since my sister's stupid boyfriend ran from the scene, there's no witnesses to prove the cop is lying about her trying to break into his house."

Bexley sighs and places my sketchbook back on the coffee table.

"I wish I could say I'm surprised. But that's usually how it goes in Chicago. New York. Philadelphia. It's not right, not at all."

"It sucks. Now that it's been a while since it happened, it's like no one remembers Katia. No one cares. Even at school, sometimes I just feel so . . . I feel so—"

"Invisible?" Bexley asks.

I nod. "And like I can't do anything to change it. I don't know how to make my own parents care about me, so how am I supposed to make the world care about my sister?"

Now I'm definitely oversharing. None of this is Bexley's

problem and I don't want her to feel like it is, just because she's an adult.

"Beau, that's a heavy burden to place on yourself," she says, handing me a napkin to wipe the tears I hadn't realized were rolling down my face.

"I know . . . but she's my sister. If I don't stand up for her, who will?"

Someone clears their throat loudly and when I look up, Madison and a couple of her friends are standing across the table from us.

They're staring at me, with these tears running down my face and my pathetic sketchbook of shitty drawings.

"Sorry if we're interrupting, Bex," Madison starts, "but we heard you'd be working here this week and we were hoping we could join you? Maybe pick your brain?"

I want Bexley to tell them we're in the middle of something and that they should go somewhere and let us finish talking alone. I have so much I wanna say, so much more I wanna ask her. But not in front of Madison. And Bexley's too nice to turn away fans.

"Oh, well, of course, pull up a few chairs. The more the merrier. I'm guessing you all know each other from art?"

Now I really regret not telling her the truth about being kicked out of class. Because now she's gonna hear it from Madison who I know is gonna make it sound way worse than it was. Bex might even put two and two together and realize it was me who defaced the mural in the first place.

Once Madison's finished weaving her bullshit story, Bexley's gonna hate me. I grab my sketchbook and stand up.

"Oh, Beau, you don't want to stay?" Bexley asks. She even

looks kinda disappointed. That's because she doesn't know me or any of the fucked-up shit I'm involved with. I knew I should have just stayed home.

"I can't. I have somewhere I have to be. Thanks for talking to me."

Before anyone has a chance to stop me, I rush through the coffeehouse, out the front doors, and into Momma's car.

I should have known meeting Bexley wouldn't change anything for me. As usual, everything I touch falls apart.

CHAPTER 24

BEFORE

I WAS LYING IN BED ONE SATURDAY MORNING, wide awake and still fuming after my big fight with Deja the day before. She was trying to convince me to come to Grady Park High for the spring semester but I said no. She called me a sell-out and I told her she was an idiot because I wasn't being paid to go to either school. We hadn't spoken since.

Katia was putting on her work uniform, a button-up and her white pharmacy tech coat.

"You think maybe I should listen to Deja and transfer to Grady Park High next semester?" I asked her.

She looked at me like I was insane. "Hell nah, haven't you noticed how happy I've been since graduation?"

"Yeah, but what if my friends think—"

"GIRLS! GET IN HERE NOW!" Daddy roared from the living room.

Katia and I turned to each other with panicked eyes.

I rolled out of bed and followed Katia into the living room where we sat down next to each other on the couch. Daddy paced back and forth across the room while Momma leaned on the kitchen counter like she was bored.

"My class ring is missing. Now I know the motherfucker didn't grow legs and walk up out this house, so what happened to it?"

My shoulders relaxed. I never even went in my parents' bedroom. I was innocent.

"I don't know what happened to it," Katia said coolly. A little too cool. Sometimes it was hard to tell when she was lying because she was so good at it. But I knew right at that moment that she knew exactly what happened to it.

Daddy turned to me. "Beau?"

"It wasn't me, Daddy!" I wasn't going to tattle on Katia, but I knew Daddy wasn't about to let it go either.

His eyebrows scrunched up tight and he looked madder than that time Momma cut up his clothes.

"Nobody know what happened to it, huh? Aight, then. Y'all are both on lockdown 'til it magically reappears on my motherfuckin' finger! Go in ya rooms, get y'all's phones, tablets, walkie-talkies, flat irons, whatever you got that runs off battery or electricity. Bring it out here NOW!"

I looked at Katia. Was she really about to let us both be punished for this when she knew I had nothing to do with it? If I'd taken it, I would have admitted it by now.

"Why don't you just tell him what you did, Beau?" she asked me.

I was so pissed I jumped up off the couch. "What?! I didn't do anything, *you* did!"

She just rolled her eyes and sighed while I stood there fuming.

"Daddy, I saw Beau wearing your ring the other day. I told her to put it back, but she wore it to school."

This. Fucking. Bitch, I thought to myself angrily.

"She's lying!" I shouted.

"Then what happened to my ring?" Daddy asked.

I shrugged my shoulders. "I don't know! But I never touched it!"

"Beau, you know I have a date this weekend. I can't believe you'd try to ruin it by blaming this on me. I told you I'd take you out to eat next weekend."

My jaw nearly hit the floor. How had she managed to make up the most convincing story within less than a minute? Her brain worked like a criminal mastermind's. She knew our parents had overheard us arguing the other day about Katia ditching our Applebee's plans to hang out with Jordan instead. I'd been mad, but not enough to do something stupid like this.

But in the end, it didn't really matter. I was just a kid and even though she still lived at home, Katia wasn't. My parents believed her.

"Katia, you're free to go," Daddy said, his red laser eyes boring into mine. I was screwed.

That night, I waited up for Katia to get home from work. Wasn't like I had shit else to do. Daddy had confiscated anything I owned that might entertain me, including all my art supplies.

As soon as Katia walked in, I was ready to fight.

"You fucking bitch," I whisper shouted. Our parents were asleep in their bedroom just down the hall.

Katia shrugged out of her pharmacy coat.

"Let me explain before you go apeshit on me, okay?"

"Explain what? How you lied on me?"

She sat down on her bed beside me.

"I'm sorry, but it was an emergency."

"What emergency?"

"Jordan was—"

"I knew it! He did it, didn't he?"

"No, I took the ring. I had to pawn it for cash. But once I get my next check, I'll buy it back."

"What did you need the cash for?"

"It's a long story, but basically, one of Jordan's friends set him up. He let him borrow his car but didn't tell him he had a bunch of stuff in the trunk. The cops pulled us over and—"

"Bail money? You pawned Daddy's ring for bail money? For Jordan's stupid ass?!"

She raised her eyebrows.

"It wasn't his fault. I couldn't just leave him in there. It wasn't safe for him, especially with who his father is? There's people he's never even met who probably wanna kill him."

I didn't care. I did not care. All I could think about was the fact that my own sister had thrown me under the bus for Jordan. And actually expected me to understand and be okay with the bullshit.

"So I'm on punishment because Jordan was an idiot and turned you into a thief?"

Her chin dropped to her chest.

"I'm not proud of what I did. You know I'm not a thief. But Jordan's trying to be better, he really is. All this shit just keeps coming at him."

"If you're really sorry, tell Momma and Daddy the truth."

Her phone pinged and she pulled it out of her pocket.

"I can't do that, Beau. If Momma and Daddy even knew he was arrested, they'd never let me see him."

"And that's a bad thing?"

She stood up and crossed the room to the vanity.

"Look, I tried to be nice about it, but you'll never get it until it happens to you," she says. "I'm not telling Momma and Daddy. I'll put the ring back next week and then you'll be off punishment."

I stomped over to the vanity and stood behind her.

"A week?! Deja's momma and her boyfriend are taking us to Medieval Times on Friday. I'll miss the trip if you don't put it back till next week!"

"Oh, whatever, you've been to Medieval Times like ten times."

"Yeah, and I wanna go for the eleventh time! You're really gonna do me like that?"

The silence between us sparked with fury as she used a makeup wipe to clean her face. This wasn't my sister. She'd never purposely gotten me into trouble before. It was her job to keep me out of it. And here she was throwing me under the bus for some stupid dude who treated her like shit!

"You're a fucking loser. Don't EVER speak to me again," I said quietly, my hands balled into tight fists.

She turned around and looked at me with this hurt look on her face. But just for a second. Then she turned back around to the mirror.

I waited for her to feel bad and change her mind, to apologize and realize that I was the one who always had her back, not Jordan.

But she just sat there at the vanity brushing her hair silently. Like I wasn't even there.

I took my pillows and blanket out to the lumpy sofa that smelled like corn chips and beer. I was too upset to sleep, so I cried into my pillow and fantasized about Jordan moving to Timbuktu.

CHAPTER 25

WHEN THE BUS DROPS US OFF NEAR THE ENTRANCE to Navy Pier, I'm already annoyed and exhausted.

"Beau, how can you be grumpy at Navy Pier on a day as beautiful as this?" Sonnet stands in the middle of the sidewalk and opens her arms wide to the sky, hot sunlight turning her highlighter into golden sparkles.

It's not that I hate Navy Pier, but it's a place for, like, thirty million tourists and their entire family. Big crowds like that make me nervous. Not to mention it takes forever just to walk through the place because everybody moves so slow, acting like they never seen a lake before.

"I just wanna find out who Murdersleuth is and get the hell outta here. With NO detours."

After we found out the Breon tip was bogus, I DM'd Murdersleuth and told him we weren't going to listen to any more of his tips unless he told us who he was. He seemed hesitant but he agreed to meet us at Navy Pier today.

I can tell from the way Sonnet has started staring at the Ferris wheel that she's gonna wanna get on it.

"What's wrong with enjoying ourselves a little bit while we're here? Don't you get tired of all this Jordan hunting sometimes?"

"Yeah, actually, I do. Which is why I've been working so hard. The faster we find him, the faster we can get Peter Johnson arrested."

I pull out my cell and send a DM to Murdersleuth.

ME: We're here. Where are you?

I get a response almost instantly.

MURDERSLEUTH99: Near Giordano's. Get a table outside and order some food. When the waiter brings it out to you, I'll join you.

ME: Whatever, fine. What are YOU wearing? So we know it's you.

MURDERSLEUTH99: You'll know when I sit down at your table. DM me when you get there.

I roll my eyes and shove my phone into the pocket of my jeans. Since Murdersleuth already knows who I am, we don't have any choice but to play his game by his stupid rules.

The sun is starting to make me sweat. I shrug out of my green flannel and wrap it around my waist, bare shoulders exposed for the first time this weekend in a dark blue camisole.

Sonnet always dresses perfectly for the weather. Today she's wearing red high-waisted shorts and a Bulls T-shirt. She fits in with the crowd of sweaty tourists we find ourselves lost in as we make our way to Giordano's.

"This seems really sketchy, Beau. He won't tell us anything about who he is, what he looks like, where he is. But he knows everything about us, including where we're going."

I bite my tongue as a group of little kids dart across our path and nearly trip me. We're trapped in a sea of vacationers, walking slow as hell and aimlessly because they don't know where anything is. We don't have time for this shit. I grab Sonnet and start pushing our way through the crowd in the direction of the restaurant. "Excuse you!" one old white guy says. But I don't care. We're here on a mission for justice, not to eat ten-dollar hot dogs and gawk over snow globes.

"He's probably afraid of someone else finding out he's helping us," I say.

"Like who? Oh—sorry, lady!" Sonnet says when she accidentally knocks someone's shoulder.

"Like maybe the cops, or the OTs."

"Why would they care?"

I take a deep breath. I wasn't going to tell Sonnet until I was sure, but she deserves to know. "Alright, I don't know for sure, but I really think this guy might be an Onyx Tiger."

"Ohmygod, really? How do you know?"

"Because it's the only thing that makes sense. Why he

would know who I am, why he won't tell us anything about who he is."

"Why would an OT wanna help us?"

"Jordan probably double-crossed him or something like he did Parker. But he knows he can't be the one to expose Jordan to the police because of his gang ties so he wants us to do it."

We pass through a line of sunburned people waiting for their turn to board one of the speedboats that takes people out on Lake Michigan.

"If that's true, he's really going out of his way to make it difficult for us."

Can't argue with her on that one. When we get to Giordano's, it's lunch hour and the place is packed inside and out. We wait in line behind a family of at least thirty people in family reunion T-shirts before the host leads us to one of the red umbrellaed tables on the patio.

"We'll have two Cokes and a medium pepperoni," I say, without even opening the menu.

"Deep-dish?" our server asks.

"Thin crust, please." I hate deep-dish pizza.

"Oh, and add anchovies and artichokes, please!" Sonnet says.

"On the whole pizza?"

"Yeah, that's fine," I say, handing her our menus before she walks back inside. I'm not hungry anyway.

"Have you talked to Champion?" Sonnet asks.

I snort. "No. Why would I? He basically called me a liar."

"But you did lie to him. More than a couple times."

I cut my eyes at her. "Whose side are you on?"

She holds up her hands. "Yours! Always. I know Champion makes you happy, so why don't you try to make things right with him?"

"Because I didn't do anything to that boy."

"Except lie to him about what we've really been doing the past few months. Champion's a good soul but everyone has their limits."

Our server returns with two big glasses of Coke. I unwrap my straw and shove it into the drink between the cubes of ice.

"Bullshit. If he was such a 'good soul' then he'd respect me when I say I can't tell him what I'm doing. I'm allowed to have privacy in my life, right?"

Sonnet takes a long sip of her Coke and smacks her lips. "Beau, be honest with yourself. If Champion bailed out of dinner with your parents over a phone call and then stood you up twice, you'd think he was seeing somebody else, too, wouldn't you?"

Probably. "Maybe, but that would be totally different. My entire life has been falling apart since Katia died. I'm trying to fix it, but people just can't leave me alone."

"I really think Champion just wants to help you."

"Yeah, well, I just want them to hurry up baking this pizza so we can see who Murdersleuth is," I say.

I get what Sonnet's trying to say, but she doesn't understand how a person like me could ruin Champion's future. People probably already looked at him funny for dating a girl from the projects. What would they think if they knew my sister was dating a full-fledged gang member before she was killed? Truth is, I do miss Champion. So bad it makes my stomach hurt. But I don't think I could handle telling him the truth and then having him still reject me after.

Half an hour and ten games of tic-tac-toe on the napkins later, our fishy pepperoni pizza arrives. Sonnet digs in immediately, long strings of cheese tethering her slice to the rest of the pizza. I grab a butter knife and cut it for her so she can put it on her plate.

"You're not going to have some?" she asks.

"Not hungry. You see anyone around who looks like they could be an OT?"

My eyes scan the tables around us and the crowds passing by, but nobody catches my eye. I sit back in my chair.

"Maybe he went to the bathroom or something. Just relax, Beau."

"I can't. What if he's sending us off?"

I send another DM.

ME: Where are you? The food is here.

I wait for a reply for over an hour. But Murdersleuth never replies.

Meanwhile, Sonnet's managed to polish off three slices of the pizza. She lets out a loud burp and then covers her mouth like she just said a cuss word. A family at a table behind her turns around with looks of disgust on their faces.

"What?!" I bark. "You never heard a girl burp before? Turn around and mind your business."

They give me a dirty look but turn back to their food.

"Beau, we've been sitting here for an hour. The pizza is gone. Whoever this Murdersleuth guy is, I don't think he's coming," Sonnet says.

"I know. I just don't get why he'd tell us to meet him here if he wasn't going to show. What's the fucking point?"

"Oooh, I got a theory! He's an undercover Giordano's employee and this has been his plan from the start to drum up business!"

I pinch the bridge of my nose. "Sonnet . . ."

"I know, I know, just trying to lighten the mood."

"You can give up because the only one thing that's gonna fix my mood is finding Jordan and clearing Katia's name. You do realize anytime anyone googles me or does a background check, they're gonna find out about the shooting and the drugs?"

"But you didn't do anything wrong, Beau."

"Do you really think that matters to the rest of the world? Everybody already thinks we're trash because we live in the projects. Now, I'm not gonna be able to do or be shit when I grow up!"

What art program would take me after everything that's come out in the news? What art gallery would even think of taking my drawings? I couldn't even paint Katia on the side of the school without parents threatening to sue the district. I didn't do anything but I'm still the one who has to deal with everything. It's not fair.

"That's not true at all, Beau. You're talented, you're funny, loyal, and honest . . . well, most of the time. This isn't gonna stop you from being what you wanna be."

"You're only saying that because you don't know what it's like for people like me."

"People like you?"

I roll my eyes. "Yeah, Black people who live in the real world."

She raises her eyebrows. "Am I not Black, too? Am I not living in this"—she gestures to the eating families around us—"real world?"

This isn't the place where I wanted to have this argument, but I knew it was coming sooner or later.

"You don't get it, Sonnet. This has all been a game to you because you've never had to deal with the kind of stuff I have! Like this weird obsession you have with *Pretty Little Liars*. Do you really think any of that shit would have happened if they looked like us?"

A couple people walking by look at us, but I don't care. I'm tired of having to explain things to Sonnet that she should already know.

"Maybe it would have been a little different, but anything is possible."

I slam my hand on the table. "No, it's not! I know you grew up in a tree house in a magical forest, but that's not real. What's real is my sister being dead, my mother losing her job, my dad lying about looking for work! That's what's happening. And looking on the bright side or whatever the fuck isn't going to change that. So it's time for you to grow the fuck up and accept the world for what it is, a shitty place where people who look like us don't get the benefit of the doubt. We don't get a break or anything like that because we don't matter to them! Now do you get it?"

I'm standing up now while Sonnet sits in her seat, glowering at me.

"Excuse me, but we're going to have to ask you to leave. You're disrupting other patrons," a waitress says to me.

I look around and everyone eating on the patio is looking at us, people walking by and shaking their heads. They don't even know what we're talking about. They don't even know anything about us.

"Why? We haven't finished our sodas. We're patrons, too!" I shout at her.

"Sorry, we're leaving," Sonnet says, pushing back from the table. But I'm on a roll now and I can't be stopped.

"No, the fuck we're not! If people don't like loud noises, they shouldn't be at Navy Pier, then!" I yell at the white diners.

"Ma'am! I'll call security if I need to," the waitress says, pulling a phone out of her back pocket.

I should be careful now. I should remember what happened to me and Sonnet after we messed up the mural. But I don't care anymore. What's the point when they're never gonna leave us alone?

I step to the waitress just like I would step to a loudmouthed Grady Park chick talking her mess. She's got a good two or three inches on me but I'm in fight mode. I start to see red and suddenly the waitress isn't who I see anymore. I see Madison. I see Blue Lives flags. I see Peter Johnson with a gun in his hand pointed at my face.

I don't move, I don't even blink. My eyes are locked on her. On them. I have to do something, or they'll never leave us alone.

Sonnet pushes her way in between us, her back to the waitress.

"Beau! Let's go!" she shouts at me.

"Move, Sonnet! I want her to tell me why she had to bother us out of everybody here?"

The scared waitress takes the chance to run back inside the restaurant and I dart around Sonnet to follow her.

"No!" she screams.

Suddenly I feel her wrap her arms around me from behind in a bear hug.

"Let me go!" I shout.

"I will! As soon as we get out of here!" Somehow, she manages to push me out of the patio area and down the pier toward the exit. I never realized it before, but Sonnet's strong as hell! I try to wriggle my way out of her arms, but she just holds me tighter, forces me to walk forward.

"Can you let go now?!" I shout once we've made it far enough from the restaurant. Sonnet loosens her grip and I walk over to the edge of the pier, taking deep breaths as the wind blows mist from the lake over my face.

Sonnet stands beside me, looking out at the water that ripples in waves.

"Thanks," I say after a minute. My adrenaline is still pumping but I understand what could have happened if Sonnet hadn't dragged me out of there.

"You don't have to thank me, Beau. We're best friends. We protect each other," she says, her usual upbeat smile replaced by a frown. I don't get why she cares about me so much, after everything I've done.

"I didn't mean any of those things I said, Sonnet. I'm just . . . tired. So tired."

Her arms are folded across her chest, but I reach for her hand anyway, hold on to it as tight as I can. With my other hand, I hold on to my necklace.

"You're not alone in this," she says.

"But it feels like I am sometimes. Everybody else can move on with their lives. I can't."

"You could if you tried."

"Yeah, right. Then who'll stop this from happening to some-body else's sister? Who's gonna protect us if we don't?"

Sonnet sighs. "I wish I had an answer besides 'ourselves.' But even if Peter Johnson goes to prison, it could still happen again."

"I know. So what do we do, then?"

"I'm not sure . . ."

As we head back to the bus stop, the world around me looks so scary. Anyone anywhere could do anything to me and prob-ably get away with it. I think Sonnet's right that I can only save myself. I just wish I knew how.

————

When I get home that afternoon, I'm hot, tired, and pissed off. I collapse face-first on Katia's bed. I roll over onto my back and pull my change from Giordano's out of my pocket. Katia's nightstand sits next to the bed, and I pull the drawer out, but it gets stuck. *That's weird.*

I sit up and start yanking on it. My own nightstand sits next to my bed and I could just put my money in there, but now I'm determined to fix this drawer. There's obviously something blocking the drawer from opening all the way. I slip my hand through the open part of the drawers and feel around. I feel change and pens and pencils in the bottom. I turn my hand over and grab on to what feels like a really thick letter. It's stuck.

I tug and yank until finally it comes loose, and the drawer opens all the way. It's a blank envelope, unsealed. When I open it, I nearly pass out. It's filled with crisp new hundred-dollar bills. I lock the bedroom door and sit on Katia's bed to count it. At first, I think maybe it's a few hundred left over from her savings. But when I'm done counting, I'm not so sure.

It's eight thousand dollars.

CHAPTER 26

I DON'T KNOW WHERE TO GO AFTER I FIND THE MONEY. I text Sonnet and she tells me not to jump to any conclusions, that just because I found it in Katia's nightstand doesn't mean it's hers. Maybe she was hiding it for Jordan. As if that makes it any better.

I put the money back in the drawer and step outside the front door for some air. I want the sun to warm my face but it's nearly dusk. Kids are in the middle of the courtyard playing and chasing one another. Tanya from Building C is braiding somebody's hair on her stoop. A couple OTs are posted up near the entrance to the complex. And my sister is a drug dealer.

I'm about to turn and head back inside when I see Breon coming up the sidewalk. Deja would kill me if she saw us talking but I don't wanna be alone right now.

"Hey, Beau! Wassup wit you?"

I wipe the tears from my face and plaster on a pathetic smile. "Nothing much, just hanging out. What about you?"

She stops just at the start of the walkway to our door. "Same ol' same ol'."

I don't know what to say to that. Where our conversations used to flow easily, now there's awkwardness, and it makes us both uncomfortable.

"I was actually 'bout to head up to the store for some chips and a pop. You wanna go?"

"Um . . . yeah, sure. Just let me get my house keys real quick."

Five minutes later, we're strolling side by side away from the Grady Park Complex. Back when we were friends, we used to have a blast just walking around the block. Now it feels like we've been walking for ages, and I don't know who's supposed to talk first or what we'd even say.

"How's school?" she asks. Lame, but at least she's trying.

"It's okay." I can't ask her about her school because I'm pretty sure she doesn't even go anymore. "How's your mom been?"

"Good, really good! She's doing great. What about your folks?"

I roll my eyes just at the thought of them. "They're annoying as hell. Momma lost her job and Daddy's sleeping on my uncle Kolby's couch." If they were better parents, if they did better in life and made more money, maybe Katia wouldn't have felt like she needed to sell or take drugs. Then I wouldn't have just wasted months of my life trying to prove everyone wrong when they had it right the whole time.

"Damn," Breon says, kicking a rock in our path, "that's a lot to deal with. How you been holding up lately?"

"I . . . I don't know. It's hard. And I just found something out that makes it even harder."

Breon's eyes widen. "What did you find out?"

I'm so deep in my feelings that I almost forget who I'm talking to. Nobody knows about the money but Sonnet and it's gonna stay that way.

"It's just one of those situations where you think you know somebody but then you find out you really don't."

I'm talking about Katia, but I could be talking about Breon, too. When she admitted to stealing Deja's bracelet, it was like she morphed into another person overnight. Before that, I would have trusted this girl with my life.

We reach a corner and wait for the light to change so we can cross.

"I know what you mean. Hey, that's pretty, can I see?" She points at my necklace.

"Thanks. Yeah, sure." I hold the purple crystal up so she can see it closer, and she reaches out and rubs the gem with her thumb.

She thinks it's just a regular piece of jewelry. If it were anybody else, I'd tell them not to touch it. But because it's Breon, it's okay.

"Where did you get it?" she asks.

"It was a gift from my aunt Pepper. It's, um . . . they made it with some of Katia's ashes." I wait for Breon to freak out and drop it, but she doesn't. She strokes it gently one last time and then lets it fall softly against my heart.

"That's really cool. Now she's really with you wherever you go."

Tears burn the corners of my eyes and I wipe them away.

"What's wrong? Did I say something? I didn't mean—"

"No, no! It's not you, it's Katia," I say.

The walk sign lights up, but instead of crossing Breon leads me to a bench next to the bus stop. She sits beside me and takes both of my hands in hers. We haven't held hands in forever, but doing it now feels good, like I'm sharing this load on my shoulders. Like I don't have to carry it alone.

"I'm sorry," Breon says softly.

I sniffle. "It's okay. I'm fine. It's just that . . ." Maybe I can tell Breon. She drinks so much lean I know she wouldn't dare judge Katia for getting involved with drugs.

"You can tell me, Beau. I know we haven't really talked in a long time but . . . I always wanted to be there for you, especially after Katia died. I tried to talk to you after the funeral, but then Deja—"

"I know. She's still not over the bracelet thing. You know that girl can hold a grudge till forever."

"Yeah, that's true. But if it's not about you missing Katia, why are you so upset?"

I take a deep breath. "I think Katia was selling drugs before she died."

"Whaaaat? Katia? How do you know?" she asks, shocked.

"I found a secret stash of money she hid. A lot of money. More than she could have made at the pharmacy. I don't know any details, but it obviously has something to do with the cocaine in the car. She had to be selling drugs."

Breon's looking down at the ground, shaking her head. "Maybe it's not what you think. You know how you always think of the worst things that could ever happen."

"Well, you tell me how you think eight thousand dollars found its way under her nightstand. I've seen some of her old check stubs. There's no way that cash is legit."

"But you don't know that for sure," Breon replies.

"The cop who killed her said she was trying to break into his house. If she'd hide eight K under a bed, who knows what other stupid shit she was doing!"

"Beau . . ."

"I should have known. She woulda did anything for Jordan and now messing with him got her shot. Got me sittin' here like an idiot tryna find some way to prove that she wasn't some thug who got what she had coming."

"Beau, stop!" Breon shouts. She holds my hands tighter, and I fight the urge to pull away. "Listen to yourself. Katia hated us hanging out after she saw me drinking that one time."

"I know, she was a fucking hypocrite, too."

"No, I'm trying to tell . . . I have to tell you something, Beau."

"About what?" Breon's looking all serious now and that can't be good.

She bites her lip and starts bouncing her knee. She's scared of something.

"Bre? What is it? Did Katia sell you drugs?"

"No! She wasn't like that, and I don't want you to think that she was."

"How the fuck would you know? You barely talked to me these past two years; you weren't friends with Katia," I snap.

"Because I bought drugs from Jordan. And . . ."

"And what?"

"I know about the Twitter page," she says quietly.

"Who told you?" I ask. Because if she knows, maybe the OTs know, too.

But Breon shakes her head. "Nobody told me. I'm ArithMy-Tick. But I can explain!"

Breon. Is ArithMyTick. What the hell? I snatch my hands away from hers.

"You're the one who's been threatening me?! The fuck?! Why? To protect Jordan?"

"No! It's a long story. Just promise you won't hate me after I tell you, okay?"

"I'm not promising you shit! What did you do? Tell me the truth. Now!" I shout at her.

"Okay, okay! I was sending you those messages to try to protect you. I knew someone had found your Twitter and was sending you fake tips to throw you off. I was never going to hurt you. I just wanted to scare you so you'd delete it and they'd leave you alone."

"The Onyx Tigers?" I ask, my throat tightening at the thought.

"Not exactly. The night after Katia's murder, I saw Jordan. He was sneaking into this girl's bedroom window, and she was helping him hide. Before I could run, they saw me. They told me if I didn't tell, they'd pay me. Beau, you gotta understand, I needed the money for something important. Otherwise, I would have never did it. I was trying to tell you after the funeral but then . . ."

No. That's not possible. "You're lying," I say. "I specifically asked you at Jacques's party if you saw Katia and Jordan that night and you swore to me that you didn't!"

Breon bites her lip. "I didn't see them that night. I saw Jordan the night *after* Katia got shot." That would explain why I didn't think she was lying at the party. Technically, she was telling the truth. Just not the whole thing.

"Breon, are you trying to tell me that you know where Jordan is? That you've known this entire time?!"

"Please, just let me finish, Beau. I didn't wanna do it at first, but she knew exactly what to say to get me to go along with it! I just missed having friends and she said that she would finally forgive me if I did her this one favor. After what I did, I thought I owed it to her. I just wanted my friends back, that's all, I swear!"

Now she's full-on sobbing, snot running down her face and the tips of her ears bright red. My brain is trying to catch up with the story and put the pieces together. But this doesn't make any sense to me.

"Okay, fuck all that other shit, where is Jordan? If you know, you have to tell me, Breon!"

"He's in Building C," she says.

"Building C?"

"Yeah. He's been hiding in the Grady Park projects."

The tension in my body loosens as I realize there's no reason to get so worked up. There's no way Jordan was walking around living his life in the next building over from mine. I would have seen him. Or somebody else would have seen him and told me. Yeah, somebody would have told me.

"Stop lying to me, Breon. How the fuck has he been hiding when we live right there? I see everything that goes on over there!"

"Not everything. He stayed in the apartment most of the time, I guess. I don't know, I didn't really ask about him after a while."

"Yeah, sure. Which unit?" I ask. Not because I believe her, but because I wanna see just how far she'll take this lie of a story.

"He's been staying with . . . Deja."

Now I know this girl is trippin' off some lean or something.

"Deja? That's the best you could come up with?"

"What do you—"

"I mean, you could have at least picked someone we don't know that well, like Porsche from Building A or somebody."

Breon's brow furrows. "I'm *not* making this up, Beau! I saw him climbing through Deja's bedroom window the night after the murder. Wasn't the first time either."

I shake my head. "I don't know why I thought we could ever be friends again. You don't care about anybody but yourself! First you steal Deja's bracelet and now you're tryna turn me against her? Just because we don't wanna be your friend anymore? That's pathetic."

I start to walk away, but she grabs my arm and pulls me back.

"You let Deja get in your head so much you can't even see what's right in your face! She's been messing around with Jordan since last summer. I'm only telling you because *she* doesn't care what happens to you. She'll do anything to protect Jordan. I don't want you to get hurt over this!"

I yank my arm back. My brain can't even begin to entertain the thought of Deja trying to play me. She would *never*. Especially not for Jordan.

"No. No, she wouldn't do that. I know she wouldn't!"

Breon takes out her cell and puts it on speakerphone. It rings a couple times.

"Hello?" It's Deja.

"It's me," Breon says.

"Duh, bitch. What is it?"

"It's about Beau's Twitter."

"Okay . . . what about it?" *What the hell?* Deja knows about the Twitter we set up?

"I don't wanna be involved in this anymore. Beau's my friend."

There's a groan on the other end of the line. "Get it straight. She's *my* friend and whatever I do or say to her doesn't have shit to do with you."

What. The. Fuck. This can't be real. Deja and I tell each other everything. At least I thought we did.

"I'm making it my business because you're a liar. In what universe do you think Beau is gonna be okay with you being with Jordan? Or the fact that you purposely sent her fake tips?" Breon asks.

"*I'm* a liar? Hello?! Did you forget you stole the silver bracelet my daddy gave me when I was a baby? I thought I could trust—"

"Get the fuck on with all that guilt tripping because I'm over it! All I did was steal a bracelet. You sneaking with Jordan behind Beau's back is worse and you know it."

"Blah blah blah. Is there a point to this call?" Deja asks flatly.

"I just wanted to see if you'd changed your mind about him."

"About who?! My man?" Deja asks.

"Do you really think Jordan is worth losing your friendship with Beau?" Breon asks, looking me in the eye.

Deja laughs. She doesn't say *I'm not with Jordan* or *What the hell are you talking about?* She *laughs.* "It's not gonna come down to that." Then her tone changes from annoyed to silky soft honey. That same tone she uses when she's lying to somebody.

"Breon, I know you're only trying to look out for her, but trust me. Once this all dies down and Beau's stopped moping about Katia, she'll understand why we couldn't tell her. She'll forgive us both. Now, I was gonna let it be a surprise, but I've got another hundred dollars with your name on it. Just for being such a good friend to me through all this. Just come by tonight to get it. We'll watch a movie and do our nails or something, k?"

Breon's quiet for a moment and then sighs. "Okay. Tonight. I'll be there."

She ends the call and I stand there next to her in complete shock. Breon starts speaking to me, but everything sounds like it's underwater. The traffic rushing by us on the street, the dudes talking and laughing outside the liquor store, my own heartbeat. I let Breon guide me back to the bench near the bus stop and I sit, still as a statue, while my brain tries to piece this fucked-up story together.

There's an explanation for this, I know it. Like maybe Breon recorded Deja's voice, or they're talking about a different Jordan, or this is actually all just a dream brought on by stress, because I heard on TV once that that happens to people sometimes.

"Do you believe me now?" Breon asks.

"I have to see him. I'm not gonna believe it unless I see him," I say, still in a daze.

"But it could be dangerous. Besides, Deja and him know you're looking for him. He'll just run off somewhere else," Breon says.

I narrow my eyes at her. "You could be right. Or you could just be saying that because you know Jordan isn't at Deja's. Maybe he's at *your* place!"

Breon blinks at me. "You know what? Fine. I'll prove to you that I'm not lying. I'll take you to see Jordan, but first, we need some backup. Just in case."

"Just in case what?" I ask.

"In case this motherfucker has a gun and decides to shoot us! Did you expect him to sit down and politely explain to you why he's been hiding out for months?"

"You're right. I know just the person to call, too," I say, pulling out my phone. I tap 'recents' and wait until he picks up. "Hey, Parker? I need your help with something,"I say.

CHAPTER 27

AN HOUR LATER, SONNET, BREON, AND I ARE SITTING IN Parker's beater at the corner of Sonnet's block. Every few minutes, I notice Breon giving Sonnet dirty looks from the front passenger seat. But I don't care. I need somebody with me I can trust and that definitely isn't Parker or Breon.

"Okay, maybe we should call somebody else for help," Sonnet says after Breon runs down her crazy story again.

"You wanna call the police? You can't be that dumb," Breon snaps.

"Not the cops. I mean, somebody who might know what to do. Like your family's lawyer, Beau?"

I thought about that, too, but I'm pretty sure Ms. Anniston's advice would be to call the police, too. She might even be legally obligated to report what she knows.

"I don't think it's a good idea," I say.

Parker groans from the driver's seat. "Why do we even need

a plan? You got me with you. Let's just bust up in that hoe and do what we gotta do!" he says.

"I'm with him," Breon agrees.

"We can't just beat him up and turn him in. We need to get him to tell the truth about what him and Katia were doing on that porch that night and whose drugs were in the back seat," I say. "If he's actually even there."

"I know my brother," Parker says. "He's not gonna wanna sit down and have a heart to heart over no damn cookies and tea. We need to roll up in there, beat his ass, then drop him in front of a police station."

"How does that help me or my sister's case?" I ask.

"I dunno. But it's either that or let the OTs pop him. I'm down to do either."

Parker's clearly out for blood, but I have more riding on this than just getting back at Jordan. If Breon's telling the truth and Jordan's at Deja's house, I have to convince him to tell me the truth. I don't know how, but I have to try.

Breon clears her throat. "We're wasting time sitting here talking about it. Whatever we're gonna do, we need to do it tonight before Deja starts getting suspicious and tries to move him."

"Okay, fine. Here's the plan. Breon will knock on the door since Deja's expecting her anyway. Me, Parker, and Sonnet will be hiding under the front window and we'll rush in after you, Breon. Parker will guard the front door so nobody can leave and the three of us will check the bedrooms for Jordan," I say.

Parker, Sonnet, and Breon wait to hear the rest of my instructions, but I don't have any more. My brain still hasn't completely wrapped itself around the fact that we're actually doing this and that my best friend in the world might have betrayed me.

"Then what do we do if we find him? Shake his hand?" Breon asks snarkily.

"We'll just play it by ear," I say with a shrug. Now I'm almost 90 percent sure Jordan isn't there. Deja would never hurt me like that. But like Sonnet said before, we have to follow up on every lead that seems even the least bit plausible. There's still that 10 percent chance that Breon is telling the truth.

But I hope to God she isn't.

———

At 10:30 P.M., the four of us enter the Grady Park courtyard. For once, it's oddly quiet and empty. No kids running around playing, nobody charring up some hot links on their grill or blasting Jay-Z from their car's stereo. Everybody's inside, except a group of Onyx Tigers posted up at their corner as usual.

"Is there a party going on tonight we don't know about?" I whisper to Breon. "Where is everyone?"

Breon only shrugs. "I don't know. But you're right. Something feels weird . . ."

I try to shake the feeling off though and focus on the issue at hand, which is searching Deja's house to prove Breon wrong. We make our way around the back of Building C, Sonnet, Parker, and me crouching down below window level so to anyone inside the building, it looks like Breon is walking to Deja's all alone.

"Okay," Breon whispers to us. "When I give you the signal"— she puts up the peace sign—"that's when you come in behind me. Got it?"

Parker, Sonnet, and I nod. We follow Breon to Deja's door and stop short just to the left of the door, where Deja won't be able to see us.

Breon knocks on the door and my heart thunders in my rib cage. We're about to ambush my best friend since childhood. But we're also this close to finding Jordan and getting Officer Johnson locked up. I'm excited, scared, angry, and sad all at once.

"Hey, Bre! Who dat is wit you?" a man calls from the sidewalk, looking right at us. *Shit.*

Breon turns around. "Oh, these just my friends. We playin' a prank on Deja," she says with a laugh.

But the man doesn't laugh and he doesn't turn to walk away.

"Oh fuck," Parker whispers, pulling his hood up over his head. I'm confused until I see the gun sticking out of the man's waistband and the group of Onyx Tigers on the corner closing in behind him.

What the fuck did we just walk into? I think to myself. Crouched behind me, I feel Sonnet start shaking in fear.

"Oh, hey y'all," Breon says nervously with a wave. "What's up wit it?"

Now I know why everybody was inside when we got here. Some shit is about to go down and we're right in the middle of it.

"Who's that nigga in the hoodie?" the Onyx Tiger asks. "Tell him to take it off."

Breon looks at Parker, but he doesn't move to stand up or take his hoodie off. Then I remember he said Jordan set him up and had the OTs jump him. If they see him here on their turf, he's dead. We're all dead.

"Nigga, stand up!" the OT yells, pulling his gun on us.

I put my hands up instinctively and watch as Parker slowly rises from the ground. Right on cue, Deja opens the door and I see Breon yanked inside quickly. Before she can slam the door shut, Parker turns and strong-arms his way in and I pull Sonnet in behind me.

"What the hell are y'all doing here?" Deja asks.

There's banging at the door. The OTs aren't backing down.

"Tell Jordan to come outside and it won't be no problems for the rest of y'all," one of the men calls through the door.

The color drains from Deja's face and then she dives across the room to turn off the lights, plunging us into darkness.

"He's not here!" Deja yells through the door.

Suddenly a dark figure appears in the doorway of the living room.

"What the fuck goin' on out here?!" I hear Jordan's voice shout.

I pull my phone out, click on the flashlight so I can see, and point it in the direction of the voice.

It really is him. It's Jordan.

He's wearing nothing but boxers and a white tank top, and he puts his hand up to block the glare from the light.

"Jordan!" I call out. Before I can say another word, Parker flies through the air out of nowhere and lands a punch right in Jordan's face. They both fall to the floor with a thud and start pummeling each other.

"Is this how you really wanna do it, Deja? Aight, bet," the OT says. The banging suddenly stops. Deja sinks to the floor beside the door, and I motion to Sonnet to follow me behind the sofa.

In Grady Park, "aight bet" doesn't mean it's over. It means something's about to pop off.

Deja looks at me, worry painted across her face.

"Beau, I can explain everything. I—"

Her sentence is cut off by the crack of bullets whipping through air.

In the darkness, I can't see anything but I hear the bullets pierce through the walls and the front window. Something glass shatters and rains shards down on the floor. I turn my head sideways and feel the heat as a bullet whizzes just a foot away. I press my body flat against the floor and pull Sonnet down with me.

The gunfire goes on for what feels like hours. But we're on the floor, as low as possible, away from the windows. I think we might make it through this, that we'll all be okay when I hear Parker shout and a loud grunt of pain. I think he's been shot.

"Jordan!" I hear Deja scream. She starts to crawl across the room to him, but Parker's holding him down, Jordan's neck trapped in the crook of his arm.

When the bullets finally stop, I think I've gone deaf. There's a loud ringing in my ears. The smell of gunpowder burns my nose and maybe it's my imagination, but I see soft wisps of smoke unfurling from the dozens of holes in the walls.

Still, we lie there for another five minutes without speaking, listening to Deja softly whimpering into the carpet and Jordan's and Parker's ragged breaths. Breon slides out from underneath the sofa. I didn't even see her slip under there.

"Is it over?" Sonnet asks me.

I grab her hand and squeeze it tight. We almost died. *We really just almost fucking died.*

"Get off him!" Deja shouts at Parker. I turn my flashlight toward them and see blood pouring out of Jordan's nose and a hole in the arm of Parker's gray hoodie, a bloodstain spreading fast.

"Call 911 and tell them we need an ambulance," I tell Sonnet.

"Get the fuck off me!" Jordan cries out in the choke hold. He tries to punch Parker in the ribs, but Parker's not budging.

"Fuck outta here. You ain't goin' nowhere, nigga! Remember you set me up? Your own brother? You lucky I don't throw your ass out that door and let 'em blast yo ass," Parker says, tightening his hold on Jordan.

Suddenly, Deja leaps on top of Parker and starts smacking him in the face, trying to get him to let go of Jordan.

"Get the fuck off him!" she screams.

I turn to Breon, who's sitting next to the couch looking scared.

"Bre, do something!" I say.

She nods and runs over to pull Deja off Parker. The two of them stumble backward onto the sofa. But Deja reacts fast. She slams her elbow into Breon's face, turns around, and grabs her around the neck.

"You! You fucking bitch! You did this!" Deja's in full-on fight mode, Jordan's blood streaked across her face and arms. She looks crazy. And desperate. I know if I don't do something, she'll strangle Breon to death. I have to fight my best friend.

I run over and try to get her to let go of Breon, who's gasping for air and whose face has turned a bright red. But Deja uses one hand to push me back and I trip over the coffee table. The back of my head slams against the floor. That's when I see it. A glass ashtray next to me that must have fell. I pick it up in my hand. It's small but heavy.

Without thinking twice, I stand up and hit Deja in the back of the head with it one good time. There's a loud crack as the ashtray breaks in two and Deja falls over and hits the floor.

"Are you okay?" I ask Breon, helping her up off the couch.

She nods, massaging the place around her neck where Deja's nails cut into her skin.

"Yes, we're at the Grady Park Complex. Please hurry, there's been a shooting!" I hear Sonnet shout into her phone.

"Check on her," I say to Breon, motioning to Deja.

"What?!" she asks, looking at me like I'm insane. "That bitch just tried to kill me!"

"Just make sure she's still breathing! I have to help Parker," I say.

I don't know a lot about first aid, but I can tell he's losing blood fast. If he passes out and Jordan gets away again . . . I don't think about that. In the kitchen, I grab a towel from next to the stove.

I kneel down beside Parker, Jordan still struggling weakly beneath him. "Parker, you're shot. Don't freak out though, Sonnet called for help," I say, pressing the towel to the wound on his arm. He grimaces but lets me hold it there to slow the bleeding.

"Bre!" I shout out, not taking my hands off Parker's wound.

"Yeah? I checked Deja; the bitch is still alive, just knocked out," she replies.

"Okay, good. Go into her room and check the bottom drawer of her dresser. There's a pair of furry pink handcuffs. Bring them here."

She gives me a strange look but nods. When Breon returns from Deja's room, she cuffs one of Jordan's arms to the heating grate against the wall and Parker's finally able to get off him.

"Help me get him to the couch," I say to Sonnet. Parker drapes his good arm over my shoulder, and we help ease him down onto the sofa. The towel I'm pressing to his wound is already soaked in blood.

"How do you feel? Are you shot anywhere else?" I ask, lifting up his hoodie.

He shakes his head. "No, I don't think so. Goddamn, I can't believe you got my ass shot out here." I look up and the corner of his mouth curls into a weak smile.

"Nobody ever said being a bodyguard would be safe," I say.

Outside, red and blue lights begin to flash and the blare of police sirens, a fire truck, and an ambulance drowns our voices out.

"Fuck!" Jordan says, trying to yank his way free from the handcuffs.

On the floor, Sonnet rolls Deja onto her back, who moans but doesn't try to fight back.

"What are we gonna say when the cops get here?" Breon asks, anxiously peeking through the peephole of the front door.

I look at the chaos around me. Sonnet pacing in the kitchen; Jordan, with a broken nose and blood all over his face, yanking away at the pink fuzzy handcuffs that have him trapped; Breon running her hands through her hair over and over again and breathing heavy; Parker still panting on the couch and squinching his face up every time I apply more pressure to his arm; and

Deja, my best friend, laid out by me on her own living room floor.

All of this so I can prove Katia wasn't a drug dealer. Nothing makes sense anymore.

I turn to Breon. "We're gonna tell the truth."

CHAPTER 28

BEFORE

THE NIGHT AFTER MY BIG FIGHT WITH KATIA, I SLEPT ON the couch. Not because I was still mad, but I was scared she might try to kill me in my sleep or something.

I still couldn't believe I'd called my big sister a "loser." And she didn't hit me or anything, she just took it. But Katia had called me a loser a million times before, so I told myself I had nothing to feel bad about. I wouldn't have even said it if she hadn't set me up over Daddy's ring.

But even though I knew those things were true, I still felt guilty, the sad kind of guilty where you start to hate yourself because you're always doing and saying stupid things and fucking up everyone's life.

"Man, that's messed up she would play you over Jordan," Breon said one afternoon at the basketball courts. It was chilly so there weren't any shirtless guys out, just me, Deja, and Breon bundled up in hoodies and watching the clouds pass over the sun.

"Right, he ain't even that fine. Can't believe she tried to say you stole the ring; you shoulda bust her upside her head," Deja said, demonstrating by slapping the air.

"Yeah, I know. I just feel like maybe I took it too far," I said.

"All you called her was a 'loser'? I've taught you better than that when it comes to cracking on hoes. Like damn, at least call her a thot or something that'll sting," Deja said.

"You didn't see how she looked at me though! I've never seen her look like that before. Like I'd just punched her in the face or something."

Breon clapped a hand on my shoulder. "That, my friend, was the look of respect. You always be letting Katia boss you around and talk to you any ol' way. Now she knows she can't do that and she's pissed about it."

I gave up trying to explain it to them. Maybe they couldn't understand because they didn't have any siblings. I thought about asking somebody else, but it didn't matter what anybody said. I hurt Katia and I felt bad for doing it. I didn't even know I could do something like that.

For the next two weeks, things at home were awkward as fuck. Katia was busy with work, so I didn't have to deal with her most of the time, but on Fridays, it was just me and her at home until Momma got off work at 11:00 P.M.

When I got home from school on Friday, Katia was in our room. She was doing something on her iPad. While sitting at MY desk.

"What are you doing?!" I snapped at her from the open doorway.

She jumped in surprise and turned toward me. "Oh, hey. I just needed to get something done really quick."

I folded my arms across my face. "Why do you have to do it there? I was gonna draw."

She narrowed her eyes at me. "It's both of our desk. Just because you put all your shit in it doesn't mean I can't use it, too."

This bitch. Suddenly my guilt went out the window and I was ready for round two. I was about to snap but before I had a chance to say anything, her cell phone rang.

"Hey girl, wassup? . . . Yeah, lemme jus go in the front room right quick," Katia said into her phone. She knocked into my shoulder on her way out.

I marched over to my desk and snatched up the iPad to see what she was working on.

It was an application. I scrolled to the top of the page. Not just any application, a college application. For Texas A&M University. No wonder she'd gotten all bitchy when I walked in. She must have thought I would make fun of her.

I sat down at my desk and scrolled through the page to see what part of her application she was still working on. But every blank space was filled out. The deadline in bold red print at the bottom of the page said all applications would be due that same day, at 11:59 P.M.

I checked my watch. It was almost 7:00 P.M. The application was done, so why hadn't Katia submitted it yet?

Because of what I said to her. Maybe I hurt her feelings so bad she actually thought she was a loser?

I would have been, too, if I'd been rejected from my top three schools as a senior. A couple years had passed since then. She probably thought she still wasn't smart enough to get into college now.

All because I told her she was a loser. I didn't mean it.

I scanned through the application one more time, just to make sure she didn't accidentally spell something wrong. Then I scrolled to the bottom of the page and pressed the green "submit" button.

If she got accepted, Katia would hug me, but if she got rejected, she'd strangle me. It seemed worth the risk, though. College was the only thing I could think of that would take Katia out of Grady Park and away from Jordan. Neither of us had ever been straight A students, but that didn't mean we had to give up on ourselves without even trying.

There wouldn't be a decision on Katia's application until the spring, but I imagined what it'd be like if she was accepted. What *she'd* be like if she was accepted. When she was being nice, I liked Katia most of the time. But I knew there were some parts about herself that she didn't like. Maybe going to a university would change that.

Not to mention, I didn't want to be the first one in our family to finish college. I wanted Katia to be the first, so then I would have help when it was my turn to go away to school.

To me, this college idea was the perfect plan for Katia. She hadn't mentioned it to me or our parents, but the fact that she'd filled out the entire application told me all I needed to know. Katia wanted to be better than she was, she wanted to be more. And she was trying this time. She was really trying.

CHAPTER 29

RUMORS FLY AROUND THE GRADY PARK COMPLEX THE weekend of the shooting. We almost die and all it is for everybody else is some juicy drama to spread around. Some people are saying Deja and Jordan were running a human trafficking ring from her apartment. Other people are saying I slept with Jordan and Parker and then they met up to fight over me at Deja's. The worst rumor is that I set up Katia's murder because I wanted Jordan for myself and then went crazy when he chose Deja instead. It pisses me off that people have time to make up all this bullshit but when I needed help finding Jordan, nobody had anything to say. But they can keep guessing. Nobody knows the truth of what went down besides the six of us who were in the apartment that night.

As I walk by Deja's boarded-up apartment door on Monday morning, hatred settles deep inside me. I thought Jordan's arrest would mean everyone would know Katia was innocent. But the one reporter who actually came out to ask questions is framing it as "SUSPECT IN ALLEGED BURGLARY THAT LEFT ONE DEAD APPREHENDED." *One dead.* That's what my sister is referred to as now. They mention a sixteen-year-old juvenile being taken to a detention center while Child Services investigates her parent. Deja's been in plenty of trouble before, but she's never been to juvie. Without me to back her up, I bet she's scared in there with all those other girls she doesn't know. I'm almost scared for her, but she's not my business. Not anymore.

When they found out about the shooting, Momma and Daddy both went off on me for what seemed like two days straight. They told me I'm on punishment for the rest of my life, but they did let me talk to Parker over the phone when he got out of the hospital two days after the shooting.

I still don't know where the eight grand in our bedroom came from, but no one's asked about it so I think maybe it really was Katia's savings. I put it under my bed, because the "get out of Chicago" plan is still in effect. One day, I'll need this money.

When I get off the bus on Tuesday morning and walk into the front doors of Millennium Magnet, my sneakers squishing from the heavy downpour outside, everyone stares at me out of the corner of their eyes. I'm like a mermaid walking on land for the first time, but not nearly as glamorous or magical. I'm something wet, dark, and ugly. Something dangerous.

I try to make myself as small as possible and snake through the crowd to my locker. If anything, I've made the rumors about Katia and my family ten times worse.

I'm pulling a book out when I feel a hand on my shoulder.

"Hey," Champion says, an awkward half smile on his lips.

"Hi," I say flatly. I'm not in the mood for his drama right now. I'm not in the mood for anything.

"I heard there was a shooting at your complex over the weekend. I wanted to call, make sure you were okay. But I wasn't sure you'd want to hear from me."

"You would have been right," I say, slamming my locker and walking away. He follows behind me.

"Come on, Beau! Damn, I'm trying to apologize here but you're not giving me anything!"

I whip around so fast he almost bumps into me.

"I don't have to accept your apology just cuz you're sorry all of a sudden! You said you were done with me."

"You didn't really give me much of a choice!"

"Champion, did you ever stop to think about how I feel? I just got shot at. I can't be worried about you right now." I turn on my heel and leave him standing there, slack jawed. He doesn't follow after me.

———

Sonnet said I should write down my thoughts before I go to visit Jordan, so that way I don't miss anything. But I tried that last night and I didn't even know what to write. It's weird. I've been waiting for this moment for over five months and I've never really thought about what I would say to Jordan. I wanna yell at him. But mostly I think I wanna know why he let this happen to Katia.

Breon said I should just mail him a letter but I know that wouldn't have been good enough. I want to look him in his eyes and hear what he has to say for himself.

After school on Wednesday, I'm waiting on the corner of my

block in a hoodie, jeans, and my Nike Air Maxes. I don't have my purse because I figure it'll be quicker to get through security without it.

Right on time, Cierra pulls up in her mom's Buick. I hop in the front seat.

"Thanks for doing this," I say as we pull into traffic.

"Not a problem. I told him I wouldn't take his calls anymore if he didn't speak to you," she says.

"You're not mad at him anymore?" Besides knocking her up and abandoning her, Jordan was entertaining a whole other girl. But Cierra shakes her head.

"I mean, I was at first, but he called me from jail and we talked about everything. He said he was scared he'd be a bad father since his was locked up from the time he was a baby. It makes sense why he didn't wanna be at the birth and everything."

No, the fuck it doesn't, I think to myself. "What'd he say about all the cheating?"

"He told me the OTs started looking for him after he skimmed a lil money off the top of their business for Jordan Jr. He planned to give it to me but then that whole shooting with the police went down. Since I wasn't taking his calls back then, he said he had to find somewhere to hide. He told me your friend Deja was just a slide. No offense."

I roll my eyes. Should have known Jordan would be trying to run game from jail. I don't even have to ask to know Cierra put some money on his books. Then Jordan told her whatever she wanted to hear. Somebody should tell her he's only using her, but I doubt it would make a difference. It didn't with Katia.

Once we get to the jail where Jordan is being held, we have

thirty minutes with him, together. We enter the beige visiting room where there are silver stools parked in front of glass windows. There are black numbers painted at the top of each visiting carrel, one through ten. The room is packed with people. I see an elderly white couple who look on the verge of tears. Lots and lots of babies, some whining, some crying with their faces pressed into the thighs of their mother as she cradles the phone in the crook of her shoulder and tries to calm them down. Nobody but me seems to be creeped out by the sterile silver feel of the room but I figure that's because they're frequent visitors. They're loved ones.

Cierra and I make our way to the only empty carrel, number eight.

Jordan is already sitting on the other side in an orange jumpsuit. There are purple bruises under his eyes and red scratch marks on his neck. I expected him to look like a shell of himself, sad, skinny, pale. But despite the bruises, he's still got that sickening swagger that drives stupid girls nuts. Even though it's obvious he's gotten his ass kicked a few times, he sits waiting for us like the king of a palace waiting for his lowly servants.

Cierra motions for me to sit on the stool closest to the phone on the side of the visiting booth, and I do. I take it off the hook and hold it to my ear. Jordan waits for a moment and then does the same.

He doesn't look surprised to see me at all. He doesn't look like he cares.

I'm so mad I start shaking. I want to scream every cuss word in the book at the top of my lungs at him. I want to pop off and let any words floating around in my head just burst out like daggers straight into his carotid. I wanna make a scene and throw things and punch people and cry.

But I already promised myself I wouldn't do that. As soon as I start flipping my shit, they'll kick us out and probably ban us.

"Hi," I say.

"Hi," he replies, the corner of his lip curling upward.

"Don't you have something to say to me?" I ask.

Jordan doesn't even flinch. "Not really."

"What about what you did to my sister?"

His nostrils flare. "I didn't do anything to Katia."

"You left her alone that night. You didn't even go back to check on her or call for help! All you cared about was yourself."

He narrows his eyes at me, and I see the muscle in his jaw twitch.

"I know you don't like me, but I loved Katia. Believe what you want but know that's the truth." If Cierra hears what he says, she doesn't react.

I laugh. "Yeah, you loved her so much that you never called us to tell us what happened. Didn't show up to her funeral. Then you had the nerve to cheat on her with my best friend! My *sixteen-year-old* best friend."

"See, this is why little girls like you are better off staying at home. You don't know shit and you're too fucking emotional. I don't care about Deja. She wanted to help me, so I let her. It was after Katia."

"So you used Deja," I ask.

"If that's what you need to hear, then yeah, I did."

I turn toward the woman in the booth next to us. She looks around Katia's age, in a flowing blue maxi dress that piles in a pool at her feet.

"He's fine," I hear her say into her receiver. "Running around the house tearin' up everything. Your mother says I need to whoop him, but I can't do that . . ."

I turn back to Jordan.

"Tell me this. If you loved Katia, how can you be okay with the man that killed her walking free?"

He sighs. "It's not like there's anything I can do about it. You made sure of that by getting me caught up in here."

"What exactly were you gonna do about it from Deja's bed?!"

He glances to his left and his right and lowers his voice to a whisper.

"I was waiting for the heat to die down. I would have *put him away*."

I'm nothing like Jordan, but I've thought about it myself, tracking Peter Johnson down and shooting him straight in the heart. It'd be a lie to say his death wouldn't make me feel good, that I'd feel even a tiny bit of remorse afterward. But him dying before he tells the world what really happened that night, without acknowledging what he did, that's not justice for Katia. It's not justice for my family.

"Not that I believe you cared enough about her to kill, but how would that have proved what happened that night? How can we clear her name if the piece of shit who shot her is dead? Did you ever think about that?" I fire back.

Jordan puts his elbows on the table in front of him and laughs.

"Beau, you really think you got this all figured out, huh? I'm facing murder charges. *Murder.*"

"Murder? You mean you—"

"No, I didn't. I'm being set up. But you don't care about that, do you? I might never get out!"

"All the more reason to tell the police Katia was innocent!"

"My pops been in the system half his life. I had a reputation in here before I even walked in the door. Like they was just waitin' on me. You really think these people are ever gonna believe shit I have to say about anything?"

"We'll never know unless you tell them."

He looks up at the ceiling and shakes his head.

"You know, what I liked about your sister was how she always pumped my head up, had me thinking I could be a rapper, recording singles with Kanye and Chance, maybe a lil Trey Songz on the hook. When I first met her that day at the basketball courts while I was hooping, I thought she was stupid. But she *really* believed in all that stuff. She thought we was gonna both be somebody."

"She was stupid for thinking that about you," I snap.

He surprises me when he says, "I know. Because I live in reality. But you and your sister just alike. It's like y'all live in some kind of fuckin' bubble and you don't wanna understand how the world really works. Sometimes it's cute but sometimes that shit can get you fucked up."

"What does any of this have to do with you telling the cops what happened that night?"

He bangs his fist on the countertop.

"You still not getting it?! The truth don't fucking matter! Not from me, not from you, not even if it came from Katia. Nobody gives a fuck about the truth when it comes to people like us."

His brown eyes burn into mine through the glass and I know

he's dropped the bullshit smug player act. He really believes what he's saying. Now, *I* don't know what to believe. He's got a point about his own history with the law, but I never thought what he had to say wouldn't make a difference. He's the only other person who was there. His story has to count, it has to mean something. I need it to mean something will change for us.

"The truth matters. It always matters," I say, but my voice trembles because if my own life these past few months has been any example, Jordan's right.

"This system is never going to pick us over some white man. Especially a cop. They're gonna believe what they wanna believe and they wanna believe that a nigga like me was out there doing some stupid shit. They already know what happened."

"What were you doing out there anyway? Why were you on that guy's porch at four in the morning?"

Jordan sighs. "We were on the way to my guy's house. The car battery died because Katia left the headlights on while we was at the club. I called my guy to come give us a jump, but he didn't answer. I knew he didn't live far so I told Katia to get out and walk with me to his house. She was gonna wait there with his girl while me and my guy drove his car back to her car."

"Okay . . . then what happened? Why didn't you go to his house?"

"I thought that's where we was at! But it was dark . . . and I was a lil faded . . . the houses on that street . . . they all look alike even in the daytime. So we get there and I'm thinking this is my guy's house. We knock and he doesn't answer. We call, still no answer. I know he's gotta be home, so I open the screen and bang on the door loud enough to wake him up. Nothing. So we just standing there on the stoop trying to figure out who we can call to get a jump when the front door opens."

I press the receiver closer to my ear and close my eyes, trying to imagine what Katia felt at that moment. Was she drunk? Was she high? Did she see it coming?

"I don't remember seeing anything. Just hearing bang bang bang! Flashes of fire. I ran as fast as I could. I thought Katia was behind me."

"Did you look?" I ask, a lump forming in my throat.

Jordan looks away in shame and shakes his head. "He was still shooting! I thought he was chasing me. I kept running trying to get as far away as I could. I ran into my dude sitting in a car in his driveway, like, five houses down, and I told him what happened. I told him we needed to go back and find Katia, but he said they would arrest me. He said she had probably just ran in a different direction."

"You believed that?" I ask skeptically.

"I wanted to. Then I thought, even if she's not okay, what I'ma do about it? I'm not a doctor. You gotta know that if I went back, either that guy woulda killed me or I'd have been arrested right there on the spot."

"At least she wouldn't have died alone!"

"So what you saying? She woulda died happy if we both bled out together on the street?"

"I'm saying you should have tried! You ran and left her there alone. Maybe there was something you coulda did, but you don't know because you're a coward!"

"Because you're a dumbass kid who's never had to worry about shit like that. You don't know what you'll do when a gun is pointed at your head," Jordan replies.

"No, because I loved Katia. That was my sister, my blood. I would never leave her alone like that and she wouldn't have left me!"

Jordan's cheeks flush red with anger. "This is my fault, right? People always gotta find somebody to blame. Not the cop who shot at us for no reason, but me. You wanna blame me. Is that what you conned my baby mama into bringing you here for? To hear me say it was my fault? Fine. It's my fault. You feel better now?"

I narrow my eyes at him. "What about the drugs in the car? Did you tell the police they were yours?"

His brown eyes flick away from mine and down toward the floor. "I don't even know what you talkin' about, man."

"I wish it had been *you* that night," I say, unblinking. My parents have always said you should never wish death on someone, but they're not here and that's what I want. To see Jordan lying in a box while his family cries over him like we had to do for Katia.

Jordan nods his head slowly. "It should have been me. But maybe I'm supposed to die here, who fucking knows. I couldn't protect Katia. I can't even protect myself! The longer you stay in Grady Park, the closer you are to getting shot. Who lives and who dies, sometimes that shit is just luck of the draw."

Behind us a trio of curly-haired toddlers begin to cry as their mother pulls them away from their chairs. One of the little girls has purple beads dangling at the ends of her braids. She stands on the stool pounding on the glass and crying as a man on the other side walks away.

"I'm not stupid," I say, turning back to Jordan. "You don't know if you could have protected Katia because you didn't even *try* to. So you can miss me with all this bullshit because I don't feel sorry for you. You got a fucked-up ass life but it's a life. Katia's is over."

Jordan leans his head on his arm like he's bored. "Anything else, little girl?"

I know I'm getting to him because the slimy smug attitude has returned to his voice. He's crawling back inside of himself to hide because that's easier than hearing the truth. But I'm not leaving here until he hears it.

"I know it eats at you, Jordan. Just because you didn't pull the trigger doesn't change the fact that you were a part of it. Katia was crazy about you. She would have done anything for you, and you knew that! But the one time she really needed you, you let her down. No matter how you try to convince yourself otherwise, you will *always* be a part of the reason my sister is dead."

I slam the receiver on its hook and get up without a look back at Jordan.

After Cierra's finished with her visit and we walk out of the jailhouse together, a light rain is falling from the purple evening sky. I exhale, thinking that big weight on my chest will finally fall off but it doesn't. There's no relief for me. But it makes me feel a little better knowing there won't be any for Jordan either.

————

The next morning, Daddy and I are sitting in Ms. Anniston's plush law office. We tried to convince Momma to come with us, but she said she was too tired, which is code for *I've given up already*.

"Chairs are nice," Daddy says awkwardly while we wait for Ms. Anniston.

"Yeah, we should get some for the house," I reply. I'm nervous as hell because I haven't told Daddy that I went to visit Jordan yesterday. I haven't told anyone because I'm still not sure what it means yet. Maybe I'd be tainting the case by letting other people know what he told me. Not that I haven't already been screwing things up since this entire thing started.

My plan is to just tell Ms. Anniston everything I know in front of Daddy. That way he'll have to wait until we get home before he kills me. But if it's good news and we can get a trial, they'll all be thanking me.

After a few minutes, Ms. Anniston steps into her office with a giant manila folder of papers that she plops on her desk as she sits down. Her assistant, a blond girl with bright red lipstick, brings me and Dad a bottle of apple juice each and two cups with ice.

"So glad you could make it in today, Mr. Willet," Ms. Anniston says.

"Absolutely. My wife wanted to come, but she needed to catch up on some rest."

"That's no problem at all. We can catch her up to speed on things later. We have a lot to talk about, Jordan Samson specifically," Ms. Anniston says, looking at me. I shrink under her gaze.

"I swear to you, I had no idea Jordan was hiding out so close to our home," Daddy says. "If I had, I woulda shot him myself!"

"I'll pretend I didn't hear that, Mr. Willet. The important thing is, Jordan Samson is in custody. I had the chance to speak with his attorney over the phone this morning."

My heart drops. *Oh shit.*

"I then had another conversation with the district attorney regarding Jordan's possible testimony."

"Did he agree to testify on the stand?" I ask, leaning forward in my seat.

Ms. Anniston purses her lips together like people do when they're about to tell you something you don't want to hear.

"He did agree to testify against Officer Johnson. As part of a plea deal for his separate murder trial."

Daddy sets his bottle of juice down and looks from me to Ms. Anniston.

"Wait, separate murder trial? Who did he murder?"

"Allegedly another gang member in southern Illinois. The murder occurred in the summer of last year, but it wasn't until Jordan went on the run that several informants came forward to identify him as the culprit."

My brain is ticking light-years faster than it used to, almost like I'm a detective. "That's too convenient. You think he was set up? By his own gang?"

Ms. Anniston nods.

"What does this mean for us?" Daddy asks.

"The district attorney presented the plea deal to the family of the victim. They refused."

Daddy and I sit staring at her waiting for more. I don't know how many times we have to tell this woman we don't under-stand what she's talking about. Although I can tell the way she looks at us, like we're sad little puppies with broken legs, that this is bad news.

"Can't he testify anyway? Without a plea deal?" Daddy asks.

"He could, but generally defendants who request plea deals

aren't interested in telling the truth for the sake of integrity. At this point, there's nothing the state can offer Jordan. They can force him to take the stand, but he'll most likely plead the fifth to every question he's asked."

Daddy starts rubbing his chin. "Maybe we can get the family to change their mind about the plea deal? Do they know about my daughter and what happened to her? That the cop is walking free?"

Ms. Anniston sighs. "I'm sure they do, Mr. Willet, but it's a difficult situation. Their fourteen-year-old son was murdered. They want justice for him just as badly as you want justice for your daughter. I don't think there's anything that will change their mind at this point."

"But he didn't even do it!" I shout, feeling my eyes start to burn. Not out of pity for Jordan, but sadness for my family, for Katia. I worked so long and so hard to get this guy and now everything is slipping through my fingers like water.

"I think there's a good chance you're right, Beau. But if the state has the evidence to put him away for this, they will. Whether he did it or not. It's unfair, I know, but this is how the law works sometimes. It's a flawed system, but that's why I'm here. To get you and your family any kind of compensation I can. We talked about this before, but it's time to get the ball rolling on filing the wrongful death suit against the City of Chicago."

"But what about the trial? I mean, can't we just go forward without Jordan? I visited him yesterday and he told me what happened that night. They were at the wrong house; they weren't trying to break in!"

Daddy turns to me and his eyes go wide. "You went where?!"

But Ms. Anniston ignores him. "Beau, I know you meant

well, but that's just not how it works. Your testimony about the event would be considered hearsay since you weren't actually there. It's not enough for the D.A. to file charges against Peter Johnson."

"Who took you down there to see that man?!" Daddy says, staring at me like he wants me to go get the belt.

"I was just trying to help," I say, sinking down into my chair and letting the cushions swallow me. I feel like I'm in a fucked-up game of Monopoly where everyone else is allowed to cheat but me. I grip the arm of my chair with my nails.

"It's partially my fault," Ms. Anniston says, looking at Daddy sympathetically. "I may have inadvertently given you all the idea that Jordan would be the key to cracking this case. At the time, I thought he was. But this was before the murder charges came to light. Please believe me, Arlen and Beau, I did everything I could. I've been in nonstop meetings with the district attorney, and no matter how many ways I flip this situation inside out and upside down, there's just no way to win. We simply don't have enough proof."

Daddy looks down at his hands like he's a child unsure of what to do with himself. A few months ago, he would have raged and shouted and maybe tossed over this giant oak desk in front of us. But I can see in his eyes that he's tired. Tired of fighting something we were never going to win.

"We could organize a protest. Right in front of the courthouse. We just need to get their attention!" I say. But even I'm starting to see that it's hopeless. Who would even show up? Everybody thinks Katia was a drug dealer. I can try to deny it as much as I want, but Katia is yesterday's news to the rest of the world. We're the only ones left who care.

"I'm not against the idea of a protest, but it won't change the prosecution's decision. Our best course of action is to file a civil suit. This money won't bring Katia back, but it will ease the financial burden of her death. We're going to sue for medical bills, lost wages, pain and suffering, everything I can get you. It might not seem like it now, but it will help you in the future."

"What future?!" I snap, standing up out of my chair.

"Beau!" Daddy shouts. But I'm done listening to him. I'm done listening to everybody who wants me to give up.

Ms. Anniston doesn't seem bothered at all, almost like she's used to being yelled at. "Beau, believe me, I did everything I could. But the legal system isn't perfect."

"It works just fine for piece-of-shit cops! So why can't you go through all these stupid books and find something to help us?" I ask.

Daddy grips my arm. "Beau Brianca Willet! You better sit your Black ass down before I sit you down myself!"

I snatch my arm away from him. "Stop telling me what to do! Beau, clean the house; Beau, help your momma; Beau, do everything for everybody!"

Daddy sighs and turns to Ms. Anniston. "I'm so sorry about my daughter. She's clearly lost her mind."

"No, I haven't!" I shout. "Why am I the only one who cares about clearing Katia's name? Or getting this cop locked up so he can't shoot any more innocent people? Why won't anyone help me?!"

Daddy stands up and clears his throat. "I'm sorry, Ms. Anniston, maybe we can do this another time. Beau, let's go," he demands, heading for the door.

I turn back to Ms. Anniston hoping that maybe my psycho

outburst changed her mind, made her understand that I can't go through the rest of my life knowing that the man who ruined it is out walking free. But she just hits me with the puppy-dog eyes again, telling me what I already know: There's nothing left she or anyone else can do about it. That's not good enough for me. It never will be.

———

The night after we talk to Ms. Anniston, I sit between my parents on the couch while we watch the news coverage of the five-year anniversary shooting death of a Black man named Diamante Jones. That cop didn't get arrested either. There's nothing on the news about Katia. Nobody cares.

To the rest of the world, it's like she wasn't even here. It's like I'm not even here. I don't know what takes over me, but suddenly I'm standing up and my fist flies into the flat screen, knocking it off the TV stand and cracking the picture.

"Girl, are you out your damn mind?!" Daddy yells. I think the sound of my fist shattering the screen snapped Momma outta her trance because she looks at me then, *finally* just looks at me.

"You must think you at one of ya lil friends' houses because in this house, you don't break shit you didn't buy! You know how much that television cost?"

"I do," Momma says from the couch. "Black Friday Doorbuster for a hundred and thirty dollars at Best Buy two years ago. Y'all remember that night?"

She stares past us, into the TV, like her memories are playing there within the cracked shards. Not like I've just destroyed our only TV with my bare hands.

"Basil, what in the hell are you talking about? Did you see what your child just did?! Who's gonna replace it, huh?"

"Who cares! We never watch it anymore, except when somebody gets killed. We can't watch TV without Katia!"

"Why not?" Daddy's voice softens as he moves slowly toward me. He thinks I'm crazy. He's just trying to get me to calm down so he can leave me and Momma alone again. Fine, then.

"Because we can't! I don't want to. Do you really think you'll ever sit on this couch again and watch the Bulls play? I can't even stand being in this house anymore!"

Momma gets up from the couch, reaches her hand out to me, but I don't take it. My parents move toward me, tears glistening in their eyes. They open their arms, waiting for me to give up. To start crying like a little punk and admit that they were right the whole time, about everything. About me wasting my time. About Katia really being snatched out of our lives forever.

No.

"Don't!" I shout at my parents. "Don't touch me, don't hug me, don't do anything. Just like you've both been doing this whole time."

"Baby, we're hurting, too! You don't see that?" Daddy asks.

"All I see is you leaving me and Momma by ourselves again! You said you wished you'd been there the night she . . . But it's been months and you *never* stay the night! You don't care if it happens again. What if the police come here in the middle of the night and try to take us?! You wouldn't be able to do shit!"

I don't know if I'm making sense anymore. My thoughts bubble to the brim of my brain and spill out of my mouth, but my lips can't keep up and everything jumbles together.

"Now don't talk crazy. Nobody's going to hurt you, Beau!"

"You don't know that! You don't know what they said to me! How they look at me, the white kids at school, that officer who punched me in the stomach and threw me on the—"

Momma's and Daddy's eyes go wide. Too late for all that get bad now, though.

"Wait a minute, those motherfuckers hit you?! You didn't tell me that!" Daddy bellows.

"Because what's the point?! What are you gonna do about it? What *can* you do about it?! Nothing."

"Beau, we just want—"

"It doesn't matter. None of it matters. You know there was only one news article online about the shooting at Deja's house? And nothing about it was on the news. I've stayed up all night the past week waiting to see if they would even say anything about it or Katia, but they didn't. It. Doesn't. Matter."

Momma's voice pleads. "I know this isn't the outcome you wanted, but baby, this is life. This is part of being alive. We're gonna be in pain, we're gonna hurt bad. But when this part's over, we're gonna live."

"Then you won't mind if I speed up this whole grieving bull-shit process, right?"

"Watch your mouth!"

I spin on my heel and run toward our, my, My, MY bedroom. With my parents hot on my tail, I snap. I wipe everything off Katia's vanity. Nail polish, creams, lotions, and serums shatter against the floorboards, stains we'll never get out.

"What are you doing?!" I hear Momma ask from some vac-uum of space drifting behind me.

"Getting rid of her stuff! The news had it right, you had it right, none of this matters, so Katia doesn't matter either!"

I pick up the white puff seat and use it to smash the mirror, its bright yellow bulbs like stars exploding in a white sky.

My hands scramble to pull every Polaroid of my sister and her friends off her wall. Some of them I tear into tiny pieces. The room is a blur, and suddenly I'm on my own side of the room, yanking drawers out of my own desk, tossing pencils, pens, old drawings to the floor. I use my favorite sketchbook to smack the lamp off my desk and the room drops into a veil of shadows, the only light coming from the last lit bulb in the vanity.

I stop then and stare at it. This one last bulb. Burning in the middle of everything I've just destroyed.

Burning.

My parents wrap their arms around me from behind, and I let myself fall into them, all baby, all cradle, all crying.

Katia is dead. She's really *really* dead.

And she left me here.

My parents and I slide into a pile on the floor. I make myself small, burrow my head into Daddy's shirt, Reggie and Crown Royale. Momma presses herself to my back and with their arms intertwined around each other, I'm safe. A kitten dangling from its momma's mouth. I'm not okay but I feel okay right now. Protected.

No one can get me here.

CHAPTER 30

REALIZING IT'S OVER FEELS LIKE BEING SOCKED in the stomach and having the wind rush out of you. I thought Katia being dead would be the worst of it, but the worst thing is that now I have to try to accept the fact that she died for nothing and there's nothing I can do to change it, fix it, or make things right again. It makes me feel useless and small.

"You're sure you want to do this, right? Really, *really* sure?" Sonnet asks me. We're standing in the empty parking lot of Rosie's Diner. The lights inside are off, the sign doesn't spin anymore, and there's weeds growing all around the corners of the building. There's a sign that says "We'll Be Back Soon . . ." taped to the inside of the front door. It's been six years since the night me and Katia ate all that cake. It didn't occur to me that the place might be out of business.

"I'm sure. Katia and I only came here the one time, but I

don't know, I think she'd wanna be here. You said you understood in the car," I say, holding on to my necklace.

"I do, but won't your parents be upset?"

"They have their own pieces of jewelry. They can keep theirs but I'm ready to let mine go," I say, pulling the necklace off over my head.

Sonnet follows behind me as I run my hand along the brick wall of Rosie's Diner. My hand catches on a brick and I yank on it till it pops out. I wrap the chain around the jewel that holds pieces of Katia and place it in the small gap. Then, I take the brick and shove it back into place. Katia's not here anymore and wearing her around my neck doesn't feel right.

"How do you feel now?" Sonnet asks.

"I dunno. Kinda weird. But mostly the same."

I wonder how my friendship with Sonnet is going to change now. She's had my back this whole time, even when shit got real. I feel like I ruined her or something by bringing her into my hot mess of a life. And using her love of *Pretty Little Liars* to get her to help was bogus as hell. But at the time, all I cared about was finding Jordan. Even if it meant hurting other people.

"I'm sorry about everything. Getting you arrested, nearly killed a couple of times," I say, squinting as the morning sun pierces through the clouds.

Sonnet turns to me.

"You have nothing to apologize for. I wanted to help you and even though it was a lot crazier than I thought it would be, I don't regret doing it. Not for a second."

"But it wasn't even worth it. We found Jordan, he told the truth, and they still don't care. We're not getting a trial and we never were." Saying it out loud doesn't make it feel any more real. But I figure if I keep saying it, eventually I'll start to accept it.

"But you tried! You didn't just sit there and give up or let it happen. You fought back. That means something."

I kick at a piece of gravel. "Yeah, it means we wasted a lot of time and energy and got our heads knocked around by those cops for nothing. You know, I see why people break the law now. You're gonna get screwed either way. Everything we did to try to prove the truth and it didn't change anything."

"It changed me."

Sonnet grabs my arm and pulls me over to the car where we both lean against the hood.

"You know why I asked my mom to let me go to Millennium Magnet?" she asks.

I shrug. "To be a better sculptor?"

"Yeah, but also to see the world outside of our family. My mom says society is corrupt and we're better off on our own for the most part. But I wanted to be able to see for myself."

I nod. "Your mom was right. There's nothing fair or right about this shit."

"Yeah, it is, and it's not going to get any better by ignoring it. Beau, we *are* powerful. We didn't get Peter Johnson arrested but we showed people that we weren't just gonna take this lying down. You and your parents showed them that Katia has a family and friends and lots of people who care about her and are willing to stand up for her. Maybe next time a cop will think twice before shooting somebody."

A strand of my hair blows into my mouth and I tuck it behind my ear.

"I guess so," I say halfheartedly. It's hard for me to care about anything these days. Seeing Jordan is when it finally started to hit me. My sister is really gone. I'll never get to be Katia's maid of honor at her wedding, she'll never be able to see me graduate high school, our kids will never grow up together. Worst of all, she won't be there with me when our parents die. It was supposed to be me and her, but now it's just going to be me. I don't think I can do this without her. Be alone in the world. I'm nowhere near as strong as Katia was.

"This whole time we've been looking for Jordan, at the funeral, even before? Ever since the night she got shot, I wasn't sure if Katia was tryna break into that house or not," I admit.

There. It's out there. I could never say it to my parents or anyone who knew Katia because it's a horrible truth. It's a horrible thing not to believe in your own sister. But how could I? Even though I loved her, still love her, Katia made so many mistakes. It's hard not to think that if only she'd been smarter or richer or kinder or just made better choices, she'd still be here with me.

Sonnet grabs my hand and squeezes.

"It's okay. Now you know the truth. Katia didn't do anything wrong that night."

I squeeze her hand back, grateful that I have her, this anchor tying me to the world because it feels like I don't belong here anymore. I just wanna be with my sister.

"Is it stupid that I'm mad at her now? For leaving me alone?" I ask, my voice cracking.

Sonnet smiles at me.

"But you're not alone, Beau. You have me." She's right. I couldn't have got through any of this without her. I've been so focused on Katia being gone that I never really paid attention to who I have left.

Later, as I merge onto the expressway for the ride back home, I imagine an alternate universe where the night me and my sister ate burgers and cake in Rosie's Diner plays on an endless loop. In this universe, it's always 4:00 A.M. and me and Katia are always together.

———

When we get back to Sonnet's house, she tells me to wait for her in the backyard near the firepit.

"Just have a seat and relax while I go get the ingredients for the world's most amazing s'more! I hope we're not out of vegan marshmallows and whole wheat graham crackers," she says.

I cringe. "God, I hope you're out of both."

"Beau, you're so funny! Be right back." I watch Sonnet skip back around to the front of the house before taking a seat in one of the wooden chairs surrounding the dark firepit.

Then I hear a boy's voice from somewhere I can't see. "Don't worry, I made her get regular graham crackers and marshmallows, too."

I turn to look behind me and Champion's walking over from behind the other side of the house, a giant heart-shaped box of chocolates in one hand and a single red rose in the other.

"Champion? What are you doing here?" I ask. Part of me wants to turn and leave him standing there looking stupid. But another part wants to wrap my arms around him.

He hands me the flower and chocolates, then sits down in the chair next to mine.

"Don't be mad at her, but I asked Sonnet to set this up. She told me," he says.

"Told you what?"

"About how you found out Jordan was hiding at Deja's house this whole time. That you and Sonnet have been working to try to find him for months."

If I know Sonnet, she only gave him the bare-bones version of the story. For a minute, I try to think of a way to save myself. To explain away just how messed up my life is. But the truth is, I'm tired of lying.

"She shouldn't have told you that," I say.

"You're right. You should have. Why didn't you just say that when I asked?"

I sigh. "I didn't want you to know what was going on because it's a lot deeper than what Sonnet probably told you. I almost got us both killed. Twice."

He gives me a confused look. "What? How?"

"It doesn't matter, Champion. I like you. I really do. But if you knew the real me, I'm not sure you'd like her very much."

He reaches out to hold my hand. "I like you, too, Beau. But I wanna like all of you, not just the good parts. I wanna get to know the bad parts, too."

"What if my bad parts are worse than other people's?" I ask.

"That doesn't matter to me."

I wanna believe him. It feels hard for me to be happy because I know it's not going to last long anyway. Something always comes along to ruin the few good things I have.

But maybe it doesn't need to be that way all the time.

"Champion," I say.

He turns to me, the bright sun reflecting the oil on his waves. "Yeah?"

"I want you to know me, too. The whole me," I say.

He smiles. "That's great because I'd been meaning to ask you something."

"What?" I ask.

"What are . . . we?"

"Oh. Uh . . . I dunno. You tell me."

I look into his eyes, and he leans over to kiss me. "If it's up to me, I think we should be together. If you want to."

I take his hand and nod. "I want to." And I do. I was so sure I'd lost Champion when I lied but maybe I had him the whole time.

"Now, back to you and Sonnet almost being killed," he says.

"I'll tell you soon. I promise. But for now, is it okay if we just . . . be here together?"

He squeezes my hand. "Yeah. Whatever you want."

A little while later, Sonnet and Ms. Bluefall come out and start up the bonfire. We roast vegan and regular marshmallows (the vegan ones turn out to be not that bad) and talk and joke and laugh. I'm having a good time, but as the sky darkens and I start thinking about home again, something changes.

It's like I hate Breon and Deja, but at the same time, I almost sort of kinda miss them. When I think about home, I'm not just thinking about our complex, I'm thinking about my best friends, too. Katia's gone, my parents are like ghosts, and now I don't even have my girls anymore. I need to make this right.

CHAPTER 31

ON SUNDAY MORNING BEFORE THE LAST WEEK OF school, I'm woken up by my parents arguing again. I thought things would be better after our little cry fest the other day, but it's the same. Momma and Daddy can't act like they care about me for more than a couple hours apparently. Sometimes I think about running away just to piss them off, but I bet they wouldn't even notice.

"You weren't here, Arlen. Of course she was gonna go hang out with that wild lil girl all the time. She misses her sister!" I hear Momma shout in the kitchen.

"You kicked me out! You were the one here! You shoulda been watching her! You shoulda been watching the both of them!"

Something porcelain smashes against a wall. More yelling and screaming and crying.

I get up and pull on Katia's old hoodie and the baby-blue joggers I wore to her funeral.

When I walk out into the living room, the screaming and shouting stop for a moment.

"Beau, where are you going?" Daddy asks.

"Arlen, leave her alone!" Momma shouts.

"Hell no! This is called parenting! All that 'leave her alone' mess is why we only got one child left now!" he roars.

As the next round of fighting commences, I slip out the front door and into the gloomy wet morning. I know they're not trying to hurt me. They're trying to break each other's hearts because they don't know what else to do. Without Katia, we'll always be missing something. This ache in my chest, I think Momma and Daddy feel it, too. I wish I could make it go away for us all. But I don't know how.

Walking to the corner store, my clothes get soaked and I feel my socks squishing in my Nikes, but nothing really makes me uncomfortable now that I've lost the two closest people to me in the world.

When I get to the store, Breon's sitting outside in her usual spot, in spandex shorts and Jordans that are about five sizes too big. She has a little baby's ladybug umbrella over her head.

I walk up to her and kick at her gigantic shoe.

"Hi," she says, looking up at me through the rain.

I hold a fifty-dollar bill out to her.

"What's that?" she asks.

"Reward money. You told us where Jordan was, so you get a reward," I say.

But Breon doesn't reach out to take it.

"Just fucking take it, Breon! Get some shoes that fit, buy some Robitussin with it, I don't care!"

But she shakes her head. "No! I don't want your money. I'm sorry, Beau, alright?"

I want her to take the money so I can be right about her. I want her to take it so I can put her in the same box as Deja, the dead-to-me box, so I can be alone in this world and accept it.

"It's wet, but you can sit down if you want," she says.

I do.

She positions the umbrella between our shoulders so we're both half wet and half dry.

I don't wanna do it, but I start crying. It just comes out all at once and I'm not even sure why. My life has been fucked up for a while; you'd think I'd run out of tears eventually.

"I heard they released Deja to her pops," Breon says after a few moments.

"Oh, fuck her. I don't even care," I lie. "Did you get in trouble with your mom?"

She shakes her head. "Nah. She doesn't come by but once a week to get the mail."

"What? What do you mean?" I remember Breon's momma working crazy hours all the time, but she usually came home, even if it was two or three in the morning.

"I mean, I been on my own since eighth grade. She still keeps everything in her name, pays the bills, leaves the LINK card with me. But she lives out in the suburbs with her boyfriend. And he doesn't like kids."

"What the fuck? So you've just been living alone this whole time? Why didn't you say anything?!"

She looks at me with red eyes. "Say anything to who? Y'all wasn't fucking with me anymore after the bracelet thing."

I shrug. "It wasn't just the stupid bracelet, Breon. You were high almost all the time. It was like I didn't know you anymore. You know you were wildin' back then." Although now, it's starting to make sense why.

"I know. I just didn't know what else to do," she says.

"Bre, if you'd told me, I would have understood. We could have helped you."

"Helped me how? Have your parents call Child Services? I didn't wanna go to a group home. There wasn't anything y'all could have done," she says.

"We would have figured something out."

The rain comes down harder, in fat drops that splash on the toes of my sneakers. I scoot closer to Breon and feel myself relax in this warm cocoon shielding us from the storm.

"I really missed you, Beau. You and Deja. I missed the both of you. When I found out what she was doing, it was like she needed me again. She'd let me come over sometimes and watch TV. I wasn't trying to hurt anybody. I just missed y'all, okay?"

I turn to her, and she smiles, then looks away like she's embarrassed.

"I missed you, too, Breon."

She turns her palm over, lets her fingers curve out away from each other a little. It's small but I know what it means. Even when I was pretending to be nice to her, I'd started seeing Breon as this creature, this thing that wasn't my friend and never had been. I let Deja talk me into forgetting one of my best friends.

Now, I stretch my fingers, slide them between Breon's.

We lock together.

CHAPTER 32

ON THE LAST DAY OF SCHOOL, PRINCIPAL MARCOS forces the entire student body to the back of the gymnasium for the unveiling of *The New Dream*. Normally, nobody would care this much about an art class, but since Bexley O took the mural under her wing, the neighborhood makes a huge deal out of it.

They've put a big white tarp over the mural with a long golden rope on one side to pull it off. The marching band is playing what sounds like "Lift Every Voice and Sing," and a dozen camera crews have their tripods trained on the mural for the big moment.

"Can they just show us this damn thing and give Madison the scholarship so we can all go home?" I say, resting my head on Sonnet's shoulder. We've been standing here at least twenty minutes in the heat, pressed up against the crowd.

"We all worked on that mural, it's not just Madison's piece.

And stop being so negative. You know you're gonna get that scholarship, Beau."

"Oh, please. Even if they'd wanted to give it to me, Marcos would have blocked that shit like Dikembe Mutombo." I try not to get my hopes up over the art scholarship, but it'd be nice to have that money.

"Ladies and gentlemen," Ms. Kubler says, "These past few months, the junior art class has worked hard to bring to life a mural designed by our own Madison Garber."

She motions to Madison, and everyone claps accordingly.

"Our mural, titled *The New Dream*, was inspired by Dr. King and the profound impact he's had on our country. We're all very proud of Madison and her classmates here at Millennium Magnet and we hope you will be, too."

Ms. Kubler gestures to Madison again, who bops over to the side of the mural where Bexley O stands. Together, they yank on the golden rope and the tarp falls.

I'm only mildly disappointed that Bexley didn't try to talk Madison out of this corny mural idea, but I have to admit, it's not that bad. Instead of black and white, the whole thing's in bright neon colors and Dr. King's face is painted Picasso-like. It's surreal to look at and I hate myself for getting kicked out of class and missing the chance to work on it. I don't feel bad for flipping out on Madison but all I really did was miss out on my favorite class. Even if it wasn't my idea, I'd be proud looking at this mural if I'd worked on it at all.

"And now," Ms. Kubler continues after the applause dies down, "Ms. Bexley O will announce the winner of this year's Millennium Magnet Art Scholarship."

"You better mention me in your acceptance speech," Sonnet whispers. I swat her arm.

"Hello, Millennium Magnet students. It's been a pleasure to be hosted at your school these past few weeks," Bexley says. "Thank you, Principal Marcos, for opening up your halls to me, and thank you, Ms. Kubler, for allowing me to share in the pride of your talented art students. Now, the moment you've all been waiting for. The 2018 Millennium Magnet Art Scholarship goes to . . ."

My heart leaps into my chest and I debate whether or not I should give Madison the finger when I get the award. Would they revoke it? Maybe I should accept the award now and wait until after graduation and *then* give her the finger.

"Madison Garber," Bexley says.

Madison jumps up and down like an idiot as Bexley holds out her certificate. Sonnet pats my shoulder and I hang my head.

Everything else this year has gone wrong. I should have seen this coming.

After Madison makes her ten-minute-long thank-you speech, Bexley comes back to the podium with a big grin on her face. I'm not mad at her. I know she didn't actually have a say in who would win the scholarship. They just had her read the winner because she's freaking Bexley O and getting an award from her feels more important than one from the principal or Ms. Kubler.

"Before I go, I'd like to announce one more winner. This is the first year of the Bexley O Fellowship Grant. Each year, one outstanding visual arts student from an Illinois high school will be chosen to work alongside me for the summer."

Sonnet elbows me in the side.

"What grant? I never heard anything about a grant," I say.

"The grant is worth ten thousand dollars," Bexley continues, "and the fellowship includes free room and board for three months, during which the fellow will work with me on slated murals in Chicago, Boston, Memphis, and New York City. The inaugural recipient of the Bexley O Fellowship Grant is . . ."

If I have to listen to another speech by Madison, I'm gonna lose it.

"Beau Willet."

No. Freaking. WAY.

"What?! I didn't even apply!" I say as everyone around me starts applauding. Well, not everyone. Madison is pouting in front of the mural, and Principal Marcos is looking at Bexley like he wants to fight her or something.

"Get up there!" Sonnet pushes me forward and the crowd parts to let me through.

Bexley beams at me, her neon braids gleaming under the sun. She shakes my hand and steps to the side so I can have the podium.

I look out at the crowd, some people yawning, others still clapping and whistling. I see Champion in the back and my heart aches for how bogus I did him. Sonnet's pressed her way to the front, and I know she couldn't look any happier if she'd won the thing herself.

I can't believe this is happening. And now I have to talk.

"Uhh . . . I'd like to thank Bexley O for this amazing opportunity. It's really great to be chosen and uhh . . . I can't wait to work with you . . . yeah, so . . . umm . . . thanks!"

I step away from the podium and get a meager round of applause again. I'm so happy I don't even know how to act. With ten thousand dollars, we'll be able to make rent and buy groceries again. I don't have to move in with Daddy in Uncle Kolby's living room.

After the principal dismisses everyone for the summer and Bexley has signed autographs for a few people, I catch up to her walking to her car in the parking lot.

"Hey! Umm . . . thank you so much for this opportunity. I didn't even know this grant existed," I say.

She smirks and sets her tote bag on top of her car.

"It didn't exist until a few days ago. After our meeting at Elena's, I mentioned you to Ms. Kubler. Let me tell you, that woman can go on for days about you. She showed me your portfolio and told me what really happened with the original mural you proposed."

"Wait a minute, you created the grant . . . for me? But why?"

She looks at me, like she's seeing *me*. Like she's seeing things that maybe I don't even fully understand about myself yet.

"Because that's how it all works. We take our gifts and we give them back to the world. Sometimes I wonder how much further I'd be in my career if I'd had someone to help me get my foot in the door. I want this fellowship to be your foot in the door, Beau."

"Wow . . . okay. Well, I don't know if Ms. Kubler made it seem like my family's struggling with money because we're not." I don't want the money or the fellowship because she feels sorry for me. I want it because she thinks I'm good enough to be an artist like her one day.

"No, nothing like that. She just told me you're one of her very best students. I still remember the sketches I saw in your book when we talked at Elena's. You have talent that needs fostering. And if you really want to do the kind of work I do, you have to get used to traveling. Unless, of course, you'd rather spend your summer at home."

"No! No way. I definitely wanna go on the road with you! I have to ask my parents, but I know they'll say yes. Thank you," I say.

I take my time walking home that afternoon, my Chucks practically floating over the sidewalk. Every few minutes I check my contacts list and find Bexley's name, as proof that this really did happen and I'm not just having a dream.

All this time I spent hating Madison and now I've got something even better than just one mural on the side of the school. Bexley O is gonna let me work with her. Bexley O likes *my* work! Finally, I did something right. And it feels good.

CHAPTER 33

"WE'LL BE VISITING THREE CITIES, BOSTON, Memphis, and New York City. I have work slated in each location and Beau will serve as my assistant," Bexley says, handing my parents an itinerary.

We're sitting in a hipster bakery on the North Side of Chicago that serves things like vegan scones and organic apple juice. Bexley's idea, of course.

"She'll be safe? I don't want her out in the streets at night in some town she's never been to," Momma says. She still spends most of the time in bed crying but every now and then, she has a good day where she gets up and makes me eggs for breakfast, straightens up the house, holds my face in her hands and kisses my forehead, days where she cares. Today, she cares a lil too much.

"Mommma," I whine.

"No, she's right to ask," Bexley says. "I promise you, Mrs.

Willet, Beau will be with me and my team every hour of the day. We won't let her out of our sight."

"Sounds like a good idea to me. I want Beau as far away from Grady Park as possible this summer. Weather gets nice and niggas don't know how to act," Daddy says, looking over the itinerary.

"Daddy!" I scold.

"Oh! Sorry, I meant *people* don't know how to act."

Bexley just smiles.

"Before we go, there's one other thing I wanted to propose to you, Beau." She pulls out a photocopy of my original mural design of Katia.

"Wow," Momma says. "Baby, you drew this?"

Daddy looks amazed, too.

"This is beautiful. Why didn't you show us?" he says.

"It's just a drawing. We were supposed to paint it on the school, but some parents called and complained because it was Katia."

Bexley says, "Ms. Kubler and I didn't think that was fair at all. We also don't think this is a picture that should go unseen. So we're going to paint it."

"Really? Where, though? Do we even have time to get a permit?"

"You let me worry about all that. I want to place this somewhere important to you. Got any ideas?"

Everyone looks at me expectantly and I only have to think about it for a moment.

"I do. But I think we're gonna need some help," I say.

———

"This looks stupid. It looks stupid, doesn't it?" Parker asks, holding his head sideways.

I stand beside him but can't see what he's talking about. He did just what I showed him.

"That butterfly is beyond perfect. Keep going," I tell him.

Bexley brings a ladder over for me so I can complete the top portion of the mural.

"Wait a minute now, that's a lil high up," Daddy says. "Let me go up there and paint that part for you."

"Dad. It's *my* mural. I'll be careful, I promise," I say, carrying my brush and pallet with me up the ladder.

He watches me with this worried look on his face as he runs his hands over his bald head. I wish Momma were here to distract him, but she said it'd make her too sad and she didn't wanna ruin it for me. It annoys me that she's not here. That she'd miss out on time with me when I need her. She's not the only one who misses Katia like hell. Daddy says we have to be patient and give her time to heal. But it's been six months already. I'm worried Momma will always be this sad, that the old Momma I know is gone forever.

When I get to the top of the ladder, I look down below me and see Breon chasing Champion with a big paintbrush dipped in purple. Sonnet is sitting cross-legged in the grass with Ms. Kubler, holding a hunk of blue crystal in one hand. Bexley's kneeling near the bottom of the mural, showing Monica and Clarice how to get just the right amount of paint on their brushes without wasting any.

I look up toward the afternoon sky and the red-orange sun blankets Rosie's Diner in its glow. I'm so high up, I almost wish I had let my dad come up here instead, but then I hear the rustle of leaves as trees sway in the wind, the chirping of baby birds ready

310

to fly, the rush of people in cars on the street heading home after a long day of work.

Then, I paint.

First, the height of her cheekbones, the slope of her button nose, the cupid's bow of her dark brown lips. It all flows straight from my heart to my arm, to my hands, through my fingertips. I'm not worried about proportions or alignment or depth because I know I won't get this wrong. I can't get this wrong.

I work for hours. Daddy says I should take a break and have something to eat. I say no. Bexley says I can finish it tomorrow since everyone's gone home for the day. I still refuse. When it's too dark to see, Champion and Sonnet come back with big flashlights and lanterns to illuminate the brick wall. Truth be told, I don't need the light. I could do this in the dark. I can see Katia's face more clearly than I think I've ever seen my own. I know she's here, somewhere in the blackness.

When I finally finish, I put my brush down and collapse into Daddy's arms. It's nearly one in the morning and it's just me and him at the diner.

"Don't you have that Grady Park High interview in the morning? You should have told me how late it was," I say groggily as he carries me on his back to the car. He hasn't given me a piggyback ride since I was seven.

"I do. If it goes well, I'll be the assistant athletic director. But I know better than to interrupt an artist at work. Besides, it's nice out tonight. Quiet, warm. Gave me some time to think."

"About Katia?" I ask.

"Yes. And you. I don't know what I did for God to bless me

with two girls as amazing as you and your sister but I'm glad he did."

We reach the car and he turns back toward the diner where the mural rests. The streetlights cast a magical purple glow over the wall, and shining in the night are Katia's eyes. Daddy doesn't talk the rest of the way home. I think he's thinking about Katia still. I don't tell him this, but he's an okay dad when he tries. I just hope that he'll keep trying. For me.

CHAPTER 34

BEFORE
JANUARY 8, 2018

"YOU SAID YOU WERE GONNA TEACH ME HOW TO contour tonight!" I whined when I smelled her fruity going-out perfume.

Katia was looking in the mirror, sucking in her stomach and smoothing down a gold minidress over her hips and butt.

"You sure? Cuz, uh, I don't remember saying anything like that."

"It was just this morning, you liar." I was sprawled out on my bed with my colored pencils and a glossy poster of Nicki Minaj for reference.

"Why you wanna start contouring anyway? You don't even need it."

"*You* wear it. Besides, you promised."

Katia walked over to me like a baby deer on her skyscraper-high rose-gold heels. They wrapped up her calves like serpents. She called them the showstoppers. I called them the Antigone heels because they reminded me of those sandals they wore in ancient Greece.

"Doesn't ring a bell," she said, sitting down on the edge of my bed.

I rolled my eyes at her.

"Whatever, trick. Which club are y'all going to tonight?"

"You the trick. We're going to the Blaze again," she said, standing up and popping her booty against the dresser.

I didn't bother asking to go because she always said no.

"Don't come back here all high and shit, wakin' me up outta my sleep," I warned her, sketching Nicki's long wavy hair.

Still popping it, Katia said, "Oh please, you love our little three A.M. drunken convos. But I'm not drinkin' tonight anyway. DD since I'm the only one with a car."

I picked up a pink colored pencil and started filling in Nicki's skintight catsuit. Katia leaned over the bed to get a closer look.

"Not bad," she said, rubbing her chin.

"You think? I feel like I didn't get her eyes right."

"Don't mess with it, it looks perfect," she said, picking her purse up off her bed. "I'm 'bout to leave. Come lock the door behind me."

I followed Katia out into the living room where it smelled like egg foo young and fried rice from the Chinese delivery we'd ordered earlier.

As she adjusted her heels, Katia's gold hoop got caught in the collar of her dress and I pulled it loose for her without snagging the fabric. She smiled at me.

"Aight, I'm gone," she said, pulling the front door open.

"See ya. Wouldn't wanna be ya," I said.

Katia stepped outside, pulling the door behind her. Before it could snap shut, she popped her head back inside real quick.

"Hey, Bozo? The contouring. I'll show you tomorrow if you remind me. Deal?" She stuck her hand through the crack in the door.

I placed my hand on top of hers. A promise.

"Deal."

CHAPTER 35

TWO DAYS AFTER WE FINISH PAINTING THE mural, Deja calls me.

It's what I've been waiting on since she got arrested. We don't make small talk or ask how the other is doing. We agree on a place to meet and then we hang up.

As I'm walking to Rosie's from the bus stop, I don't know what I'll say to her. I've imagined our meeting plenty of times, but over the past couple weeks, each encounter I imagine becomes less and less violent.

When I get to the parking lot of Rosie's Diner, I finally get to see what my mural looks like without a bunch of people and paint buckets in front of it.

Surrounded by pink and blue butterflies that look ready to pop right off the bricks of the building and float away, is Katia. Not a Picasso version, but my version. The middle part wearin', Cheetah Girl lovin', drunk pep talk givin' Katia. She smiles down at me and everyone who passes by on their way to live their life.

It hurts to see her like this still. I don't want my sister to be painted on a wall. You can't hug a wall. You can't tell a wall to stop calling you Bozo. You can't ask a wall if she can drive you to the mall.

When I see Deja coming up the street, my heart leaps into my throat.

She stops when she gets a few feet away, and she looks afraid of getting too close. But I'm honestly not even on that fighting stuff with her.

"Hey," I say.

"Hey," she replies.

Silence overtakes us and it's strange because we never used to have moments of silence. Even if we had, they wouldn't have been uncomfortable. But we're not the same people we were before. We'll never completely be those girls again.

"Where'd they take you?" I finally ask.

"Juvie. Then an emergency shelter till my dad came to get me. We've been staying at a motel across town."

"Oh," I say.

"Yeah. How you been though? I heard you're going on tour with this big-time tagger."

"Yeah, in a few weeks. We're going to Boston, Memphis, and NYC. It's gonna suck having to come back home when it's over."

Deja twists her mouth awkwardly. The betrayal is a huge elephant in the room that we both insist on tiptoeing around.

"You painted this?" she asks, noticing the mural on the side of the diner.

"Yeah. Me, Bexley, Sonnet, Breon. It was a group thing, kind of."

She looks down and shakes her head.

"I should have been there . . . ," she whispers.

"Nobody wanted *you* there," I snap, surprising even myself.

"No, I meant I should have been there for you. Instead of doing what I was doing."

My mouth dries up as I glare at her.

"Not the first time you chose a dude over me. But Jordan? Of all the dudes you could have, you just had to pick him. Even after all the shit you knew he put my sister through, you still went after him!"

"It wasn't like that. He chased me!"

"You really are an idiot," I say.

Her ears perk up at the word.

"What did you just call me?"

But I'm not backing down. The Grady Park force is in full effect and there's no stopping what comes out of my mouth.

"You heard me. All the shit people say about you is true. Katia told me to drop your ass a long time ago and I should have listened to her." I turn to walk away but she pulls my arm back.

I yank away from her. "Don't touch me, Deja! I swear to God, I'll—"

"Beat my ass? Fine! Do it!" She closes her eyes and stands there with her hands at her sides.

"What the hell are you doing?"

"I'm standin' here waiting for you to do what you need to do to get over this. Go ahead! It can't be any worse than getting hit with that ashtray."

I think about hitting her, how that'll make us even somehow. But deep down, I know it won't change anything.

"Why did you do it, Deja?"

"I don't know. I just wanted someone who was gonna be for me. He needed me. Or he said he did."

"He did. Who else would hide a criminal?"

"I asked him what he saw that night your sister was murdered. He said she was fine when he left. He was gonna come back but he saw all the police cars and he got scared. He didn't know what they would do to him."

"Katia was scared, too. And alone. She wouldn't have left him to die alone."

She sighs.

"What do you want me to say, Beau? What do I have to do? It's over between me and Jordan."

I roll my eyes.

"Of course, it is, because he's going to prison! But if he wasn't, you'd be right back with him. I know you would."

"No, I wouldn't! I can handle being without him, but I can't handle being without you. You're my day one. Literally the only person I can trust."

"But I can't trust you."

"Yes, you can! I admit it, okay? I fucked up. I'm always fucking up. But I promise I'll never hurt you again. Ever."

She looks up at me with pleading, tearstained eyes, but I don't respond.

Her shoulders slouch as she starts to back away from me.

"Okay, I get it. I'll just go. But I really am sorry. I just want you to know that." She turns and starts walking back the way she came.

I should let her go. I don't need people like her in my life. People who make dumbass decisions for dumbass dudes. But then the sun catches the glitter of the purple paint we used for Katia's shirt. I look up at her, larger than life and beautiful as ever. I should let Deja go.

But I can't.

"Wait!" I call out to her. She turns around and wipes her face on her T-shirt. I wanted an apology, but I know it's not going to make it hurt any less. It's not gonna magically turn us back into the team we used to be.

"I really am sorry, Beau," she says, the pain in her eyes a reflection of the pain in mine.

"I know. The OTs aren't still after you?"

"Possibly. That's why we're at the motel, figured it's safer."

"Right. That's good."

More silence.

"Last night when I was walking home, I saw Jacques sneaking out Miss Odella's back window," I say.

Deja's eyes widen like I knew they would. "Girl, you lyin!"

We settle into an easy rhythm of conversation, updating each other on what's happened in our lives and in Grady Park since we last talked. We don't talk about Jordan anymore. We don't have to.

We talk in front of the mural for a whole two hours. Sitting down cross-legged on the asphalt of the parking lot, we get to know each other again. It's just as we're getting up to leave that a strong wind blows the white seeds of the dandelion weeds up into the air.

Suddenly, I realize I can finally answer my own question. That question that has been eating at me for months. Deep down somewhere, I think I've known the truth this whole time.

Katia didn't do anything wrong. And even though she was dating a terrible guy, lived at home while the rest of her friends were at college, and wasn't sure what her future was going to be, none of it matters. It never did.

She did *not* deserve to die.

———

The two weeks before my fellowship are the best I've had in a long time. Everything still feels strange, like I'm walking through milky fog. But even though I can't always see, I keep going. I keep sifting through the fog.

On my bad days, I lock the door, turn off my phone, and cry in a ball under Katia's sheets. On my good days, I'm the glue that holds my friends together.

The night before I'm scheduled to leave, we get together for a slumber party at Sonnet's. Ms. Bluefall sets up a cozy space in the open field near the side of the house. Big colorful velvet throw pillows cover a large blue tumbling mat. There's blankets, a radio, veggies, fruits, and hummus with chips.

"This stuff tastes like an armpit. What is it?" Deja asks before spitting her mouthful into a napkin.

"Mashed chickpeas," Breon says. She's wearing the dark green flannel pajama set I loaned her before Daddy dropped us off earlier. I'm glad I got the grant when I did, because without it, there's no way we would have been able to give Breon a home with us. I sleep in Katia's bed now, and Breon sleeps in mine. It's not the same, obviously. But sometimes that's okay. Not the same is sometimes just enough.

"Okay, first we fill up our mason jars," Sonnet says, setting a glass jar in front of each of us. Ms. Bluefall brings out a big pitcher of water and we pass it around.

Sonnet and her mom both say it's lucky that my trip is starting the morning after a full moon, that it means more good things are coming for me. I wanna believe that's true, even though I'm nervous about being away from home, especially after everything that's happened. Before, I talked a good game about escaping Grady Park but now that it's actually about to happen, I'm not ready.

"Y'all . . . what if sometimes happens when I'm gone?"

Breon drums on the lid of her filled jar. "Like what?"

Sonnet reaches over and puts a hand on my shoulder. "You're nervous about the trip, aren't you?"

"No, I'm just not sure now's the right time for it. We've been having so much fun, I don't want this to end," I say.

"I know what this is about," Deja says. "You're not afraid things here will change, you're afraid *you* will."

I laugh. "Here you go, being philosophical and shit," I say.

"Nah, that kinda makes sense though. I remember back when I found out I was in the running for valedictorian in eighth grade. Nobody stood a chance against me. But the idea of winning didn't make me excited. It stressed me out and made me anxious as hell," Breon says.

"Why? Being valedictorian is an amazing thing," Sonnet asks thoughtfully.

"Not when you feel like you don't deserve good things happening to you. What made me any better than any of the other kids? And if I did get it, I knew people would expect me to be high school valedictorian, then graduate top of the class from Princeton and cure cancer or somethin'."

"But you were—you *are* smart enough to do all that if you want," I say.

"I didn't see it like that back then. I couldn't see how I could ever really win anything with my momma barely around and me still living in the projects. One way or another, I was gonna fuck it all up and end up right back where I started, so I figured, why bother trying?"

It's almost like Breon's telling my story for me. "Yeah . . . yeah, that's exactly how I feel. I don't feel like I did enough to deserve this. Bexley probably only gave me the award because she felt sorry for me. I would have felt sorry for me, too," I admit.

Ms. Bluefall lights tea candles and places them around our circle. Sonnet turns to me. "Beau, did you ever think this was all meant to happen because it's your path? I believe in luck, but I also believe in destiny. I mean, what are the chances that we—I mean, *someone* would deface the mural and that Bexley herself would volunteer to come help repair it?"

"Yeah, Beau, don't you see that you deserve all this? You deserve even more," Deja agrees.

My friends are all looking at me with love and suddenly it's too much. I bury my face in my hands. Say what's really in my heart.

"Why should I get to leave Grady Park when Katia never will?"

I start to cry and feel several pairs of arms wrap tightly around me.

"But she has," I hear Ms. Bluefall say softly. "She's not trapped in Grady Park and neither are you. She'd want the best for you. You don't have to feel guilty about wanting it, too."

I know she's right. Katia would call me dumb for even thinking about not going. She'd want this for me, I know she would. It just sucks that I'll never get to hear her tell me herself.

A fresh wave of sobs racks my body, and my girls hold me tighter. I feel warm, sad, angry, happy, hatred, and love all at the same time under a sea of white stars. Katia's never coming back but I still have Deja, Breon, and Sonnet. Maybe tomorrow, it won't feel like enough. But tonight, it is.

ACKNOWLEDGMENTS

THIS BOOK WOULDN'T HAVE BEEN POSSIBLE without the amazing team that supported me.

To my agent, Patricia, thank you for believing in my story and me as an author.

To my editor, Kat Brzozowski, thank you for helping me transform my story into its best possible version.

To the Tulsa Artist Fellowship, thank you for giving me the time and space to work on my book and changing my life for the better. And my Tulsa homies, Steve Bellin-Oka, Kenichi Bellin-Oka, and Zoie.

To my friend and mentor, Dr. Erika Wurth: Thank you for nurturing baby writer Juliana so I could become the writer I am today. I hope you know I'm one of your biggest fans. Thank you for everything you've done for me.

To my best friend, Audrey Gradzewicz; thank you for always being there and for being the loving, thoughtful, awesome, brilliant person that you are. You've stood by me in my darkest times and I'll forever be grateful for you. To my other best friend, Quarchea, thank you for always going the extra mile for me and helping me learn to be kinder and softer. You are without a doubt the kindest person I have ever known and I don't know where I'd be without our friendship.

To my family members who aren't here to see my childhood dream come true, my aunt Marcia Balciar; my grandmothers, Peggy Goodman and Willa Onayo; and my grandfathers, Charles Onayo and Jesse Wiley: Thank you for believing in me when I didn't believe in myself. Thank you for loving me unconditionally. I hope this makes you proud.

Special shout-out to my crazy cat, Pickle Bickle, and my favorite boy, Artie Partie, my late-night writing buddies.

Thank you to the rest of my family, my brothers Brian Wiley and Chaz Gross, and my niece Zoey Wiley.

To my mother, Ginger Wiley, aka Gidget: Thank you for letting me dream. I think you knew before I even did that I wanted to be an author and that one day it would happen for me. Thank you for being my first example of a successful Black woman and for helping me to become one, too. I love you, Mommy!

To my big sister, Jillian: I saved the best for last because there's no way I could have written a book about sisters without my own sister. The love Beau has for her big sister Katia is the same love I have for you. Even when we get on each other's nerves, I know you'll always be there for me, and I hope you know I'm always going to be here for you. Thirty-one years in the making, nothing could ever break our bond. Thank you for being honest with me and loving me. I love you, J Gizzle #1.